CoasttoCoast

CoasttoCoast

JAN MINSHULL

transita

Published by Transita
3 Newtec Place, Magdalen Road,
Oxford OX4 1RE. United Kingdom.
Tel: (01865) 204393. Fax: (01865) 248780.
email: info@transita.co.uk
http://www.transita.co.uk

British Library Cataloguing in Publication Data
A catalogue record for this book is available from the British Library

ISBN-10: 1-905175-21-3
ISBN-13: 978-1-905175-21-5

Produced for Transita by Deer Park Productions, Tavistock
Typeset by PDQ Typesetting, Newcastle-under-Lyme
Printed and bound by Bookmarque, Croydon

ABOUT THE AUTHOR

Jan Minshull grew up in a Kentish seaside town with her six sisters and brother playing 'imagine' games and writing prize winning compositions in school. After the failure of her early marriage, she married her graphic designer boss and has lived happily ever after, working together in the advertising business in Canterbury, adopting cats and dogs and walking wherever and whenever they could. After a year of dithering, at the toss of a coin, they sold the business and moved to the Lake District where her husband is now a professional artist and Janet manages an idyllically located hotel on the shores of Ullswater: a perfect job for a writer, providing interesting characters and four winter months of writing time.

ACKNOWLEDGEMENTS

My very sincere thanks go to …

my husband, Mike, for being a survivor and for
his encouragement and enthusiasm for my writing
endeavours

my parents, sisters, brother, step-daughter, their partners
and offspring, for commiserating with my downs and
celebrating my ups

the membership of The Romantic Novelists' Association
for their friendship and support and especially to the
organisers and readers of the New Writers' Scheme, whose
generosity in time and experience has been invaluable in
bringing me to the point of publication

Laura at MBA Literary Agency for things yet to come

my friends and neighbours for sharing the Champagne

and Jack and Dottie, the only two real characters in this
book, whose sense of fun and loyalty will never be
forgotten.

The Coast to Coast walk is a recognised route and all the places mentioned are real. Some of the hostelries and hotels exist but as this is a novel, not a guidebook, most are fictional and are not based on any establishment in the towns where I have put them. All the characters, major and minor, are fictitious, with two exceptions: the personalities and brilliance of the two dogs, Dot and Jack, are based on my own two border collies.

CHAPTER 1

THE WHOLE THING WAS TRIGGERED by the sort of pathetically small marital dispute that most people have from time to time.

Linda was in bed, reading a delightfully amusing novel about an old woman wryly reviewing her life and relationships: it had been quite some life, packed with unlikely romantic adventures, all a far cry from the reality of Linda's life, or any real person's life for that matter. Anyway, it was giving her a much needed giggle or two when she heard the scrunch of the big BMW on the gravel, the quiet thud of the closing door, the crunch, crunch like munching cornflakes as her husband walked from the drive to the front porch. Nearly at the end of a chapter, she carried on reading, half-listening to his progress, the key in the lock, the opening and shutting of the door. Her attention slid from the book when something she still expected didn't happen. Up until a few weeks before there'd have been a gentle woof and thumping of plumed tail on banister rails, and Jim's quiet voice responding to Dottie's enthusiastic nuzzling with her wet black nose, telling her to stay down because he didn't want her long hairs on his smart business suit. Thinking of the elderly border collie dog still brought a lump to her throat. For nearly fifteen years Dot had been welcoming the family home and she'd been something responsive to talk to in the otherwise unoccupied house and garden. Unlike the kids and Jim, Dot never argued or stomped off in a huff, Dot was never too busy to listen. She wondered if Jim felt the absence as he went through to the kitchen where he would leave his briefcase and check the mail. Within a few minutes he was switching off lights and coming up the stairs.

'Good meeting?' she asked, as he came into the bedroom.

'Okay. Yes. Good,' he replied, bending to exchange a peck of a kiss. She could smell wine on his breath but had no reason to worry: he was always responsible about drinking and driving. 'Usual crowd. All on good form. Interesting speaker, just back from India and hoping to raise funds for a school.'

As a vicar's daughter, she had grown up with missionary tales of hardship in Africa and India and found it depressing that, despite all the saving of ship-ha'pennies, jumble sales, and 'adopting' of orphans and whole villages, things seemed to have become worse rather than better in the half century of her life. She wasn't indifferent to what was going on, but had reached a point of acceptance that nothing she could do was going to make a jot of difference. If he heard her say it, her father would look at her large, comfortably furnished, five-bedroom house and shake his head sadly.

'All well at the office?' she asked, having not seen nor spoken to him since his departure for work at seven-thirty that morning.

'Yes, fine.' Whilst pulling off his jacket and tie and unbuttoning his shirt, he gave a brief account of the day's events. He had always revelled in the cut and thrust of high finance and had the sort of charisma that motivated people, so it was no surprise that he had made it to Chief Executive and fully expected, by the end of the summer, to be appointed Chairman of the investment consultancy where he'd been a rising star for nearly thirty years.

He undressed without thinking, folding his trousers into the trouser press and hanging his jacket on the hanger, dumping his shirt, underpants and socks on the floor and pulling on his sky-blue shortie pyjamas. He was still a good-looking man but weightier than he used to be. When people commented about his increased girth, he laughingly blamed her for being too good a cook. She always accepted it with a smile and a shrug but really it was down to his lack of self-discipline when eating out, and too little exercise. His dark-steel hair was still thick and only slightly receding from his temples; his bright hazel eyes, cheerfully edged with rays of little lines, declared his friendly, humorous personality. He disappeared into the en-suite bathroom, as always without quite shutting the door, from whence came the ritual noises of peeing into the pan from a great height, flushing cistern, teeth cleaning, gargling and face splashing. She envisaged the soapy splashes that would be left halfway up the mirror and around the back of the taps, the toothpaste tube without its cap, abandoned on the glass shelf, the towel slung over the edge of the bath instead of the rail.

He flicked off the light and shut the door as he came back into the bedroom. 'You'll need to make a diary note for the first weekend in July. For the Dutch return visit. Three days, as usual.' His thoughts had obviously reverted to his Rotary meeting.

'Dutch visit?' She distinctly remembered telling him that if a return visit was planned, he could count her out.

'I meant to tell you last week. Unfortunately, we'll have to stay with the Van Hopstrops.'

And that's what started it. It was the 'I meant to tell you'; not 'I meant to ask you', but *tell* you, that made her particularly angry.

'I thought I'd made it plain that I didn't want to go,' she said, as his weight upset the equilibrium of the bed. The previous year's experience of entertaining the then president of the Rotary Friendship Club and his hypochondriac wife had made for an interminably long, long weekend. Because of her various allergies and intestinal disorders, Gerda Van Hopstrop had been unable to eat anything Linda put in front of her; she couldn't sleep with a down duvet, or on a firm bed; she didn't trust tap water but was allergic to Perrier. Nobody had thought to forewarn Linda about any of this. And if that hadn't been bad enough, Gerda could only travel in the front of the car, didn't trust the air conditioning not to be recycling everybody's germs, so had to have the windows open. Linda had been consigned to a buffeting draught in the back alongside Claus Van Hopstrop, unable to hear any conversation and with her vision limited by the front seat headrest and Gerda's enormous shoulders. She had made it very plain to Jim, immediately upon the Hopstrop's departure, that under no circumstances was she going to accept the inevitable invitation for a return match.

'We have to go,' he said, neither admitting nor denying his recall of events. 'As immediate Past President, I have to.'

'You go if you feel you have to, but I'm not the Rotarian: I don't have to.' She pulled her pillows from sitting to sleeping position and thrust her head into their softness.

He sighed. 'We'll talk about it in the morning.' Turning his back, he pulled the duvet over his shoulders and reached to switch out his bedside light.

'There's nothing to talk about,' she responded, yanking back her share of the duvet. 'I'm not going.' And because she was angry, she added, 'And I'll tell you something else, I'm not going on your proposed golfing holiday with your friends, either!'

'Oh, for Pete's sake! What's brought all this on?' He turned over, supported his head on his hand and scowled down at her.

'You,' she answered, glaring back at him. 'You keep doing this. You're always making arrangements to do things that you want to do with your friends, without ever *consulting* me.'

'I thought they were *our* friends.'

'Jim, why don't you *listen* to me? You play golf with the guys, you all have fun, but during the day I'm stuck with their wives who are not friends I'd choose to spend a whole week with. They're fine in small doses, at dinner parties and the like, but not all day, from breakfast to dinner, every day for a whole week.'

'What's wrong with them?'

'Absolutely nothing ... '

'So what's your problem?'

'I've told you before. They never want to *do* anything. All they want is to lounge by the pool sunning themselves or to be pampered in the beauty parlour.'

'I thought you enjoyed that. That's why we always go to places with those facilities.'

'I don't not enjoy it, but given the choice, I'd rather do what *I* want for my holiday.'

'Which is?'

'Dammit, Jim, you know very well. I've been telling you for years. I like walking holidays like we used to do with the kids. I want to go back to the Lake District, I want to go to Scotland, I want to do the Coast to Coast walk.'

'It's you that doesn't listen. I keep telling you, those sort of jaunts will have to wait until I retire. It's not something you can undertake unless you're fit for it and I haven't got time to get the practice in.'

'Huh! You find plenty of time to practice golf!'

'Humph!' he grunted, throwing himself onto his side with his back to her.

End of conversation.

In less than five minutes the rhythm of his breathing changed and she knew he was asleep. He didn't stir as she reached to turn out her light. She couldn't sleep. She lay on her back staring into the darkness, wondering if she was being selfish and unreasonable. He worked hard, had provided well for the family and for years had gone along with the idea of family holidays and doing what was best for the kids. Now that they were no longer a consideration, why shouldn't he have the holidays that suited him? But, by the same token, she also worked hard so didn't she qualify, just once in a while, to have a holiday of her choice? She eventually slept, but on and off, and during her long periods of wakefulness found herself anguishing over the cause of their tiff. By the time dawn broke, she had made up her mind that compromise was the answer. He should do his thing and she would do hers. She reasoned that as she had no problem with him going away on his Rotary weekend and golfing holiday, why should he have any objection to her going in another direction?

The next day, being Saturday, she let him have an extra couple of hours' sleep beyond that of his working day while she went for her ritual morning walk. Dot's lead was still on the hook by the back door. Whenever she was asked if she would have another dog, which was often, she said no. They'd bought the puppy for the kids but in reality the dog had become her responsibility, and her soul-mate. Right from the start it had been her with whom Dot had identified, which was understandable. In those days the kids had been at school, Jim at work, and she had been the one at home all day to take the dog for walks and feed her. None of the others had had to give the dog a second thought as they went their separate ways, but for her, when she went to catering college and then to work, the dog had been a major consideration. And at the end, it had been Linda who had been left with making the decision to have the dog put to sleep, and only Linda who had been there to hold Dot when she released her last long breath. She didn't feel she could go through all the anguish and pain again. Still feeling the loss, she pulled on her coat, laced up her shoes and headed up the lane alone.

The Kent countryside was not as challenging as Scotland or the Lake District and she managed the five mile circuit, which included a long steepish hill, without difficulty. As she walked, she planned her holiday. A week in the Lake District was favourite, maybe Keswick, revisiting the fells she had walked with the kids.

She felt better when she arrived home, invigorated and determined. She made a pot of tea and took it, along with the half rainforest of morning papers, up to their room.

'Morning,' she said cheerfully, opening the curtains to let the spring sunshine flow across Jim still cocooned in cream cotton duvet.

He yawned and turned onto his back, squinting at the light and stretching out his dark-haired arms, no doubt looking forward to the day ahead. Golf, of course, a few hours of rugby or football on television and then some Rotary friends for dinner in the evening. Linda's day would be spent cooking and preparing for the evening, which wasn't a problem; she actually preferred the preparation bit to the live entertaining. They were always a good double act: Jim was a brilliant host, very affable, generous with the drinks, attentive, and ever ready with an opinion or anecdote to entertain if the conversation flagged; Linda concentrated on the presentation of the table and the food.

'I've been thinking,' she said, as he sat up and settled against the pillows drawing the papers onto his lap. 'About holidays ... '

'Oh, Linda,' he groaned. 'Not now. Not first thing in the morning.' He unfolded the bundle of papers, looking for the finance supplement.

'Okay, but let me just say this, so you can think about it.'

He raised pained eyes from the headlines with a look that said, 'If you must'.

'I think that as we both want different things for our holidays, we should go our separate ways. That way we'll both be happy.'

He took a long patient breath, then released it slowly as he said, 'My initial reaction is that a holiday without you isn't my idea of happiness. Like I said, let's discuss it later.'

'Right-oh.' She smiled, determined to remain cheerful. She hadn't expected immediate concurrence, in fact, quite the reverse. Obviously he would need time to weigh up the pros and cons of this deviation from their norm.

*

There were several occasions during the day when he could have brought the matter up: like when they were sitting in the conservatory with pre-golf coffee and toast, but he appeared to have forgotten all about it and sat reading the paper, as he habitually did, while she did the crossword in the previous day's paper and waited patiently for his considered response, and later in the afternoon when he returned and she took him a cup of tea and home-baked cake, but he was too interested in channel-hopping and catching up with the latest football scores to talk to her about anything.

Whilst lying in a bath full of bubbles she thought irritably about the lost opportunities. It just about summed up where she fitted in his life: somewhere after the newspaper, television sport, golf, etcetera, etcetera. Certainly her needs weren't rating very highly. What really irked was that he seemed to have forgotten all about the previous evening's altercation and her proposed compromise; there was absolutely no evidence that he was giving it even so much as a passing thought. He hadn't appeared to notice that she had been silently waiting for him to raise the subject, or that during those moments of contact throughout the day she hadn't made any of the usual little pass-the-time-of-day comments, nor made any more than polite responses to his observations on the content of his newspaper or progress of the rugby match. Sometimes she wondered whether he was really aware of her presence: she was something like the dog, something to toss a passing remark to without having to listen to a reply. Well, she resolved, scrubbing furiously at the hard skin on her feet, if he thought she was going to come to heel on this one, he had another think coming.

'You look lovely,' he remarked as she came down the stairs wearing a shift-style cornflower blue dress that flattered her still firm and shapely curves.

'Thank you.' That's it, she thought, pat me on the head. Good dog. Dog to be proud of. Healthy diet and regular exercise had ensured that she remained in good shape, if not the sleek size twelve she'd been when she married, but a shapely size fourteen which was in proportion to her five foot six in height. Her complexion was good and her blue-grey eyes still bright; her hair, which had been long and natural honey-blonde when they met, was now a nape-length bob liberally streaked with silver and more often than not tucked behind her ears. A lot of their friends had been surprised to learn that her birthday last June had been the big five-0, boosting her ego no end by saying she could easily pass for forty. It was nice of them to say so, but sadly it wasn't true; she wasn't blind to the lines around her eyes and mouth, nor the wrinkles in her neck, nor the thread veins in her legs.

There were last minute things to do in the kitchen and then their guests arrived. They were all sitting in the large, restfully beige lounge with pre-dinner drinks when, inevitably, the subject of the Dutch trip was raised, as she knew it would be. The four guests, Michael and Maureen, Keith and Barbara talked enthusiastically about previous exchange visits and how well they'd got on with their hosts or guests.

'You, poor things, had the frightful Gerda Van Hopstrop to deal with,' Barbara recalled sympathetically.

'We'll give as good as we got on the return visit, won't we Linda?' Jim smiled across the length of the coffee table, his eyes holding hers. Recognising in his bright and breezy comment that he had been waiting for this moment to corner her into capitulation, she tilted her head and smiled as though to an exasperating but endearing small child.

'But darling, I told you last night: I shan't be going.' She slid her smile slowly from him to their guests and shrugged apologetically. 'I've made other arrangements.'

'Oh, no!' Maureen cried, 'You can't … You must come.'

Michael laughed, 'Aha! The dreaded Gerda too much for you, eh?'

'I don't know how you survived it,' Barbara shook her head.

Pleased with this unsolicited support, she smiled triumphantly at Jim. Arguing in public had never been their scene and she knew he wouldn't make an issue, at least, not immediately. She didn't feel bad about making her point in front of their friends: after all, hadn't he just tried to use them to manipulate her?

'We'll miss you,' Keith said, patting her thigh.

'Well, don't you worry about Jim,' Maureen laughed and slid her arm through his, 'I'll look after him.'

'Thank you, Mo.' Jim put his arm around her shoulder, hugged her and kissed her cheek. She blushed and fluttered her dark eyelashes at him.

He was that sort of man: women flirted with him and came over all unnecessary when he responded. Linda felt sorry for them. She supposed they imagined him to be as near perfect as his looks. All the indicators were there: successful career, lovely home, smart car, three good kids – well, she thought they were good even if he didn't entirely agree – and although he was perhaps not quite the athletic sportsman he once had been, he was still in reasonable shape and oozed charm. Did they imagine that as everything else about him was so good, it followed he would be the perfect mate? Did they fantasise about swapping their place with Linda? She would love a fiver for every time she'd heard one their friends tell her how lucky she was. Once upon a time she would have agreed with them.

She laughed. 'Well, I shall leave him in your capable hands.' The timer on her oven beeped. 'I think we could go through for dinner now.' She didn't need to escort them to the dining-room, they knew the way and would arrange their own seating based on who sat where and beside whom at the last dinner they'd all attended.

Jim followed her to the kitchen. His smile had gone. 'Thank you for that! You might have waited until we'd discussed it before making your announcement.'

'Like you discussed it before making yours?' she said more light-heartedly than she felt. 'Don't be so grumpy. You'll be amongst friends. Anyway, I doubt my absence will be noticed.'

'I'd notice it.' He changed tactics, putting his hand gently on her arm, pulling his brows together in perplexed concern and saying softly. 'What's got into you, Linda? This isn't like you.'

It would have sounded pathetic for her say that actually, she hadn't been feeling herself for several weeks, not since she'd had to have the dog put to sleep. It would probably sound contrary, considering Dot's perambulations had been gradually reducing over the last year, but now that the dog had gone she felt a desperate need to get out of the house. She wanted to get away, but from what, she wasn't really sure. Tears stung the back of her eyes, so she turned away to concentrate on taking the tray of salmon and dill tartlets from the oven. 'Nothing's got into me, Jim. I just don't want to go to Holland, and that shouldn't be a surprise to you because I told you so last year. Excuse me.' She moved round him with the hot tray.

He drew a deep breath and silently shook his head in a way that said he didn't understand. She wondered just what she would have to do to make him understand what seemed like a very simple to comprehend statement. Letting it pass, she quickly placed the tartlets onto the plates already dressed with a little salad and gave him two to carry through to the dining room.

*

The dinner party had been a success and other than a parting remark from Keith to the effect that he hoped she would change her mind, nothing more was said about the Dutch trip. Surprisingly, none of them had asked what her prior engagement was. It rather underlined her opinion that as long as Jim was there, whether or not she was made very little difference. By the time their guests had gone, they had been tired and the subject remained dormant. Feeling that she had said her piece, she didn't bring it up again and neither did he. She had no doubt that as far as he was concerned she was just having a little puff, and that in the end she would go with him to Holland. Besides, it was too lovely a morning to be spoilt by discord and he seemed happy enough, whistling along to an old Mark Knopfler CD,

Local Hero, a long-standing joint favourite, whilst polishing the glasses.

Morning sun streamed across her pale green kitchen. It was her domain, the only room in the house where she had had one hundred percent say in its design and decor. She had flatly refused to have an Aga, however trendy and however much their friends raved about how wonderful they were; as far as she was concerned, hers was a modern house with a functioning, productive kitchen, open plan to a family room which had perfectly adequate central heating. As they had designed the house themselves, well, Keith had been the architect but they'd told him exactly what they wanted, she'd opted for a walk-in pantry rather than lots of wall cupboards, which left plenty of wall space for pictures and shelves for her cookery books and ever-growing collection of pottery jugs.

The phone rang while she was emptying the dish-washer. Jim picked it up.

'Hello, darling!' His delighted greeting told her that it was Fiona, their eldest daughter. He would hotly deny that he had a favourite amongst his children, but his tone when speaking to Fiona was quite different to that which greeted Suzy, their youngest, or Rob, their only son and middle child. Fiona, the career girl, spoke his language. He discarded the tea towel and strolled into his study with the phone attached to his ear, laughing and chatting about stocks and shares. About fifteen minutes later he wandered back into earshot through the sitting-room and into the kitchen, still talking and smiling. 'I'll pass you over to your mother. Nice to hear from you, darling. Love you. Lots of kisses.' Smiling proudly, he handed over the receiver and departed through the back door into the garden.

'Hi, Mum.'

'And hi to you, stranger.' It was weeks since she'd seen Fiona although they exchanged a call at least once a week. 'I'm fine. And you?' She stopped wiping down the dark green worktops to stand by the sink, looking out through the window and watching Jim stroll down to the pond, bucket of fish food swinging from his hand, apparently blind to the burgeoning progress of the herbaceous border as he went. She could never step into the garden without finding something exciting to stop and wonder at: the first snowdrop, the first daffodil, lupin, rose, or a weed that needed pulling, or a snail that needed relocating, or something self-sown to be identified.

'Brill. I've just been telling Dad, I've been promoted to Business Manager. I'll have my own portfolio of clients, some really big ones. Not bad, eh?'

Not bad indeed for a girl of twenty-six. It was all a far cry from her own days in the bank when the lads got all the available promotions and girls were left on the tills.

'Congratulations. Are you staying with your branch?'

'For now, yes, which is great. I like being in London.'

'Takes all sorts,' Linda laughed.

'Mu-um..?' Fiona's voice was hesitant. 'Are you sure you're all right? Dad seems to think you're out of sorts. He suspects you're having a mid-life crisis.'

She laughed to cover her irritation. 'A man's answer to everything when he has failed to understand his wife after over a quarter of a century of marriage!' A quarter century. It sounded such a long time. Jim had reached the pond and was scattering handfuls of the food across the top of the water, no doubt counting the koi carp as they emerged from beneath the lily leaves. Personally, she couldn't see the fascination for what to her amounted to big goldfish: they had no personality, not like dogs.

'Is everything all right?'

'Yes, darling. Everything's fine.'

'Are you really thinking of doing the C to C, or are you just winding him up?'

Linda opened her mouth, then shut it. The Coast to Coast walk had been only one of several options she'd thrown into the frame during Friday night's brief tiff, but because Jim had latched onto the most extreme in order to rally the support of his daughter, she decided to play along with it. 'Yes. I'm serious. Ever since Rob did it, I've been saying I'd like to do it.' She grinned and added, as a challenge, 'I don't suppose you'd like to do it with me, would you?'

'Er ... no, actually, I've outgrown the pleasures of tramping around in the rain and besides, I've already got my holiday planned. I'm going on a vineyard tour of Italy in August.'

'That'll be nice.' She listened as her daughter rattled confidently through an itinerary that should ensure alcohol poisoning by the end of it.

'It's a pity Rob's not about,' Fiona reverted to the pre-Italy topic, 'he'd have gone with you. Where is he now? Have you heard from him?'

'Australia, last we heard, which was a week ago. He was grape-picking. He plans to go from there to New Zealand for a couple of months.'

'Doesn't sound like he's any nearer to getting himself a proper job,' Fiona echoed her father's oft-repeated opinion.

'No, darling, but he's gaining a wealth of experience. It's what he wants to do. He's supporting himself and not harming anybody so … '

'Just worrying the life out of you,' Fiona chipped in critically.

She chuckled. 'Well, I do worry, yes. I worry about all of you, for different reasons.'

'Why do you need to worry about me?'

'Because you're my daughter.' She didn't want to get into conversation about the daily threats that faced over-confident, pretty young blondes in big bad cities: the spectre of Suzy Lamplugh often walked the winding corridors of her mind on sleepless nights.

'I worry about you, too, Mum. That walk isn't a Sunday afternoon stroll, you know: it's nearly two hundred miles across the country's wildest terrain.'

'Sounds wonderful. If Rob survived it, and enjoyed it, I'm sure I will.' She hadn't the slightest intention of doing it, at least, not unless she could persuade Jim to join her and there was more chance of pigs flying than him doing that.

'He was still at uni, a fit young bloke of twenty. You're middle-aged.'

'Thank you for that, dear. I'll have you know that people in their seventies complete the walk, and probably older. I'm only fifty and fit. I can read a map and use a compass.'

'But you're not going to carry all your gear on your back and sleep in a tent, like Rob did, are you?'

'For heaven's sake, Fiona, don't you remember the holidays we had when you were small? We walked for miles with kids and packs on our backs.'

'Not tents and things ... '

'There are such things as Hotels, Inns, B&Bs and hostels.' She assumed there were, anyway. Maybe tomorrow, when Jim was back at work, just out of curiosity, she'd go onto the internet and look into it. The idea of teasing him into believing she was serious was beginning to sound more and more appealing, as was the fantasy that she could persuade him to join her.

Fiona spluttered. 'I can't imagine you dossing down in a hostel dormitory with a load of schoolgirls!'

'And why not?'

'Well ... you've become used to better things.'

'In my time I've done my fair share of roughing it. I camped with the Girl Guides and the church youth club. I actually enjoyed it.' And the truth be known, she looked back on those holidays with far more pleasure than some of the more recent ones in five-star hotels.

'What about Dad?'

'What about him?'

'Who'll look after him?'

'I don't believe I'm hearing this! Not from you, of all people! Miss Millennium Independent Career Girl is actually suggesting that a woman's place is in the home looking after her man? Or is equality okay for the under thirties, but Mums, well, they're different!'

'Keep your hair on. I didn't mean it like it sounded ... '

'Look, darling, I'm a big girl, not yet in my dotage and quite capable of looking after myself, and Daddy is a big boy. He'll go off and have fun with his friends, and when he comes back he knows just where to find all he needs to keep body and soul together for a few days. I promise that before I leave, I'll put a load of stuff in the freezer and give him a crash course on how to use the microwave oven. Okay? Unless, of course, you'd like to come home to look after him?'

'That's not what I meant. It's just, well, you two always do things together. You're such a couple. It just seems so odd for you to go off on your own.'

'If Daddy wanted to join me, I'd love to do it with him, but it doesn't appeal to him ... '

'He says he will do it, when he retires.'

'Darling, trust me, I know him better.' She knew him well enough to know that he didn't want to do it, ever, and that he believed if he delayed long enough she would give up the idea. She chuckled to keep the conversation light-hearted. 'He really is happier playing golf.'

'But ... '

'Okay, darling, let's drop the subject. You can tell your father that you did your best.' She laughed but it rankled that he had discussed the issue with their daughter, having deliberately avoided discussing it with her.

Fiona growled in defeat. 'Okay. So, have you seen Suzy lately?'

'Of course. I see her most weekdays. Why don't you call her? She'd love to hear from you.'

'I do, sometimes. It works both ways, you know,' she said, defensively. 'She doesn't often call me.'

'She tells me that she does, but always gets your answerphone and you don't call her back. Anyway, she and the children are fine. I'll probably see them tomorrow on my way home from work.'

'Good old Granny!' Fiona chuckled.

'Get lost!' Grandma she'd accept, but Granny sounded ancient!

'I love you too! Nice talking to you, Mum, even if you are going round the bend!'

'And nice talking to you, daughter, even if you are the most opinionated little wotsit.'

After affectionate farewells, Linda put the phone down and wondered how two girls from the same two parents, who had lived in the same houses and village, who had attended the same schools from nursery to grammar, could turn out so very different. Fiona had been one of those children who, if she fell from her pony, would get up, brush herself down and get straight back into the saddle to tackle an even higher jump. Suzy, on the other hand, was easily defeated. Whereas Fiona had sailed through school, passing exams with apparently little effort, Suzy had swotted and struggled and worried and still failed to get the grades for the university of her choice. Having no heart to fight on for another year to improve her grades, she'd dropped out and, for once going against her father's expressed wishes, had taken a job as general assistant in the local pub, cleaning, waiting and serving in the bar. There she met Phil, a monosyllabic, ringed and studded, motorbike-mad farm labourer. Within two years she was living with him and Daniel was on the way, and less than two years later Ruth had followed.

Now out of the frame in the competition for her father's approval, Suzy seemed perfectly happy with her lot, but Fiona, nearly four years her senior, made no secret of her opinion that her sister was effectively sticking her fingers up at her family because she didn't have what it took to have a 'proper' career. It would probably come as a surprise to Fiona to know that Suzy, genuinely, did not envy her sister her smart city flat, career, clubs, circle of girlfriends or the ever-changing men in her life. Whatever Fiona thought of her sister, Linda recognised that in Phil Suzy had found something which forthright Fiona might later in life find herself envying. She hoped, for Suzy's sake, that her dreams and ideals would survive the pressures of life better than Linda's had.

CHAPTER 2

'I STILL CAN'T GET USED TO DOTTIE not being with you,' Suzy's sad gaze rose from the floor by Linda's feet.

'I know. I keep looking for her, too.' She hugged her daughter and for a moment they held each other just a little longer than their usual greeting. Of all the children, Suzy had been the one who most related to the dog, possibly because Dottie had arrived when she was only seven, and, as Suzy had stayed in the same village, Dottie had remained very much part of her life.

'The kids are both asleep.' Suzy indicated that they were upstairs with a flick of her starkly plucked, ring-pierced dark eyebrows.

'I won't disturb them.' Linda smiled. 'Not yet, anyway.' Tough though she looked with her exposed upper arms crawling with tattooed insects, she knew that Suzy would be disappointed if she didn't go and coo over the little angels in their crib and cot. Her role as grandmother was one she was not yet comfortable with, which was surprising considering she had advised and supported Suzy throughout both pregnancies, and had been outside the delivery room when both the babies had been born. It hadn't quite sunk in that Daniel and Ruth were her *grand*children. She supposed she sort of accepted it because that's how she referred to them when speaking to her friends, but she didn't feel old enough for the title of grandmother. When Suzy said things to Daniel like, 'Take it to Grandma', it always took a moment for her to realise that Suzy meant her, not her own mother or mother-in-law.

'You're not serious, are you, about this walk thing?' Suzy filled her battered old kettle and placed it onto the hob of the ancient, solid-fuel Rayburn, where it spat and hissed like an angry cat as water dripped from a hole in the seal of the spout. 'Fi told me. She phoned *me*, amazingly!'

'Yes, I'm serious.' She hadn't been, but the more Jim lined up the troops against her, the more determined she was to give him a run for his money. She shrugged off her jacket and draped it over the back of a purple-painted chair at the dining end of Suzy's compact cottage kitchen.

'It does seem rather odd, after all these years.' Suzy was frowning as she dropped two tea bags into a floral-patterned teapot, no doubt one she'd picked up for next to nothing in a boot sale. Avoiding looking up, she asked with unnatural awkwardness, 'Everything's all right between you and Dad, isn't it?'

'Of course.' She smiled, out of habit protecting her children by smothering her own woes. 'He'll be okay when he gets used to the idea.' Like Jim, she would deny that she had a favourite child. Suzy was not favoured, but right from her premature birth she had needed much more support than the others: at only five foot two, she was the smallest, and had always been the one most prone to ailments and allergies, which, perhaps, explained and excused her lack of courage and confidence.

'Have you spoken to Rob about it?'

'Not yet.' She wondered how long it would be before Rob got to hear about it, and how her son would react. Suzy poured the tea into delicate china teacups with saucers, none of which matched, and brought them to the pine table. Warm sunshine spread from the glazed kitchen door. Outside, a kaleidoscope of tulips and primulas competed in the happy colour stakes with a kiddie's swing, slide, sandpit and wooden sit-on toys, all hand-made by Phil and painted by Suzy.

'Do you remember when we went to the Lakes and the others were determined to conquer Helvellyn via Striding Edge?' Suzy asked as she sat down, stretching her bare slender legs to the warmth of the sun, the tight sheath of her denim skirt only just concealing her knickers.

Linda smiled. 'Oh, yes. They were always so gung-ho, weren't they?'

'But you weren't. Or was it only because of me that you didn't do it?'

'Oh, darling, I can't remember now. You were very small.' It was a good question, though, making her wonder if perhaps she had used Suzy's fear to hide her own temerity.

Suzy chuckled. 'No change there, then.'

She smiled. 'I don't go along with the idea that kids should be pushed into doing things that they don't feel comfortable with, at least, not when it's potentially dangerous.' Whatever her feelings for her own safety had been, that at least was true. 'Daddy, Fi and Rob enjoyed challenges, but you were different and I wasn't going to spoil your holiday, or mine, by making you do things that terrified you.'

'I was always the wimp.' Suzy swirled her tea with a spoon.

'You were the youngest. As you'll find out when Dan and Ruth are a little older, even a two-year gap can sometimes seem huge.'

'I wish I could come with you.'

'Really?' The wistfulness in the remark worried her.

'Mmm. I remember Rob saying there were several ways of doing it, that you could choose your own route.' She grinned. 'He, naturally, diverted to take on every peak; I'd accept the challenge of finding us the easiest, lowest level paths.'

Linda laughed. 'I don't expect I shall be making life any harder for myself than is necessary.' She studied her daughter closely. 'Would you really like to do it?'

Suzy lifted her shoulders. 'I like the idea. Obviously I can't do it now. I was telling Phil last night, about Fi's call, and he said that one day he'd like to do it. It's an ambition for the future.'

She reached across to touch her daughter's hand. 'Don't leave it too long into the future. Whenever you and Phil are ready and want to leave the kids for a bit, to do something together, you know I'm here to take care of them.'

Suzy's green-flecked amber eyes looked quizzically at hers, but she didn't voice her obvious concern. It was just as well, because Linda wasn't quite sure that she could explain. The comment had been instinctive but it came with a creeping realisation that she was warning her daughter about something, even if she didn't know exactly what.

A demanding call of 'Mummy,' from above caused them both to look to the ceiling.

'I'll go.' Linda left the table, opened the latch door and went up the narrow, enclosed staircase. At the top was a protective gate and two doors leading from the small square landing. She peeked into Suzy and Phil's room with its stripped pine furniture and patchwork-quilt covered bed. Baby Ruth was asleep in the fairytale rocking crib at the foot of the bed, all but her head and tiny hands covered in a white baby suit, her dark-lashed eyes closed. It didn't seem twenty-two years since Suzy had looked just like that. She crossed the landing to where Danny, wearing only a nappy, was standing in his cot, his little fists impatiently shaking the rails.

'Ganna!' He grinned in delight and stretched his arms, wiggling little chipolata fingers, so eager for her to lift him from the cot that he tumbled backwards and bumped his head. He looked surprised then giggled and very quickly wriggled onto his knees and back to his feet. This was Jim's grandson to a T. She lifted him out and hugged his warm softness to her.

'Wet,' he said.

She could smell it. 'You're horrible.' And to prove just how horrible, she snuggled a kiss into his neck. Automatically she went through the process of laying him on the single bed and changing his nappy, poking his navel and telling him, 'Big boys don't wet nappies.' He gurgled some sort of response which obviously made sense to him. He was a bonny boy, pudgy but not fat, dark like his mother, but with his father's bright blue eyes. She picked him up, settling him onto her hip, her arm curled around him, hand under his bottom, and carefully carried him down the stairs. It came so easily, as if there hadn't been a twenty-year gap between him and his mother.

By the time they reached the kitchen, Suzy had warmed a cup of milk for him. With a cursory 'Ta', he grabbed it and stuck the spout into his mouth, content, just for a few minutes, to sit on Linda's knee and guzzle greedily.

'Ruth's still asleep.'

Suzy smiled contentedly, obviously happy with her babies and her little rented house and taciturn partner.

Other than the usual attention-seeking strops and battles of wills, Linda hadn't had problems relating to her children: she'd worked hard at it, determined to be more in tune with them throughout their childhood, and beyond, than she'd been with her parents. Her own childhood had not been particularly unhappy, but looking back on it, she felt it had been a non-event. She didn't feel that her parents had put any effort into it: they told her things, taught her right from wrong, but never discussed things, consequently there was no rapport and visiting them was a duty which, as they lived only twenty miles away, was one she felt had to be observed at least once a month.

'I shall be going to see Grandma and Granddad next week, would you like to come too? They haven't seen Ruth yet.'

Suzy drew in her lips and Linda knew exactly what it meant. 'Like' wasn't the word her daughter would use to describe a visit to her grandparents. It would be a duty but, she wondered, did she see it as a duty to her mother or grandparents?

'Of course, but … ' Suzy paused awkwardly, 'could we make it an afternoon trip? Maybe we could have a picnic on the beach, and see them in the afternoon?'

Linda chuckled. Her mother's cooking had been the subject of family humour for years. Most people of her mother's generation boiled vegetables to a tasteless pulp, but not Mrs Ramsey: she had been serving *al denté* vegetables for as long as Linda could remember, not because they were deemed to be healthy, but because they took less cooking time, therefore less fuel. Unfortunately, the same went for her pies which were whiter than white and her meat which was so rare it didn't require gravy, but also so cheap that sharp knives and good teeth were essential.

The gift of a microwave oven should have solved the problem, but it had proved too suspiciously scientific for her mother to adapt to; in the end it had been donated to the church hall. Fortunately, Mrs Ramsey didn't bake cakes or biscuits, deeming them luxury self-indulgencies that were unnecessary to keep body and soul together, and besides, her husband was fed quite enough of them on his pastoral rounds. It was just as well for Jim and her children that Linda had learned the rudiments of cookery at school. Not that her culinary skills had been anything to write home about: she'd learned a great deal more from her mother-in-law, and when the children were through primary school, she and her friend

Jenny had enrolled on a City and Guilds course. Since then her interest in food had blossomed.

*

When visiting with Suzy, Linda hadn't told her elderly parents about her proposed solo holiday, it seemed premature when her plans were still so vague. Jim, however, found it necessary to mention it to his father during his dutiful hour on his way back from the golf club.

'He's naturally worried,' Jim reported when he came home. 'He's come to rely on you calling in every day, to check that he hasn't fallen down the stairs or had a heart attack. It gives him reassurance to know you're around.'

'I don't call in every day,' she responded, splitting hairs, 'only on days I work, which is only four out of seven.' She could have added that it was three more visits a week than Jim found time for.

'But you cook dinner for him every day. He looks forward to it.'

True, whilst she was there she did cook him a meal, and often took him leftovers from the café where she worked, and always made sure there was something in the freezer for the days she didn't call. She didn't do it for him so much as for her deceased mother-in-law to whom she had promised that she would look after Fred. 'He manages without complaint when I'm away with you.' She tilted her head and raised a brow to make him realise that she knew exactly what he was up to.

Jim shrugged. 'Maybe it's his way of saying it seems an odd thing for you to be doing. Perhaps it makes him feel insecure.'

'Does it make you feel insecure?' she asked, hoping it did.

One dark eyebrow raised quizzically, confirming that the thought hadn't entered his mind, probably because he had every confidence that he would talk her round to complying with his plans.

He shrugged. 'I daresay Suzy will pop in to see him from time to time, if we ask her.' He made it sound like acceptance, but Linda knew what he was up to: he was well aware of her concern that, because Suzy lived in the same village and had no career, she was heir apparent to the role of family dogsbody.

She responded lightly, 'She already does, on a regular basis, to read his paper to him. He also has neighbours who stop by for a chat, and he still sees well enough to totter across the green to the pub for his daily pint.' To bring the conversation to a close, she said. 'Dinner will be ready in an hour, if you're thinking of taking a shower.'

'Okay, but seriously, we are going to have to start thinking about looking after him.'

'Oh, *we* are, are we?'

He stopped by the door and looked back, took a breath as though to say something, then changed his mind.

'My point is, Jim, that *I* do look after him.'

He brought his lips together, nodded and left the room. She bit back the urge to shout at him to come back and say what was on his mind.

*

Her daughters both seemed to share their father's opinion that she was suffering some sort of mid-life crisis and had to be humoured. She didn't confess to anybody, other than her friend Jenny, that she hadn't originally planned to do the Coast to Coast walk, but as a result of Jim's machinations it was becoming a challenge. Jenny, one of the few women who wasn't a member of the Jim Challoner fan club, was all for it.

'Give the bugger something to worry about,' she said. 'Teach him not to take you for granted.'

More out of devilment than real intention, she had checked it out on the internet. There were several sites offering all sorts of guidance regarding accommodation, route variations, preparation, kit, and one where people who were looking for groups or walking companions could introduce themselves and make contacts. Group walking had never appealed and the idea of walking with a stranger was equally alien.

Over the years, since Jim had taken up golf and the children had left home, she had become accustomed to walking alone, alone with the dog and her thoughts. If Jim couldn't be persuaded to join her on this, or any sort of walking holiday, just the two of them, then she would rather go it alone. But something as big as the Coast to Coast alone was, for her, one hell of a challenge and she had serious doubts that she was really up to it. However, still tempted to at least look into it, she sent away for books and maps and the more she read, the more appealing it became.

She was becoming so used to friends and family being against the idea that when Jim brought the telephone into the garden and told her that it was Rob calling from Australia, she was half prepared to allow herself to be talked into something perhaps a little less ambitious by the one person she knew who had done it. As she had heard the phone ring some ten minutes earlier, and Rob and Jim weren't known for their long conversations, she concluded that her husband had used the time to appraise their son of the situation. With a small shrug and a half smile which indicated that the lack of rapport with his son wasn't for his lack of trying, he retreated to the conservatory.

'Hi there, Mum. How ya' doin?' His voice was deep and slow. She could imagine his wide smile, the creased, bronzed cheeks and soft puppy eyes. He was a good-looking young man, dark like his father, with similar light brown eyes, but taller, six foot three and bean-pole thin, having inherited his structure from her father. Despite being something of a dreamer, he had done well in school and obtained a place at Oxford university to study modern languages, but having flunked his second year exams he'd dropped out, packed his rucksack and set off to see the world. That was four years ago and since then he had never been home, not even for Christmas.

'I'm just fine. And you?' It was her standard reply, regardless of how she really felt.

'Bonzo. Still at the vineyard in Western Oz. Will have to move on soon though, or I'll become a total dipso.'

'From what I hear you'd be in good company with Fi. She's off wine-tasting in Italy next month.'

'So I hear. And you, I've just been told, are planning to do the C to C?'

'It's the front runner of several options,' she conceded, leaving a door open.

'Go for it, Mum. You'll love it. It'll do you the power of good. You'll find yourself.'

'I don't think I've lost myself, yet.' She laughed because she really didn't believe she needed to find herself, but inside she did feel a need for something, and it was something she couldn't easily define beyond a feeling of frustration. 'Anyway, if you haven't found yourself in four years, what chance have I in two weeks?'

'Hmm,' he responded enigmatically, then moved on, as he always did if they skirted close to his real reason for going. 'Have you thought which way you're going to do it?' he asked, his voice on the phone sounding as clear as though he were by her side. Wishing he was, she waited for the slight delay before answering.

'The oracle, Wainwright, advocates west to east, apparently that puts the prevailing weather behind you. I've bought the OS strip maps based on his book. They're very informative.'

'Yeah, that's the way I did it. His book's in my room somewhere, if you want it. I realised afterwards, though, that it was probably better the other way. True, you might get wind and rain in your face, but starting on the comparative level of the North York Moors will get your legs walked in before you tackle the Cumbrian mountains. The Helvellyn range on the third day is a tall order if you're not used to that sort of walking.'

'I'm not sure about tackling Helvellyn at all, particularly on my own,' she admitted.

'Then go round it.' He hesitated a moment before adding in a voice full of meaning, 'You're good at that.'

'Sometimes it's wiser to work around a problem.' Wiser or easier, she wondered. Easier at the time, maybe, but in the long run?

He grunted. 'I told Dad that he should be doing it with you.'

'To which he no doubt responded that he will, if I'm prepared to wait until he retires.' She laughed to keep it light-hearted.

'I don't know why you put up with it.' Rob's voice almost disappeared into a grumble. 'Anyway, you'd have to do something really daft to get into trouble, and you're not daft.' His tone lifted again. 'Just take your time. I don't need to tell you what you were always telling us ... if in doubt, don't. You don't have to take the tough routes. And in early July there'll be lots of walkers about. That's another advantage to going the opposite way: you'll meet people who've been where you're going; they'll warn you about things to be avoided or looked out for, and where to go for a decent pint.'

'Robbie, you're wonderful.' His confidence boosted her courage and tipped her mental scales in favour of going for it.

His motives for not supporting his father might be questionable, but there was no way he'd be encouraging her if he thought there was a serious risk to her safety. 'I know that persuading your Dad to come is a lost cause, but can I ask you, please, to call Suzy and put her mind at rest?'

'It's a done deal. And Mum, if you want anything from my room, books, gear, help yourself. There's nothing in there I wouldn't want you to see. At least, I don't think so!'

'Bless you, darling. I'll call you when I'm on my way.'

'Good luck. Love you.'

*

Despite another long telephone conversation with their son, the raking out of maps and books from his room, and the acquisition of a few more, Jim still did not seem to believe that she would, in the end, leave him to go to Holland on his own. It became a bit of a joke, he even teased her about it, recalling incidents from their walking holidays when she'd needed to go for a pee, miles from the nearest convenience, in a vast open space with no tree cover, and the fuss she'd made about finding the right place, where nobody, not even somebody with binoculars on a distant mountain, would be able to see her drop her trousers and squat, and even when a crag, boulder or corner in a wall had been found, the family was posted on all compass points to keep an eye in every direction in case another hiker suddenly appeared within a mile.

'How do you suppose you'll manage on your own?' he asked, a sparkle of mischief glittering in his eyes.

Pelvic floor exercises had ensured that her bladder control was a great deal better than it had been following the births of her children, so she felt fairly confident that she wouldn't have a problem. 'I know you think I'm a wimp, but you don't think fear of getting caught short is going to put me off, do you?'

Unconvinced, he flicked his brows.

The matter came to a head two days before they were due to leave in their different directions. He came home from work to find her in their son's room with a large rucksack surrounded by the paraphernalia that she would be taking with her. In neat piles on the single bed were t-shirts, knickers, socks and bras, sufficient for a week. At the halfway mark she intended to visit a launderette. There was also a zip-fronted fleece jacket, a lightweight but guaranteed breathable and waterproof jacket and over-trousers, a second pair of cotton trousers, wash-bag with basic necessities, a loo roll and packet of wet-wipes, maps and pocket-sized guide book, compass, first aid kit, survival bag, camera, notebook, pencil (with rubber) and, to entertain herself on evenings alone, a paperback book of cryptic crosswords. She had already packed them all into the rucksack and knew they would fit with just space enough for a day's provisions and water bottle, and that, despite its considerable size, once on her back the pack was comfortable. She had even hiked it, fully packed, for a twenty-mile stretch of the North Downs Way, just to be sure.

'Okay,' he said, leaning against the frame of the door, still in his white business shirt and dark grey trousers, but tie loosened and jacket hooked over his shoulder by its loop on his forefinger. 'The joke's gone far enough.'

'It's no joke.' She went to kiss him. He returned the peck as a matter of course. 'If you want to change your mind about joining me, it's not too late.'

'I was hoping that you would change your mind about joining me,' he said levelly.

'Hoping, or expecting?' She had no such expectation, just hope.

'All right,' he said crossly, slinging his jacket on top of the things on the bed. 'You've made your point. I made a mistake in making the arrangement without telling you first ... '

'Your mistake, Jim, was ignoring my specifically stated wishes and taking it for granted that I'd go along with you whether I like it or not, and then, when I objected, doing your damndest to manipulate me, even to the point of using our friends and children.'

His eyes met hers and held them for a moment, then he dropped his head and nodded. 'For which I apologise, unreservedly. I was wrong.'

'Apology accepted. And thank you.'

'So you'll abandon all this.' He swept his arm to indicate the gear piled on the bed.

'No.'

He dropped his head wearily against the door jamb and sighed. 'Lindy, I know you: you don't want to do this. Not really.' Lines of concern creased his forehead.

He was half right. She didn't want to do it on her own. She wanted him to want to come with her. She wanted him to want to be gallant and escort her. She didn't want to ask him to do it; she wanted it to come from him because *he* wanted to do something for her.

'I've put my itinerary on the dresser. All typed up with intended routes and the places I shall be staying, telephone numbers, etcetera.' Ever hopeful that at the last minute he might change his mind to please her, all the rooms she had booked were doubles, and as much as possible, in the sort of places that he would find acceptable. 'I'll have my mobile.'

He said nothing, but the movement of his eyes and slight twitch of his mouth showed that a lot was going on in his head. She suspected he was controlling frustration, or even anger.

'And I've scheduled in a weekend break in Kirkby Stephen, that's just over halfway.' She stopped herself suggesting that even if he couldn't face the walk itself, he might like to join her there for the weekend. As a further hint, she added, 'I haven't booked accommodation for the second half. I can do that from the Kirkby Stephen tourist info office. I'll see how I get on.'

'You mean you have doubts about doing the difficult bit?' he asked, just a hint of triumph in his voice.

Her chest tightened as she met his challenging eyes and she could hear a wobble in her voice. 'I've never done anything like this ... entirely on my own. I won't know until I get there whether I'll want to go on. I'm not out to prove anything so there'd be no point in going on if I wasn't enjoying it.' There was a lot he could, and should, read into it. He held her gaze as if he was trying to understand her meaning but seemed unable to come back with a reply. Maybe, in that moment, she had just begun to get through to him what it was that she really wanted.

'Darling,' he appealed in a low voice. 'I know I can't forbid you, but I can ask you, beg you, please ... The kids are worried about you. I'm worried about you.'

'Then come with me,' she answered softly. In the small delay before he spoke again, she wondered whether he really was considering doing just that.

'I'll do a deal. You come with me on this trip, and we'll take a walking holiday sometime later in the year. I promise.'

She resisted the temptation to stamp her foot. 'I've already booked the time off work. I can't mess Jenny about.'

He flicked his arm impatiently. 'You can have as much time as you like. Jenny won't mind.'

'The fact that I work with a personal friend doesn't give me leave to treat her business as a hobby that I can pick up and put down as I please.'

'Oh, come on, Lindy, be real, that's all it is. What you make out of it is peanuts. It's not as though we need the money. It's just another hassle you can do without.'

'Correction. It's a hassle that *you* can do without.' Controlling her frustration was becoming difficult.

'Oh, for Pete's sake! What the hell's got into you? Why have you got to challenge me every time I open my mouth?'

'Maybe it's because every time you open your mouth you come out with something crass. I can't believe how selfish and insensitive you've become.'

'Me selfish and insensitive?' His voice rose in disbelief. The widening of his eyes left her in no doubt that in this instance he saw her as the guilty one. With a final incredulous shake of his head he snatched up his jacket and left the room.

She sank onto the bed and wondered whether, for the sake of marital harmony, it would be best if she were to accept his deal and go on his bloody trip. Nearly everybody she had spoken to thought she was mad: mad to contemplate such an arduous expedition on her own, and even madder to want to do it in preference to a sociable weekend in the company of her handsome and amusing husband.

Was she making a mountain of a molehill? She didn't think so. His dismissal of her work and loyalty to her friend just added insult to injury. Why, she wondered, did he deem it so difficult for him to withdraw from the purely social Dutch visit, but so easy for her casually leave her friend without someone to cook and serve in the café? Sometimes she wondered if he knew her at all. True, her income compared to his was peanuts, but she used those peanuts to buy personal things for herself and presents for the kids. To her it meant something that the presents she bought for him were bought with money that she earned. Her money. Huh! If he felt like that about her working four days a week in the café, what was he going to think if she bought it, as Jenny had suggested? It was a tempting proposition, on two fronts: one because she liked it, the other because he wouldn't.

Why she should make a stand now, after all the bigger issues she'd shirked in the past, she couldn't explain, not even to herself. What she did know was that he was right about one thing: she didn't really want to do the walk on her own. What she had wanted, and it had taken her a while to realise it, was for him to demonstrate that he cared about her by giving her just two weeks: two weeks doing what she wanted, and now, when she wanted it, not at some later date. Was that so much to ask? It would have been nice if he'd recognised what she wanted, but he hadn't. There was only one thing more she could do. She left her son's room and went to find him.

*

Having changed from his office clothes into cream chinos and polo shirt, he was pouring himself a drink in their sitting-room.

'Jim,' she said softly. 'If you care for me, please come with me. Even if we only do half the walk now, and complete it another year.'

'What do you mean, *if* I care for you? Surely that goes both ways.' He pointed to the antique sideboard which served as a drinks cupboard. 'Drink?'

She shook her head. 'I've always done what you want to do, to keep the peace and make you happy, but I don't see much coming the other way.'

'Only because you've changed your mind about what makes you happy.' He took his drink to the coffee table and sank into the squashy softness of the sofa, obviously tired.

'That's not true and you know it.' Struggling to hide her disappointment, she perched on the arm of the other sofa.

'Look, Lindy,' he adopted her tone of quiet appeal, 'I have to go to Holland. It's a commitment. I can't back out now.'

'Exactly why not? Do you really think that your absence will make such a huge difference to the group's enjoyment of the event? You've been telling all and sundry that your wife is having a mid-life crisis, well, maybe I am. Surely they'll understand if you pull out to be with me?'

He studied her for a moment then raised his gin and tonic slowly to his lips. 'I think that's called emotional blackmail.'

Coming from him that was rich, but seeing she wasn't going to win, she let it pass. What hurt was that he still couldn't see what it was she wanted from him, not even when she spelled it out. It never even occurred to him that perhaps he owed her that small bit of consideration. Defeated, she retreated to the kitchen to serve their dinner.

*

The mood of quiet stalemate persisted throughout the evening, and the following one as they went about their separate preparations. They went to bed, but were both so locked in their feelings of the other's unreasonableness that any attempt at affection, let alone intimacy, was out of the question. She slept badly and woke early feeling guilty for rocking their usually calm boat. When he joined her in the conservatory he was cool but polite throughout breakfast.

'So, that's it,' he said as he drained his second cup of coffee. 'You haven't changed your mind?'

A great lump stuck in her throat. She shook her head.

'And you're really going on that walk, on your own?'

'If you won't come with me, yes.'

He closed his eyes in a God-give-me-patience manner.

'I'll be okay. Rob isn't worried …'

His chair scraped the tiled floor as he stood. 'Well, if Rob's happy with your preparations, I suppose I have to be satisfied. He is, after all, the family expert when it comes to walking out on responsibilities. I suppose he had to be good at something!'

Instinctively she wanted to defend Rob, to tell him that he had only himself to blame for his son's rejection, but, as always, she side-stepped the issue. 'You'd better get a move on.' She gathered the breakfast things onto the tray, keen now to get this bit over with. His party were convening at Keith's house, from where they would travel to Stansted for their flight to Amsterdam. They would be in the air when she boarded her train in Faversham for her complicated journey to Whitby.

'It doesn't feel right,' he said, calmer now, coming to stand close to her, sliding his arms around her shoulders to pull her to him. She could have cried. 'Are you sure I can't persuade you?' He tilted her chin, looked intently into her eyes and kissed her more seductively than he had for a very long time. Squeezing her eyes to hold back her tears, she pulled away from him.

CHAPTER 3

W ITH SHALLOW RIPPLES OF LOW TIDE just washing onto the welt of her sturdy walking boots, Linda stood among the flat limestone rocks surveying the wide arc of Robin Hood's Bay. A cascade of red-tiled rooftops spilled from a cleft between steep, grass-topped ridges of buff coloured sandstone and grey clay cliffs. Behind her, somewhere to the south east, across the ribbed, pewter expanse of the North Sea, was Jim. She hoped that now amongst his chums he was feeling happier than he was when they parted. She sighed, knowing in her heart that apart from the residual sting left by the unaccustomed experience of being checkmated, he was probably hardly aware of her absence. After all, on those sort of jaunts didn't he usually leave her to entertain or be entertained by the other wives?

Behind her, also, was the first challenge of her walk: getting to the starting point. Nobody had volunteered to drive her nearly four hundred miles upcountry, which didn't surprise her, and she hadn't expected it. Suzy had taken her to Faversham station, and from there she'd taken the train to Victoria and humped her rucksack through the grim-faced crowds on the underground to Kings Cross. Too busy with their urban lives, nobody had batted an eyelid at the sight of a woman, obviously past youth, dressed in pale blue shirt and navy cotton trousers, toting a sizeable rucksack on her back, hiking in substantial walking boots through the pedestrian tunnels from station to station. She had boarded a train to York, changed to another for Middlesbrough, then another to Whitby, and after one of the best fish and chip suppers she'd ever had in her life, she had walked five miles to Robin Hood's Bay. In all it had taken just over nine hours and was the most complicated journey she had ever undertaken alone. Her admiration of her son, who had hiked solo half-way round the world and was intent on hiking his way back via the Eastern continents, went up a hundredfold.

Although for most of it she had been sat on her bottom, she had been exhausted by the time she arrived at the quaint bed and breakfast cottage that she had pre-booked. As with all the accommodation she had reserved, it had been picked in the hope that Jim would be with her, in the hope that it would remind them both of their early days, when they'd had little money and been happy just to be together.

This one, with its tiny rooms and faded chintzy decor, was heart-achingly similar to the one in Hastings where they had spent their honeymoon. Her tiredness, she decided, was not only because she'd been unable to relax during the journey for fear of falling asleep or the trains being delayed, either of which could cause her to miss her various connections, but also due to the emotional stress of the past few weeks. On that topic, once on the train to York, she had lectured herself on the futility of regret. She had made her stand, made her point, so now she must put all the aggravation behind her and enjoy the holiday. After text-messaging Jim, the children and Jenny, to let them know of her safe arrival, she had settled between the laundry-crisp cotton sheets, in the middle of the double bed, and been asleep within minutes. After eight uninterrupted hours, she had been woken by the seagulls yelling at each other from the rooftops and couldn't wait to get started.

The weather forecast was for sunshine and showers and as she stood with her back to the sea the latter looked more likely. The sky was uniformly grey, broken only by wisps of lower white clouds like stray puffs of smoke from an invisible steam train. Whatever, it mattered not; she was prepared for anything with waterproofs and sunhat packed at the top of her rucksack.

She bent to pick up a small grey flinty stone which she clutched tightly in her palm; it was her little piece of Yorkshire rock which she would carry all the way to St Bees. She checked her watch, it was eight-thirty in the morning, and with a slow, deep breath of moist, salty air she took the first symbolic step.

She was not entirely alone. There were joggers, and dog walkers throwing stones into the sea for their dogs to chase, and some people digging for worms in patches of sand, but she was the only person with a pack on her back, for which she was relieved, having feared that there might be scores of Coast to Coast walkers starting off at the same time, or that she might end up attached to a group not of her choosing. Perversely, having been apprehensive about doing the walk solo, she was now beginning to relish the idea.

She planned, initially, to stick pretty closely to the reversed Wainwright's route because he made it sound so marvellous and easy. The first leg would be nineteen miles, starting on a cliff-top path, branching inland across summer-flowering meadows, and then through lush green woodland, climbing to a small heather moor, then descending for a stroll alongside the river Esk to the village of Glaisdale where she was to spend the night. Along the way she expected to encounter pretty villages providing refreshment and the all-important comfort stops, waterfalls, and several sites of environmental, historical or archaeological interest. She would also experience the first few of many ascents and descents, good practice for the more arduous climbs that were to follow.

Excited to be on her way, she navigated around the sea-weedy rocks and rock pools to the heavy-going shingle of the upper beach and the cobbled slope that took her to the steep main street of the old fishing village. Too precipitous and narrow for vehicles, it was a pedestrian maze of tiny lanes and alleyways which smelled of fish and salt and brought to mind the bygone days when patch-eyed smugglers and scheming press men had lurked in dark doorways. By contrast, despite the weather, the present reality was quite cheerful with gift shops and cafés not yet opened, and flint and stone cottages, many with B&B signs, colourfully decorated with hanging baskets and window boxes. Young seagulls strutted on the rooftops, calling raucously to their parents returning from the shore. It was the first steep climb, an anthill compared with the hills and mountains to come, but exhilarating enough to make her heart beat faster and cheeks tingle.

The map directed her to the main road which was busy with traffic. People were going about their Saturday lives, travelling to work, to shops, taking kids to weekend pursuits, delivering goods, visiting clients. Every car and lorry contained a life or several lives, every one with its own joys, concerns, hopes, ambitions, frustrations, loves, heart-aches and tragedies. It was a levelling thought that compared to her own domestic difficulties, some would have far bigger problems to deal with. The thought brought a wry smile. That was a bit of her mother in her: it didn't matter how great one's pain, there was always somebody worse off to make one's own complaints seem trivial. It was, of course, true, but somehow her mother's dismissal of Linda's childhood wants and woes had led her to believe that her mother didn't really care, or understand. They had never connected. Rebellion, she supposed, had been inevitable. Not that she'd done it in a big way, nor with any deliberate intent to wound: it had been more about making a statement that she wasn't going to be the person they were trying to mould her into.

The biggest wound she had inflicted on her parents was insisting on being called Linda. She had been christened Grace, and hated it. She had hated the sniggers at school every lunchtime when the dining-hall full of children had been called upon to say grace. She hated the nickname, 'Amazing Grace'. She hated the implication that she was somehow more God-given than any other human being, but that was how her father saw her: an unexpected miracle. The miracle was that her other-worldly father's passion had ever risen sufficiently for her mother's sense of wifely duty to be called upon!

The name Linda came from a girl she had known in primary school, and, sinfully, envied. Linda Anderson was American, her father was in England on business. Linda Anderson had pretty, full-skirted dresses with flounced petticoats, white ankle socks and dainty white sandals that tapped on the stone corridor as she walked. Grace Ramsey had limp, jumble-sale frocks of war-time vintage, grey socks with not enough cling to stay up around her skinny legs, and sensible brown shoes with squeaky crepe soles. Linda Anderson's hair was fair, soft and wavy; Grace Ramsey's golden tresses were long, plaited and crossed over the top of her head like Gretel of Hansel and Gretel. Linda Anderson had returned to America at the end of primary school and letters had been exchanged for a few years but then Linda Anderson had found new friends and forgotten the old.

Grace Ramsey emerged from grammar school very aware that compared to her friends, even those in the same church youth club, she was a frump. Until she had money of her own, to buy her own clothes, there was nothing she could do about it beyond, when she was fourteen, in a fit of rebellious frustration, taking the kitchen scissors to her plaits. As punishment she'd had to live with the resulting mess for two weeks until her mother relented and allowed a friend's mother, who was a hairdresser, to tidy it into something resembling a short waving bob. Seeing her new image in the mirror, she decided she looked a bit like her old friend and began fantasising that she was Linda. When she left school, at sixteen, she started work as a shorthand typist in a builder's merchants' office and saved her earnings until she had enough to buy an old Singer sewing machine so that she could make her own clothes. They were mostly easy-to-make shift dresses, not too short, nor too tight, so as not to offend her parents, and even if the zips and seams were a bit wobbly and the hem stitches showed, at least they were new and reasonably fashionable.

Her real break came when her father transferred from his Sussex village parish, to south east Kent. As she was only seventeen, there was no question of her staying in Sussex on her own, even if she had wanted to, which she didn't. Moving to an area where she was unknown gave her the opportunity to present her new persona, introducing herself to all her new friends as Linda and refusing to respond to anybody, including her parents, if they called her Grace. Assuming it was a temporary teenage thing they had humoured her, but Linda she became and remained.

Strengthened by the memory, she turned onto a grassy track which narrowed to a path enclosed by hawthorns and led to a kissing gate. Here she paused. Kissing gates had been part of a family ritual. In her mind's eye she saw Jim going through first: a bronzed young father in short-sleeved, open-necked shirt and shorts, rucksack on his back, holding the gate closed until Fiona paid the toll, a kiss, then the pair of them kissing Rob to let him pass, the three of them kissing Suzy, the four of them kissing Dot on the white blaze on her head, and then all kissing her as she came through last. Jim's kiss had always held something special that recalled past intimacies and the promise of more to come. She smiled to herself, remembering how displays of parental pash always brought a chorus of amused distaste from the kids. They had been happy days, silly days, and she sighed regretfully at the passing of them.

Enjoying the memories, breathing deeply of the salty air, she strode on along the cliff path, climbing a little, until she could see Whitby harbour and the ruins of the Abbey. The sky was clearing as she turned inland to follow a well-worn track across flower-studded grassy pastures to a campsite. It was not yet fully occupied as the schools had a couple of weeks to go before breaking up for the holidays. More happy memories slipped through her mind.

The family walking holidays had been instigated by her. In those days, when Jim's feet were on the bottom rungs of the management ladder, funds had been short and camping, caravan, and later, holiday cottages, had been the only holidays they could afford. It had never occurred to her to book the family into even a small hotel, probably, she decided, because they had so much fun being just them, playing their silly games and being as noisy as they liked without fear of disturbing anybody else. Neither of them had come from moneyed families; Jim and his brother had camped with the Scouts and she with the Guides, so it was a natural progression.

She couldn't recall that there'd ever been a problem or discontent that had brought an end to that sort of holiday; it had simply been that Fiona, and then Rob had left school for university and chosen to travel and work abroad with their friends during their vacations, and with finances less stretched Jim, who had by then travelled overseas quite a lot with his work, had wanted to show her more of the world, and they'd taken Suzy to France and Italy. Then Suzy had decided to do her own thing and for the last five years they'd teamed up twice a year with his golfing friends and been to various European, American and South African golfing resorts. She had suggested Scotland for a change, where there were numerous golf courses and areas where she could have walked, but she had been outvoted because of the uncertain climate.

Her thoughts drifting easily, she hiked into an area of heather moor where the dense, closely knit plants obscured the path and required thigh-aching lifting of feet to avoid being tripped, but the effort didn't detract from her enjoyment of the magnificent views across miles of wild moorland and distant green and yellow pastures. The terrain, similar to the Devon moors that she'd tramped with the Church youth club, took her thoughts back to her young days.

University had not been an option for her. O-levels had been sufficient to get a girl a reasonable clerical job in those pre-computer days when there'd been such things as filing clerks and typing pools. The concept of career or job satisfaction didn't come into it: she had to have a job in order to pay for her keep until such time as she married. That was the way it was. Her parents, who made a virtue of being humble, had not encouraged her to aim high, but were content that her honest labours contributed toward the household. Much of that money, she later discovered, had been put into a savings account for her, and subsequently paid the bulk of the deposit on her first home when she married. When she had moved to Kent, she had deliberately looked for a job outside the immediate area of her father's parish in a conscious move to disassociate herself from their parochial lifestyle, which was how she came to be junior secretary in a bank in Canterbury, a ten-mile bus ride away.

City life, albeit a small city, was new to her and might have been daunting had she not started work at the same time as Carol Austin, a native of the area. Carol, one of the tellers, introduced her to ballroom dance classes. Carol's mother had said that girls who wanted to get on in life should know how to dance properly, and Carol wanted to get on. At least, she wanted to marry somebody with the earning potential to keep her in a life of luxury, about which she daily fantasised, but had not been born to. With insufficient time to get home for tea between work and dancing, they went to the coffee bar and supped frothy coffee whilst listening to popular music on the juke box.

At seventeen Linda wasn't entirely green: she had studied biology and had always been a keen reader, and, like others in her class, had secretly read books that would have appalled her parents. She had even struggled through *Lady Chatterley's Lover*, just for the naughtiness of it, but had to admit to finding the less literary *Angelique* books far more stimulating. Even so, her full understanding of sex and what could and couldn't make a girl pregnant had remained confused enough for her to be wary of getting too kissing-close to boys. Dark-haired, gypsy-eyed Carol, second eldest in a family of ten, knew it all and eagerly gave lessons in the art of flirting and snogging.

Carol's sisters, brothers and friends seemed always to know where there was a party or dance on a Saturday night, and within a year Linda had become one of their crowd. Her father had quietly disapproved of these friends he'd never met but left it to her mother to try to guide her back to what was expected of a vicar's daughter. Full-scale rows had never been the Ramsey scene but her mother had a way of making censure felt. It involved quite a bit of lip-pursing, disapproving frowns and deeply disappointed sighs when Linda declined invitations to assist with Church bazaars and Sunday school, and quietly spoken warnings to the effect that girls who dressed like tarts would be treated like tarts and bring shame to their families. It had some effect. By the standards of many of her friends, her hemline was demure at only a couple of inches above the knee, and she did avoid being separated from the crowd so as to prevent the risk of a boy thinking she was game to go all the way.

She and Carol had been good friends for two years when James Challoner started work at their branch. She would never forget that Monday morning ...

*

'Have you seen him?' Carol asked, her almost black eyes wide with wonder.

Her first thought was that Elvis Presley or one of the Beatles had walked into their branch. Carol was potty about all of them. 'Who?' she asked.

'The new bloke, upstairs.'

'How could I? I've only just arrived.'

'Good. Then I saw him first, so keep your hands off.'

Linda shrugged. She had boyfriends enough of her own without fighting with her friend for another. She went up the stairs to the office she shared with three other secretaries. Alison, Lesley and Anne were already there, and from the excited chatter she deduced that they were proposing to draw straws as to who would take dictation from the new Mr Challoner when he required it.

'Oh, for heaven's sake,' she said, 'count me out.'

'You obviously haven't seen him.' Alison held her powder compact close to her pasty face and pursed her lips together to seal the newly applied, pale pink lipstick.

'The epitome of tall, dark and handsome,' sighed Lesley, 'with a body just made for snuggling close to.' She curled her shoulders sensuously.

Anne sighed hopelessly. 'He's probably already got a girlfriend, or even married.'

'He's not married. Mr Crisp told me.' Alison, pleased as always to be the one in the know, went on to tell the others. 'He's come from the Faversham branch. Management material, Mr Crisp says. He's just passed his Institute exams with flying colours and will be taking over our stocks and securities department when Mr Morris moves on.'

'A bit young for that, isn't he?' Lesley's over-plucked brows raised.

Linda laughed. 'I suppose that depends when Mr Morris moves on. He's been in the post for decades and isn't due to retire for years yet.' She took the plastic cover off her typewriter and opened her drawer to take out her shorthand notebook. There were a few documents still to be typed that hadn't been done on Saturday morning but had not been deemed urgent enough to warrant overtime. Leaving the others to their conversation, she drew three foolscap pieces of paper from the packet and interleaved them with two sheets of carbon, knocked them together on her desk then inserted them into the platen. Closing her mind to what the others were saying, she started to type. Absorbed in her work, listening only for the ting of the bell on her typewriter, she wasn't aware that the others had fallen silent.

'Ladies ... ' Mr Crisp's voice behind her made her jump. She turned quickly and stared straight into the light brown eyes of a politely smiling stranger. 'I'm sorry if I startled you, Miss Ramsey,' Mr Crisp, the senior clerk, known behind his back as Mr Creeps, was standing beside the stranger. He put his hand on her shoulder and gave it a gentle squeeze creating a scuttling spider sensation down her spine. 'I want to introduce Mr Challoner to you all.' He went round the room indicating the girls sitting at the desks: 'Miss Smith, Miss Case, Miss Andrews and Miss Ramsey.'

Lesley smiled at the new man. 'Otherwise known as Lesley,' she bobbed a funny little curtsey, then pointed to the others, 'Anne, Alison and Linda.'

Mr Crisp beamed his sugar-coated smile. 'They are all handpicked for their charm and beauty but, amazingly, some of them can also take dictation and type.'

Mr Challoner's handsome tan went a little pink. 'Good morning. Forgive me if I don't immediately get your names right. It's a big branch.' He smiled apologetically, his eyes moving to each in turn as though mentally logging the name and face, settling finally on Linda's. 'So many people to meet all in one day.' His voice was calm, assured, deep. She could see why all the others were knocked out by him. He'd be about twenty-six: the body beneath the dark suit and crisp white shirt appeared to be in good shape and his pale tan, dark hair and light brown eyes glowed with oomph. Feeling a touch overawed, she flicked him a bit of a smile.

'Nice to meet you. I hope you'll be happy here.'

'Thank you.' He inclined his head slightly.

Remembering Carol's prior claim, and her workload, she dragged her eyes away. 'Excuse me. I have to get on.'

'Of course.'

She went back to her typing.

Much to the disappointment of all the girls in the bank, it transpired that James Challoner already had a leggy blonde girlfriend in Faversham. He was extremely polite to everybody, but as the months went by she noticed that he sometimes betrayed a touch of irritation at the obvious attempts some of the girls made to attract his attention. Sadly, Carol was one of them.

During their lunch break visit to their usual café, Linda tried to warn her that she was doing her cause no good by constantly creating pathetic reasons to be in his path.

'It's all right for you,' Carol swept her tongue over her froth-covered upper lip, 'you're upstairs and see him every day, several times a day. You even get to be alone with him, taking dictation,' she sighed enviously, as though she could think of nothing more heavenly to do.

'It's my job. I can't help it. But I can assure you there's nothing going on.'

Carol narrowed her eyes. 'He likes you, though. Lesley says he uses you far more than the others.'

'Probably because instead of gawping at him, I get on with the job.'

'Er-er, get you!'

'I do like him. Who wouldn't? He's dead dishy. He's also very good at his job. Very particular. He wants to get on.'

'Told you that, did he?'

'Yes.'

'So you do talk about things other than work, then.'

'Yes, I suppose we do, a bit.'

'What else has he told you?'

She lifted her shoulders as though it was inconsequential. 'I don't know … His father works on a fruit farm. That's where he lives. He has a brother who's married and plans to emigrate to Canada, and he plays cricket for his village on Sundays.'

'And I suppose you just happened to tell him all about yourself.'

'Not much. You know how it is. People ask if you've had a good weekend, you say yes, or no, and they ask what did you do, so I tell him I went to a dance with you and the gang, or went for a walk on the cliffs, or whatever, and he told me he went to the pictures and played cricket. Big deal.'

'Does he ever mention the girlfriend?'

'No.' It was true, he hadn't mentioned her and she hadn't asked.

Carol looked appealingly across the café table. 'Couldn't you put in a word for me? Couldn't you tell him that your friend fancies the pants off him?'

'Oh, Carol, how could I say that, or anything like it?'

'You could. For me, you could.'

She really didn't want to. She couldn't see how she could go about it, but for Carol she decided to bite the bullet and determined that next time she was called to his office to take dictation, she would mention it.

She was called in that same afternoon.

He smiled as she entered his small shelf-lined office packed with lever-arch files and box files. 'There's quite a lot, I'm afraid.' He was standing by the long, Georgian window, surrounded by afternoon light.

She shrugged but avoided looking him straight in the face. 'That's all right.'

He put his head slightly on one side. 'Are you all right? You seem ... uncomfortable.'

She felt her colour rise. 'I'm fine.' To hide her awkwardness with an illusion of efficiency, she quickly sat in the chair by the old leather-topped desk stacked with orderly piles of papers. He didn't pursue it but sat down, gathered his papers and started to dictate. It must have been her anxiety about what she was going to tell him, but several times she had to ask him to repeat what he'd said because she couldn't keep up. Normally she had no problem. When, after about an hour and a half, he came to the end of a letter, he said, 'I think that's enough for now. I could give the rest to one of the others.'

'It's all right. I'll get them done,' she said quickly, hating him to think she was incompetent.

'I wouldn't want to overburden you,' he answered kindly, his eyes slightly teasing, bringing fire again to her cheeks.

'I'm sorry if I'm not quite up to speed this afternoon … but … . actually, I have something to ask you … tell you … ' Her mouth felt dry.

One eyebrow lifted very slightly. 'Do you?'

'It's a bit difficult … embarrassing, actually … ' Her cheeks flamed.

'So I see.' His eyes flicked across hers, making her realise, all of a sudden, that she really didn't want to steer him in the direction of her best friend.

She gulped on her disloyalty. 'Actually, it's about my friend. Carol. She thinks she's in love with you.' She dropped her eyes as she forced the words out. 'I wondered if … perhaps … you'd ask her out or something. To put her out of her misery.'

'Ah,' he said, sounding disappointed and sitting back in his chair. 'That's awkward.'

'I know. I told her you already have a girlfriend.'

He ran his finger around the collar of his shirt. 'Actually, I don't have a girlfriend, not any more. The thing is, I was going to ask you if you'd like to come to the pictures with me on Saturday. We could perhaps have a coffee or something first.'

She stared at him. 'She'll kill me!'

'I doubt it.' He smiled his devastating smile. 'But I doubt you'll still be her best friend when you tell her.'

She shook her head. 'Thanks for the invite, but I couldn't do it. We have an arrangement ... She saw you first.'

'If the boot were on the other foot, do you think she'd turn me down?' His brows raised with complete confidence of the answer.

She got up. 'But the boot isn't. She's the one that fancies you.'

'And you don't?' The surprise in his tone unnerved her.

'It ... it's not that I don't ... ' she flustered, uncertain exactly how she felt. Up to now she'd always thought the others were rather stupid because he was so obviously out of their league, and hers, but now that he had declared his interest in her, she realised that her feelings weren't as ambivalent as she'd pretended.

Still sitting at the other side of the desk, he looked at her with a small apologetic smile. 'I'm not interested in Carol. Never was, never could be.'

'I know, but she's my friend. I wouldn't want to upset her.'

He grimaced and flicked his dark brows. 'Trust me to pick the one girl in the bank that isn't interested.'

'It's not that I'm not ... ' she felt her cheeks go warm again and quickly gathered her pad and pencil. 'I must get on.'

She didn't tell Carol.

That evening, after her tea with her parents, she set out for a walk on the cliffs, as she often did if she hadn't got a date or anywhere else to go. It was better than sitting at home listening to the ticking clock and the occasional flutter of a turning page as her parents sat in their chairs with their edifying books. They didn't have television and the radio was only turned on twice daily for the news and weather forecast and morning service. Conversation with her parents was difficult: they talked of people in the parish that she didn't know, or want to know, or of books she had no intention of reading. After a year of trying they had given up suggesting that instead of frivolous parties and dances she might make more valuable use of her spare time assisting with the youth fellowship or Sunday school.

She closed the door of the Victorian vicarage and walked down the path between overgrown laurel bushes to the wrought iron gate that squeaked as she opened it. Preoccupied with her thoughts, she turned automatically to the left alongside the high yew hedge, heading toward the sea, then nearly jumped out her skin when she rounded the corner and collided with a young man in jeans and big black sweater. As it was so unexpected, it took a second or two before she realised who he was.

'Hey! That was lucky,' James grinned. 'Two minutes later and I'd have missed you!'

She was too stunned to speak.

'You said your Dad was the vicar. I didn't need a degree to work out you must live at the vicarage.'

'But ... I said ... '

'I know, but I think we need to talk more about it. Away from the bank. I want to tell you why it is that I particularly like you. I want to get to know you better, and maybe, when you know a bit more about me, maybe you'll change your mind.' His smile ensured that there was no maybe about it.

On that first walk on the cliffs above Whit Bay, he had taken her hand and squeezed it in a way that made her legs go wobbly. Nearly thirty years later she couldn't recall the content of the conversation, or even if he did tell her what it was about her that attracted him. Much later she would realise that it was simply that he had a penchant for slender blondes. She would, however, never forget the magic of the night she had fallen in love with James Challoner.

When they came to a cliff-top bench he had suggested they sit to watch the setting sun. It had shimmered in a sky of copper and rose onto the glistening sea. He had put his arm across her shoulders and pressed his face into her hair which was, at that time, silkily framing her face in the style of Sandie Shaw. As the sky darkened and the lights of the ships in the channel had started to twinkle on the horizon, he had pulled her close, turned her face to his and softly kissed her lips. Every word she'd ever read about the electrifying effect of a lover's kiss couldn't describe the sensation as that long, soft kiss warmed and stirred every erogenous part of her body. Every girl in the bank had dreamed of this; she had always accepted he was out of her reach, but here she was, with his strong arms around her and his warm lips on hers, her breasts tingling in anticipation of his touch, her lower regions sinfully damp and pulsing.

After that, they met regularly for evening cliff-top walks followed by drinks in a pub, which was very grown up. On Saturdays they went to the pictures or theatre in Canterbury and on Sundays, after she had dutifully attended church with her mother and listened to her father's interminable sermons, she would take the train to Faversham, where Jim picked her up and took her to his parents' house for a Sunday roast lunch before she watched him play cricket. She didn't understand the game, and even when it was explained she found it rather boring, but if he was bowling, or in to bat, or at the receiving end of a catch, then it became exciting. He was, of course, the team's star all-rounder and looked doubly delicious in cricket whites.

Inevitably, it didn't take long for Carol to work out why it was that Linda was no longer interested in Saturday night parties and dances with the old crowd. Feeling betrayed, she left the bank and Linda never saw her again. Her social life took a different turn. The functions she attended were more formal and revolved around his cricket club, the village in which he had grown up and the Round Table which brought her new friends and regular invitations to dinner parties.

• Most parents would have been delighted at their daughter's association with an up-and-coming young man, but hers were stiff with him and wary. They'd never been too happy about her job in the bank, probably because it smacked of capitalism, and James was obviously aiming high. His mother, on the other hand, was delighted. Linda was the daughter she hadn't had and Nancy Challoner was much easier to relate to than her own mother. From the very beginning they got on well. Nan, as she preferred to be known, was happy to have Linda in her kitchen, showing her how to cook the sort of things that Jim liked, and Linda was eager to learn and to please.

Being in the first throes of youthful love, it was difficult to remain professional at work. In the uncertain privacy of his shared office, if there was nobody else about, they did indulge in the occasional snogging session, but anything more than that was reserved for his VW Beetle or the bench on the cliffs. Even then it was only intimate petting, sometimes serious, deliriously delicious, heavy petting which left them both tingling with satisfaction, but 'all the way' was too big a risk for her.

Two years after his arrival at the bank in Canterbury, impatient with lack of promotion opportunity, Jim applied for a more varied job with an investment management company in London. Moving from the safety of a big bank was a risk that she and his parents were doubtful about, but she was even more afraid that his working in London might herald the end of their relationship: she feared he'd meet new, more worldly-wise girls, but, when he was offered the job, he surprised her by going down on his knee and asking her to marry him.

By then she was twenty-one and free to accept without reference to her parents, but still took their advice and waited another year before she married, to be sure, and to save some money for their first house, a three-bedroom end of terrace cottage in the village adjacent to Melling Leas. By then Jim was nearly twenty-nine and had been promoted to stocks and securities manager. Their social life changed again and she was expected to attend company and client functions in London. Within a few years Fiona, Rob and Suzy were born and she became involved with pre-school groups, then schools and all the diverse sporting and social activities that the three kids took up. Looking back, she was amazed at the energy she'd had. They had both been busy, busy, busy all day but still looked forward to the time every evening when the ten o'clock news finished and they'd lock the doors, check the children were all comfortable, switch off the lights, and relax in each others arms.

She had thought that everything was perfect, well, perhaps not totally perfect, like every couple they had their disagreements, but she had felt secure in the belief that they were working, if in separate corners, for their common good. She saw now that she had always lived for the present, coping with present problems, her sights set no further than launching the children into careers or loving relationships. She had never considered what the common good would be once the children had left home. She wondered now if part of her problem was that she had lost all focus for her life. Jim had spoken vaguely of retirement, and then in terms of time to play more golf or see more of the world, but he was in no hurry for it, his sights still firmly set on chairmanship of the company. But where did that leave her?

Her thought process had been fragmented over the miles, frequently interrupted by references to her map, the occasional exchange of greetings with other walkers, and long pauses to admire the beauty of the landscape as she picked her way from the heather moors, sauntered through flowering pastures and verdant woods, stopping now and then to identify unfamiliar wild flowers. She was still in the woods, three miles from her destination and with plenty of time to spare, when from behind her came the familiar scuffle of running paws, panting and a jingling collar. Instinctively, she turned.

CHAPTER 4

THE BROWN AND WHITE DOG galloped towards her, its delighted face dispelling any concern that she was about to be pounced upon. It had a white tip to its wagging tail, a white chest and white blaze between its eyes that reminded her of Dottie. It was a border collie in build but its chestnut and cream rather than black and tan colouring was unusual. It circled around her, stopping for a moment and lifting its white-socked front feet as though tempted to jump up but knowing it shouldn't, in just the same way that Dot used to. It was uncanny. He was a young dog: she could tell by the leanness of his build, his eagerness and agility and the brightness of his unusual golden eyes. He barked an excited 'woof' then shot off again, retracing his steps to the bend in the path where he paused, woofed again, as though to tell somebody out of view that he'd found something interesting and they should hurry up before it disappeared.

It reminded her of the days when the family had been out walking and she and Suzy had fallen behind the others and Dot had run back and forth between those in front and those lagging behind, doing her best to keep the party together. From the edge of a coppiced little clearing in the woods, with the sun shining through the trees onto a patch of brilliant green grass spotted with buttercups and daisies, she looked back up the path but there was nobody in sight. The dog charged back to her and danced in front of her, successfully preventing her from walking on.

'I think you've mistaken me for somebody else,' she said to him, laughing and bending to offer her hand in friendship. He nuzzled rather than sniffed her hand and his tail went round in a circle. 'Are you with somebody, then?' she asked. Silly question, and not one a dog could answer, but he bounced around in front of her, making it obvious that he wasn't at all concerned about anything. He didn't recoil when she bent to stroke his head. She didn't get the feeling that he was lost or alone and his chestnut coat was gleaming and silky, so he was obviously an animal that was well cared for. She ran her hand down his head to his leather collar and tracked it down to the silver identity disk but she couldn't read it without her reading glasses. She was about to fish them out of her pocket when a man's voice called.

'Jack? Jack? Come 'ere, yer daft bugger!'

She looked back along the track. A man had rounded the bend. He was alone, average height, sturdy build, grey-haired, trim-bearded and pleasant-faced, with a heavy rucksack complete with bedroll on his back. Jack left her and ran toward the man, his tail circling rather than wagging.

The man put his hand down to the dog and rubbed his ears. 'Good boy.' He looked up and called across the fifteen or so yards that separated them. 'I hope he wasn't troubling you.'

'Not at all,' she called back, waiting for him to catch up.

'He's very friendly,' the man said as he drew nearer.

'So I see.' She smiled to allay any fear that she was annoyed or distressed. 'He's a lovely dog. Is he a border collie crossed with something?'

The man smiled. 'I suppose there might be something in his ancestry that's not kosher, but both his parents are working collies. Every now and then my brother's bitch throws out a brown 'un.'

The dog circled happily around them.

'Sit!' the man commanded. The dog sat, his tail swishing the gravel on the stony path, his eyes on his master waiting for the next command. The man shook his head as though exasperated. 'He's enough to make you giddy. He's got a lot to learn.'

'But he's keen,' she smiled, 'you can tell that. He wants to please you.'

'Aye,' the man smiled, 'he does that.'

'Do you think he'll let me get on now?' she asked.

The man grinned. 'Aye. If you want to get on I'll hold him back, but as we're heading in the same direction ... ' he left the statement hanging.

'By all means,' she responded. 'You're obviously on a long trek. Where are you headed?'

'I'm doing the Coast to Coast,' he answered.

'So am I.' She smiled and nodded toward his pack. 'But I'm travelling lighter. You're camping?'

'Some and some. I camp for a couple of days then treat myself to the luxury of a hostelry, a bath, a comfortable bed, a few beers and real food.'

They fell into step. The dog stayed in front of them, weaving back and forth across the path, investigating the smells left by previous canine travellers on the bases of the trees, only now and then looking back to ensure that his master was still within earshot.

'How far are you travelling today?' he asked.

'I'm stopping at Glaisdale. The Arncliffe Arms.' She'd chosen the pub rather than several farmhouses suggested in the guide book because it was the one most likely to appeal to Jim.

'I'm planning to camp at a farm t'other side of Glaisdale. Do you mind walking with me or shall I hang back and let you get on?'

'No, I don't mind.' It was only another three miles or so and he seemed a pleasant enough chap.

For a while they didn't speak again. It was rather an odd situation, walking with a stranger. A couple appeared on the path, walking toward them. They all nodded and agreed it was a nice day as they passed. It occurred to her that they probably thought she and the man were, as they said in modern parlance, an item.

'How are you feeling, after your first day?' the man asked, as though he felt they ought to be talking about something.

'Incredibly well. Nothing aches. My feet feel fine. Mind you, I did put in a lot of training before I left home.'

'Where's that?' he asked.

She told him she lived in Kent, in a village, but didn't go into any personal details about husband and family and diverted further questions with one of her own.

'I gather from your accent that you're from the north?'

'Aye. I live not far from Shap.'

Although she'd never been there, she knew where Shap was because it was on her route, on the edge of the Lake District National Park. 'You'll be passing your doorstep then, or are you doing the walk in two halves?'

'I'll probably go the whole way. I've done the St Bee's to Shap, and Shap to Robin Hood's Bay in two different sessions before, but I've never done it East to West, nor in one lump.'

'You walk a lot then.'

He smiled. 'Aye. It's what I do. I'm a sort of professional guide. People hire me to take them on sight-seeing tours or walking trips. Mostly around the Lake District.'

'What a wonderful way to make a living!'

'Yes and no. It depends on the client, and the weather. You'd be amazed how often I'm stood down at the last minute.'

'So this is a busman's holiday, is it?'

'Sort of. I'm researching the possibility of guiding or servicing East to West walkers. There's companies that do it t'other way about, the Wainwright way, but nobody doing it in reverse.'

'Is this the way you prefer?'

'I don't know yet, but it seems logical to me that doing the relatively easy bit first gets you walked in, so to speak.'

'I get the feeling from Wainwright's books that he was a bit of a challenge-freak. He never seemed to see things as difficult.'

'For him, they weren't, I suppose. He was a seasoned walker and possibly out of touch with the average townie. I wouldn't knock his books, though. He had a wonderful feel for the landscape and was, I think, very much part of it. More in touch with it than with people.' His smile was very slightly lop-sided. 'I think it's ironic that someone so in love with solitude did so much to introduce people to the land he loved.'

'A bit like Wordsworth,' she commented.

'Aye,' he agreed and smiled again.

They walked on in silence for quite a while, their combined pace, whilst slower than when she had been walking alone, was still a comfortable stride rather than a stroll. She found herself wondering about him. Was he married? Did he have children? Was his family at all interested in his wanderings? There was no reason why she shouldn't ask these questions but somehow it didn't seem right. It would have been all right at a cocktail party or if they'd been introduced by mutual friends, but somehow, to show such interest in a total stranger, casually met on a woodland path, it seemed ... well, just not right. She'd put him down as being a few years older than her, nearer sixty. His hair was mostly grey with streaks of dark, his complexion above the trimmed grey beard reflected his outdoor life in that it was lined and weather tanned. There were deep, squinting lines beside his eyes, which were a somewhat serious nondescript grey. He wasn't good-looking in the way Jim was, nor was there any feature that was especially unattractive. He was, she thought, basically a plain man, or maybe comfortable was a better word for him.

After half an hour or so of intermittent chit-chat about the trees and flowers that appeared by the way, and the occasional 'mind your step' as they passed across over-used stone slabs, which, the man explained, had been laid as part of a pack horse route, and patches where the previous week's rain still lay in deceptively deep puddles, the path veered around a bend and dropped quite steeply to the river that had periodically gurgled or rushed on their left, sometimes hidden from view, sometimes sparkling in the sun that dappled through the trees. The track took them over the river on a steeply arched, stone footbridge. As she always did on bridges over water, she stopped to look over the side, looking down at the water flowing deeply between the trees.

'A lot of water's flowed under this bridge since it was built in 1619,' he said, leaning beside her.

'Beggar's Bridge,' she nodded. 'I read about it. It was built by some poor lad who wasn't deemed worthy enough to marry the girl he loved, so he left home to seek his fortune, but on the night of his departure the river was too high for him to say goodbye to his sweetheart. He pledged he'd build the bridge on his return.' She smiled. 'It's good to know he did return, but what I want to know, and none of the bits I read said, is did he get the girl in the end?'

'A search of parish records might tell you,' he suggested helpfully.

'I like happy endings. I don't think I'd want to know if this is a memorial to lost love.'

He chuckled.

Jack had taken himself over the bridge and slipped down the bank into the water. They watched him happily dog-paddling in circles, frequently turning and looking up at his master.

The man sighed, 'Oh, all right,' and withdrew a ball from his pocket which he then threw a little way upstream. Delighted, the dog turned in the water and paddled furiously, his nose homing in on the ball his tail going like a rudder behind him. He grabbed the ball and headed for the nearest negotiable bit of bank, dragged himself out, up the bank and streaked up the track toward the bridge with water streaming from his long coat.

'Stay!' the man commanded and Jack skidded to a halt just a few feet from them. The man was smiling at the dog. 'I know you, you villain.' Jack appeared to be smiling, too, as well as he could with a yellow ball clamped firmly between his jaws. Linda knew exactly what this was all about and felt again the deep ache of loss. The man stepped forward toward Jack. 'Drop it,' he said. Jack dropped the ball which rolled away down onto the track. 'Fetch it here.' The man said. Happily, Jack did so, and when he returned, before the man had a chance to tell him to sit again, Jack shook himself, corkscrewing his body at high speed the way dogs do, wringing a shower of water all over his master.

'Yer booger!' the man laughed, shielding his face from the spray. Despite the ache in her chest, Linda laughed, too. It was so Dottie, so border collie.

The man picked up the ball and threw it again into the water. Jack streaked off to retrieve it. It was a game that Dottie never tired of.

They backtracked over the bridge and he led the way under a railway bridge to a junction of minor roads. Without consultation, both stopped to visually get their bearings. In silence, with the warm breeze just kissing her cheeks, her eyes were drawn to the valley on her left, where pastures sloped steeply down to a scattered village of grey-roofed terraces, interspersed by patches of green and clusters of trees. The air smelled clean with just a hint of wood-smoke and freshly mown hay. A tractor purred in a distant field, towing an implement which flipped the grass into neat lines. It was beautiful and peaceful. She felt at peace. Even Jack, damp now from his visit to the river, was content to sit and wait and draw breath in readiness for the next stage of his adventure.

'It's hard to believe that for a brief moment in history, this was a busy industrial town,' the man said, his voice deep and easy, his eyes slightly squinting against the sun as he looked at the landscape. 'In the mid-nineteenth century they found iron ore on these moors.' He indicated the surrounding terrain with an easy sweep of his hairy, sun-tanned arm. 'Victorians, being the entrepreneurs they were, rushed in with the money to sink shafts and build blast-furnaces. They built the cottages for the workers. There'd only been about six hundred farmers and quarrymen before, but the population rose to over two thousand. It's reckoned that the ore from here and nearby mines were what made Middlesbrough the major steel centre it was. For Glaisdale, though, it was a short-lived boom, over in about ten years.'

She'd read a little about the places she would be visiting, but it was nice to hear a more comprehensive history from somebody who obviously knew his stuff. 'I suppose you've learned all this for the edification of your clients?' She smiled up at him to show her appreciation.

He smiled back, a warm, relaxed smile. 'I'm not sure which came first, really. I've always been fascinated by industrial and social history, ever since school.' He shrugged comfortably. 'Doing what I do is combining two things I like: walking and re-visiting history. I think both put one's own life into context.'

Putting her life into the context of a much wider picture wasn't something she'd ever thought about: maybe, on this walk, away from all the people and things that usually occupied her mind, she'd have that opportunity. His statement aroused her curiosity about him. 'Have you always done this sort of thing?'

He shook his head. 'Believe it or not, I used to be in banking, in London.'

At that point she could have said, quite naturally, that her husband was also involved in the finance sector, but she didn't. She didn't want to talk about Jim. 'I can understand you liking this better,' she said, smiling again. 'I imagine that the compensations for having to be nice to people you don't like very much are far greater.' As soon as she'd said it, she found herself thinking: greater than what? What did Jim see as his compensation for putting up with the aggravations of his work? What was her reward for putting up with all that she did? The thought disturbed her previous feeling of peace.

'Aye, that's true,' he agreed. 'When you can breathe air like this and see miles of open space ... ' He didn't finish the sentence, underlining the fact that the negatives of his work, whatever they were, were not worth bringing to mind on such a perfect day. She wondered if he really was as content as he seemed. She wished she could find that same sense of being at peace with oneself and one's place in the scheme of things.

After another few minutes of restful silence, he slipped his thumb under the strap of his rucksack. 'Well, shall we press on, then?'

Jack was up like a flash, dancing around them, trying to anticipate which road they would take, his eyes bright, his tail wagging.

She felt a sudden tightening in her chest and blinked at the rising water in her eyes. 'Golly.' Her voice husked as the words forced through her throat, 'he does remind me so much of my dog when she was young.' She swallowed hard, feeling the need to excuse the sudden rush of emotion. 'She died a couple of months ago. She was fifteen. I had to ... '

Her companion put his hand out to hers and gave it a quick squeeze. 'If you feel the need, don't hold back on my account. I understand. They become good friends, don't they?'

She nodded and fished a tissue from her sleeve. 'Sorry about that.'

'Don't be. If you can't feel free to let the pressure off out here, where can you?'

She nodded again, blew her nose hard, wiped her eyes and determinedly put her tissue into her pocket. Jack pushed his damp brown nose onto her hand, making the tears rise again. 'They know, don't they, when you're upset. Dottie was always there, offering consolation when I felt frustrated or ...' She had been going to say sad, unloved, unappreciated, but stopped herself. It was too much information. She ruffled the dog's ears and bent to kiss him on the white flash between his honey-coloured eyebrows in the way she used to kiss Dot. More tears slipped down her cheek onto the dog who mopped them up with his tongue.

'What breed was she?' the man asked.

'Border collie, smaller than Jack, tri-colour, mostly black with tan and white. She was bought for the kids, but became very much mine.'

'They know which side their bread is buttered.'

She straightened, wiped her face again and took a deep calming breath. 'Right, having got that out of my system, let's proceed.'

Had she been on her own she would have consulted her map, but without thinking about it, she left it to him to lead the way. He seemed to know.

He turned into a narrow lane with hedges either side, a mix of hawthorn, ash and goodness knows what else. Perfect for nesting birds, she thought. Stinging nettles and sticky grass grew through the hedge, tall golden buttercups, scarlet poppies, white Michaelmas daisies and twining purple vetch added patches of colour.

'This is sandstone country,' the man said. 'It's said that the stone for Waterloo Bridge came from here.'

'Wouldn't you think they could find something cheaper closer to hand?' she asked.

'They had railways by then. The world had begun to get smaller.'

*

The Arncliffe Arms was unpretentious but clean and welcoming. Her room was warm and comfortable, simply furnished with modern light oak furniture and a standard double bed. The decor was a sort of terracotta pink. Linda liked it but couldn't be sure that it would have pleased Jim. Once upon a time it would, but his tastes had changed. Not for the first time, she felt a sort of guilt that the fault for their discord was not his for changing, but hers for having failed to adapt to their increased prosperity. She thought of the man she'd walked with and how at ease he seemed with himself, as did Jim, but her? No, she didn't feel right. She shook her shoulders to dispel the gloomy feeling that had crept like a cloud across her otherwise wonderful day. It wasn't the man's fault. On the contrary, she had enjoyed his company, but he had made her think a little more deeply about who she was. It was ironic, she thought, that they'd spent nearly two hours together but neither had introduced themselves. He was a passing stranger, one of many that Rob had said she would meet. Although both headed in the same direction, on parting they had made no plans to meet again or walk on together.

She checked her watch. It was just after five, a good time to call Jim. The group would probably have returned from their day's outing and be retiring to their rooms to prepare for cocktails at six. The ritual rarely varied. She dreaded to think what the hospitality would be like at Gerda van Hopstrop's house. Somehow she imagined it to be Spartan, all stainless steel and plastic, or leather so that nothing allergenic could be harboured. God knew what Jim would be offered to eat that was egg-free, wheat-free, fat-free, blood-free, etc., etc. Oh lucky Jim! She fished her mobile phone from her pocket and checked to see if he had answered the text she'd sent him before setting off. He hadn't. It seemed he was still miffed. She pressed the code for his mobile number. It rang a few times before he answered.

'Hi, Lindy!' he sounded really cheerful.

'Hi. You sound as though you've had a good day.'

'Marvellous. We've been on a tour of farms and factories, not as boring as it sounds, and the girls have, of course, been shopping.'

Linda stifled her yawn at the thought. 'And how are the van Hopstrops?'

He chuckled. 'Sadly poor Gerda has been struck down with some allergy or other and was unable to accommodate me. So, you see, all your evasive action was for nought!'

'No wonder you sound so cheerful!' She decided it was futile to try to explain, again, that Gerda van Hopstrop had very little to do with her refusal to accompany him.

'How's your day been?' he asked with just a hint of reluctance.

'Wonderful. I can't begin to tell you all the things I've seen. I've walked nineteen miles and didn't get lost once.'

'I still think you're mad. Did you meet up with anybody to do the walk with?'

'No. I didn't want to. I met a few going the other way, and exchanged pleasantries, and walked the last couple of miles with a chap and his dog. It's like Rob said it would be: meeting lots of people but essentially being on one's own.'

'Maybe we now know where Rob gets it from.' His comment was just audible over the crackle of a none too steady airwave. She wondered what 'it' he meant, but let it pass. She'd never been confrontational and over a mobile phone, when half of what was said would need to be repeated, was hardly the time to start.

'I'm going to have to go, Lindy. I'm in the garden with the others. As you've often observed, talking on the mobile to somebody else isn't polite in company.'

'Absolutely,' she agreed. 'Have a good time.'

'And you.'

'Bye, darling.'

'Bye.' Click. Gone.

She sent text messages to Suzy, Rob, Fiona and Jenny to let them know that she was safe and enjoying herself. She would have loved a nice long soak in a bath, but the en suite only had a shower. Jim would have approved, he never bathed, but for her showers were quick and clean, and a bath was pure relaxation. When the kids had been young, a bath had been her escape route: somewhere she could legitimately lock the door and be unavailable for an hour. She smiled. That had been the theory but in reality it hadn't stopped them shouting through the door with their complaints and requests.

After her shower she changed into clean undies, t-shirt and the reserve pair of trousers which she had decided to keep for evenings unless the day pair became too hopelessly wet and mucky for comfort, and after creaming her feet to keep them soft and blister-free she slipped them into lightweight loafers.

Going into a pub alone was still something she was uncomfortable with. In her youth, women who went into pubs unaccompanied by males were considered to be tarts. She supposed that even at fifty-one years old, a woman could still be a tart. Amused by the thought that she was not quite past her sell-by date, she went down the stairs into the warm bar. There were a few men grouped at the counter, locals judging by their broad Yorkshire accent, and several sitting in twos and fours on reproduction Windsor type chairs at dark oak square tables. Somebody was smoking a cigar, its pungent smell overriding the typical pub cocktail of beer, chips and cigarettes. The building was old with beamed ceiling and open fire, laid but not lit, candle wall lights on the bare stone walls.

She went to the bar and asked for a glass of red wine, and after selecting her supper from the menu chalked on the blackboard, took her drink to a vacant table by the window. She had brought her guide book down with her, more so that she would feel less conspicuously alone than for something to read, but she left it unopened on the table and picked up the *Daily Express* that somebody else had left on the neighbouring table. Looking up as she turned the page, she noted that another single lady had come into the bar. She was the tall woman who had checked in just before her and they been shown to their rooms together. She, too, had been kitted with full walking gear. They'd only nodded and smiled at the time. Catching her eye, the other woman smiled and headed toward her. Men's eyes swivelled over their beer glasses as she navigated between the tables and chairs, ogling her sleek dark hair, her pert little breasts cupped in lacy white bra, tauntingly visible beneath a fine lawn shirt, which was tied just short of her tiny waist and tight, flat belly and hipster linen trousers that clung to her long lean legs. She wasn't beautiful, and past the age of prettiness, but definitely striking.

'Hi, are you expecting company?' Her face was tanned, dark eyebrows plucked to a thin arc over thickly-mascaraed, long-lashed, brown eyes.

'No. Feel free.' She indicated the other chair at the table.

'I'm Jacquie. Jacquie Letts.' She stretched out a tanned hand with long fingers tipped with square-ended nails. It was a style of manicure Linda still found odd, but then, if she couldn't get past fifty and be a bit oldfashioned, what could she be?

'I'm Linda Challoner.' She took the hand for a brief, business-like shake.

'God! I hope dinner won't be long coming. I'm starving!' Jacquie looked as though she could do with a good feed: slim bordering on anorexic to Linda's mind, but obviously fit and healthy. Just watching her movement at the bar, the way she'd scanned the room and come across had suggested a woman full of confidence and nervous energy.

'There's nothing like fresh air and exercise for building up an appetite.' Linda smiled. 'Obviously, you're on a walking holiday. Are you doing the Coast to Coast?'

'Yes. You?' She took a good sip of her red wine.

'Yes. I started at Robin Hood's Bay this morning.'

'Really? Me too. What time did you leave?'

'Eight-thirty.'

'And you didn't get here until five?' Jacquie raised her brows into her feathered fringe. 'I must have overtaken you somewhere along the line. I didn't leave until ten. Nineteen miles in seven hours, that's less than three miles an hour. Not good enough. Mind you, I did stop for half an hour's break.'

Mmm, competitive, Linda thought. 'What's your hurry?'

'I'm not in a hurry. I've allowed myself two weeks. That's what the books reckon, isn't it? But fourteen days to do a hundred and seventy eight miles, that's just under thirteen miles a day. Anybody reasonably fit, and you wouldn't be doing the walk if you weren't, should be able to do at least three miles an hour, so in a six-hour day you should cover twenty miles. I reckon it should be possible to do the whole thing in ten days.'

'On the level, maybe, but this isn't a level walk. Far from it.'

'But for every uphill slog there's a downhill trot, so you should be able to keep up an average of something close to three miles an hour.'

Linda laughed. 'You might, but what's the point? Why make a race of it? Unless, of course, you're aiming to be in the *Guinness Book of Records*.'

Jacquie lifted her shoulders cheerfully. 'I don't know. One just does. There has to be a challenge, something that makes the effort worth it.'

Linda was tempted to ask why there had to be a challenge. She wasn't doing it because it *was* a challenge: her reasons for doing the walk were a personal issue. She wondered why just doing it, being there, enjoying it, wasn't enough. It was patently obvious that Jacquie liked to be one better, go one step further, faster than anybody else. She was a woman who felt she had something to prove. To whom, though? Somebody in particular, the world, or just herself? She smiled across the table at the younger woman, younger by a good fifteen years, she guessed. 'For me just doing the walk is challenge enough, however long it takes. I'm not even bothered if I don't complete it. I'm doing it simply because I enjoy walking. I'm hugely enjoying the environment and the opportunity to stand and stare, and to absorb,' she shrugged, not certain she could quantify what it was she wanted to absorb, 'everything and anything that comes my way.' It sounded a bit lame and she wasn't surprised that Jacquie just tilted her eyebrows in a vaguely 'if that's what you want' sort of way.

In unison, they both picked up their glasses and sipped at their wine for a while.

'So, where are you from?' Jacquie asked.

Linda gave a quick resumé that encompassed home, husband and nature of his employment and the three grown-up kids: enough to give information, but not to bore, and finishing with the fact that her husband was away on a Rotary trip as though it was quite normal for them to go their separate ways.

It wasn't exciting enough for Jacquie to ask questions, she immediately launched into her own potted history. 'I grew up in Suffolk where my life was as flat as the landscape. I wanted to go to uni but the parents wanted me to work in their greengrocery shop. There was a lot of pressure, fifth generation and all that. Just as well I didn't because it went down the chute when the supermarket opened. I got a job as an estate agent's clerk but quickly rose to negotiator. With a few years' experience under my belt, I moved to London and got a job there. I was good at it. I realised there was money to be made and I wasn't getting it, so, at the tender age of twenty-six, I set up on my own.' Her chin was high and her dark eyes glowing. 'Within ten years I'd expanded to four branches, all in London, and last year I branched into foreign property. You know, people from England buying old farms and derelict mansions in France and Spain.'

Crikey, thought Linda, no wonder she'd been unimpressed by her lack of achievement. 'You didn't mention husband or partner, or children?' She mentioned it just in case it had been a case of them being less important than her career.

'No kids, and nothing permanent relationwise, but that's not to say that I've led a nun's life.' Her full lips parted in a smile that left no doubt that she knew how to play. 'I work hard, but I play, too.' It occurred to Linda again, as it often did, how quickly things had changed from her day, how acceptable it had become for girls to play the field, sleep with blokes, live together, without any stain on their character. It had been going on in her youth, she knew, but it had still been frowned upon. Even her own daughters had embraced the trend in their different ways. She was about to ask Jacquie if she'd ever wanted children, when a waitress arrived at their table with two steaming plates.

'Veggie lasagne?' she asked.

'That's me,' Linda said, moving her glass to make way for the plate.

'Medium steak and salad,' the girl said as she put the other plate in front of Jacquie.

'I didn't have you down as a veggie.' Jacquie seemed surprised.

'I'm not, but I'm married to a born and bred carnivore, so a veggie meal now and then is a real treat.'

'He dictates what you eat, does he?'

'No,' Linda laughed and hoped she didn't sound defensive, 'but I cook what I know will please him. It's what wives do.'

For a while they concentrated on their meals, the only conversation being words of appreciation and Jacquie ordering two more glasses of wine from the waitress when she returned to ask if her steak was all right. Jacquie ate at speed and had finished before Linda was halfway through hers.

'I sometimes think it would be nice to have a child. It is, after all what being a woman is about, isn't it? I get the feeling that I haven't quite done the job unless I've reproduced.'

'A box to be ticked?' It had slipped out before Linda could stop it.

'Not exactly.' She didn't take offence and smiled. 'I think I'm experiencing the Bridget Jones dilemma. You know, aware that the body clock is ticking but not yet having found the right bloke to give me the child I want.'

Like picking one off a grocery shelf, Linda thought, and wondered again what the world was coming to. 'Are you intending that the father does any more than fertilise the egg?'

'I don't know. I'm still thinking about it. The only thing is, if I decide I do want a child, I'll have to do it soon.'

Linda finished her meal and decided that when she'd drunk her wine she would plead tiredness and retire early.

She had just tilted her glass for the last drop, when she saw the man she'd been walking with come into the bar. He scanned the room, saw her and waved.

'Your husband?' asked Jacquie.

'No, just a man I met this afternoon. He's doing the Coast to Coast, too.'

CHAPTER 5

LINDA WOKE EARLY THE FOLLOWING MORNING, which was surprising as she'd been tired after her all-day walk and it had been ten-thirty before she had eventually parted company with Jacquie and Nick. It was interesting to reflect on how the evening had progressed, primarily because Nick had not responded to Jacquie's assumption that he'd be bowled over by her charms. On realising that he was a professional guide, Jacquie had sidled up to him, expecting him to be impressed by her route planning and her determination to do it faster than the average. He wasn't. He pointed out to her that she'd miss historical, industrial and natural gems, not to mention the opportunity to meet people from very different walks of life to her own. It was, he said, a walk through life's rich pattern: history, geography, topography, geology, sociology, you name it, it was there to be observed and enjoyed.

Linda felt she'd scored one over the go-getting career girl and it felt good. She stretched and sat up. Nothing ached from the previous day's exertions. She felt fit and ready to go. Checking her mobile phone, there were text messages from Suzy, Rob and Jenny, all basically pleased to hear that Day One had gone well and wishing her well for the next. Typically, Fiona was too busy doing her own thing to find time to respond, and there was nothing from Jim. His schedule would be for a sociable morning in Holland, some sort of civic lunch, and then departure during the afternoon and home during evening. She wondered how he would feel returning to an empty house. Almost certainly one of their friends would offer him dinner, but eventually he would go home. There'd be no dog nor wife nor child to greet him. It would be a very rare occurrence for him. Her own feelings of guilt were quickly quashed by the memory of the many, many evenings she had spent entirely on her own while he had been occupied on business jollies, golf club or Rotary activities.

When saying goodnight to Jacquie and Nick, there'd been no plan to meet the following morning to walk together. She knew that Jacquie had booked at a hotel that would collect her from a lay-by on the Great Broughton road. Linda had enquired at the same hotel, thinking Jim would prefer it, but they'd been fully booked so she'd opted for a farmhouse offering bed and breakfast: it claimed to be only a couple of miles from an inn where evening meals were served and, by happy coincidence, Nick was planning to camp at the same farm so hopefully they would meet again.

The next stage of the walk was about seventeen miles to Clay Top Bank, or nineteen, depending on which guide book she looked at. According to Jacquie's calculations it could be done in just over six hours. Linda's reckoning was that it would take between seven and eight, possibly more with the planned stop at The Lion Inn on Blakey Moor. It would be a fairly arduous walk to start with, climbing onto the high North Yorkshire moors. One of the books she'd read painted a fairly gloomy view of walking in drenching mist, but the forecast was for a mostly sunny day so she expected to enjoy some fine long-distance views.

She packed her rucksack, double-checked her route and then went down for breakfast, hoping that she'd get away before Jacquie rose from her bed, but she'd only been in the dining-room for a few minutes when Jacquie appeared.

The table was laid for two, so Jacquie sat down without further invitation. 'Hi. I hoped I'd catch you before you left. I thought we might set off together.'

'By all means,' she replied, 'but I'm not in a hurry so I won't be offended if you decide I'm too slow and you want to press on.'

Jacquie smiled. 'After what Nick was saying last night, I'd feel I was missing out if I didn't stop now and then to study the environment.' She opened her guide book. 'Mind you, it doesn't seem that we'll see much today. Just miles and miles of moorland.'

'There are the moorland crosses,' Linda pointed out, 'and for a bit we'll be walking on an old railway line.'

'Ye-es,' Jacquie responded, indicating that she couldn't see anything interesting in lumps of stone roughly carved into crosses which had been standing since the early Christians had put them there in the seventh century; nor could she find anything to wonder at in a railway that had been laid to carry iron ore from the moorland mines. She seemed to have no idea what a challenge and achievement these things would have been for the people involved, no fascination in the lives and motivations of her ancestors.

'We'll see how we go,' Linda said charitably.

They set off at nine, striding at a good pace along the dale road which gradually climbed onto the route of an ancient highway. Bearing in mind Nick's comments about putting oneself into the context of history, Linda talked about the sort of people who would have traversed the track over the centuries: the monks on pilgrimages, the farmers, the quarrymen, all of whom led very simple lives.

'We think we're so clever in this day and age, with all our technology, but don't you sometimes wonder if all we've done is make life difficult for ourselves? In those days all that was important was to be sheltered, warm and fed. Today that should be so simple, but we want so much more.'

Jacquie had the grace to consider the statement before responding. 'I know what you mean, but can you imagine a life that simple, now? Could you do without an automatic washing machine and tumble drier? Could you manage with only a couple of outfits in your wardrobe?'

Her immediate thought was that her parents could, but, to be honest … 'Washing machine? No. Wardrobe? I feel sure there's a compromise. In fact, my younger daughter, Suzy, rather proves the point. She and her partner grow their own vegetables, all organic. They don't eat meat. They have a few chickens for eggs. They don't have television. They cook on an ancient Rayburn which keeps the chill off the whole house but their life isn't austere. They do a lot together for the children, make things, play with them.'

'But is that lifestyle dictated by limited income, or is it choice?'

'They're both intelligent, quite capable of getting the necessary qualifications to earn good money, but they choose not to. Phil works on a fruit farm, he's also very good with wood. With his pierced ears and eyebrows, he might not look like my first choice for a son-in-law, but I like him. I'd even go so far as to say I'm proud of him, and Suzy, for being the people they want to be.'

'Really?' Jacquie didn't sound convinced or even really interested. After quite a long pause she asked, 'Are you the person you want to be?'

She had to think about that for a while, then answered, quietly and honestly. 'Yes and no.' There was no time to qualify her uncertainty because Jacquie jumped in with her own interpretation.

'Unfulfilled. I know what you mean.' She didn't look at Linda but scanned the distant horizon as if the answer might lie somewhere out there.

Unfulfilled wasn't exactly the word Linda would have used to express how she felt, but Jacquie's comment aroused her curiosity. 'Is that how you feel? Despite all your business achievements?'

She, too, scanned the landscape which, high on the moors, was an apparently endless emptiness with only small variations in the colour of low-growing foliage. The unexciting flatness of it was rather how she saw her future. It was like she had climbed a long hard hill, which she had, only to find there was nothing rewarding at the top of it.

Jacquie sighed. 'I feel something's missing. I think it must be that I haven't done the natural thing. I haven't had a child.'

'You mentioned that last night.' Linda paused and continued carefully. 'I know I don't know you, but I don't really see you as a mother figure. From what you say, you enjoy your job, work long hours, go abroad a lot. Could you give all that up?' One day, she thought, in another ten years or so, she could be having this conversation with Fiona.

'Would I have to?'

'That begs the question: is your urge to have a child purely biological? It's probably stating the obvious, but babies grow up. However much you try to shape them, outside influences come into play and they form their own ideas, create their own problems. A child who feels in the way, or unloved, can become a much bigger problem than a frustrated biological urge.'

Jacquie's pace slowed then stopped. Linda also stopped, a few paces ahead and turned round, afraid that she'd been too blunt and caused offence. Fiona would certainly have accused her of interfering, but she wasn't, not really, because Jacquie had invited her opinion. She must have known it would be different from that of her similarly-aged circle of friends who would, no doubt, be sympathetic, and were possibly experiencing the same dilemma.

'You don't pull your punches, do you?' Jacquie said. 'You've as good as said that you think I'm too selfish to give a child a life.'

'That's not what I said. I said that I thought you'd have to make some adjustments to your current lifestyle.'

'I could name quite a few very successful women who have children.'

'I'm sure you could and I'm certainly not of the school that says a woman shouldn't have a career and a family. The thing is, though, are their children happy? If they are, look closely at how the mother juggles her career and family. Ask yourself if you can do it. If the children are difficult, try to identify why.'

Jacquie started to walk again, her eyes on the grassy track a few yards ahead. 'You know, none of my girlfriends would have said what you've said. I'm glad I met you.'

As she couldn't honestly return the compliment, Linda asked, 'Have you discussed this dilemma with your mother?'

'Good Lord, no! She wouldn't understand.'

'By understand, do you really mean that your mother would advise against it, and that's not what you want to hear?'

'I haven't really talked to my mother in years. She's never forgiven me for going my own way. She seems to think it's my fault their business went bust. The stress of it all caused Dad's heart attack, so his death is my fault, too.'

Linda thought that was very sad. 'Isn't she proud of what you've achieved?'

'You know, I don't think she is. She seems to see it as a criticism of her.'

'Has she said as much or is that your interpretation?'

Jacquie laughed. 'You know Linda, you missed your vocation. You should have been a shrink!'

'Perish the thought! It's just years of being a mother and dealing with problems.' Her children used to discuss their plans and problems with her, and still did to a degree. Whilst she might stop short of actually telling them what she thought they should do, she felt she was pretty good at finding ways to make them think about the pros and cons, so that they could reach their own conclusions. It had been easier when they were children and adolescent, but now that they were older and their life experience so different, she felt they were growing away from her. At least, Fiona and Rob were. She still had a good rapport with Suzy.

They walked on for quite a long time in thoughtful silence. Jacquie's pace was faster than Linda's, not dramatically, but just enough to make her aware that walking was more of an effort than it had been the day before. In many ways, Jacquie reminded her of Fiona and she could quite see that in another ten years or so, Fiona would still be single, her social life would still revolve around meeting her girlfriends in the gym, bistro and wine bars; her motivating force would still be her career. There would be boyfriends along the way, there always had been with Fiona, ever since she was fourteen, but they'd never interfered with her studies or career. It seemed that the men in her life were there only to add a touch of sexiness, as and when she felt the need. Having a boyfriend, going steady, planning a future with a bloke, didn't seem as important as it had been in her own youth.

She wondered if this is what Jim wanted for his daughter. Who had got it right: the girls who kept their independence, their careers, and even had babies without the added complication of being in love with and sharing it all with a man, or women like herself for whom husband, home and family had been the be-all and end-all? Given all that had happened and how she felt, was she really qualified to give advice to this young woman? Thinking about it, she felt that on the subject of motherhood, if not marriage, she was qualified. Children were a commitment for life. Even when they'd grown up and left home, even if they rarely made contact, the bond was still there, the feelings of angst when they had problems, the joys at their achievements didn't stop and would be there to the day she died. As far as her children were concerned, she had no regrets: she hadn't been presented with a career opportunity and didn't feel that she had missed out. She didn't envy Jacquie or Fiona the lives they led. Jacquie, it seemed, was already aware that there was something missing, but was it a child or possibly something deeper?

She broke their thoughtful silence. 'You talk of having a child, but haven't mentioned a special man in your life. I mean, from what you tell me of your social life, it seems to be all gym and girlfriends ... '

Jacquie laughed. 'I've lots of men friends, too. I have a good time. If I'm a bit sceptical about giving my all to one man it's because I know what they're like. They want to dominate your life but they'll be unfaithful at the drop of a hat. Believe me, I know. I've had a fling or two with married men. In fact, the only man I ever felt I could sacrifice all for was married. He talked about leaving his wife, but when the crunch came ... ' She shrugged and sighed as if to say, *c'est la vie*. 'Swearing he'd always love me, he disappeared into the sunset never to be seen again. I cried a lot. I really did love him. But I got over it.'

But did the wife, Linda wondered? Trying not to dwell on that hornet's nest, she surveyed the scenery around her. They had been steadily climbing and were now high on the moor surrounded by miles and miles of heathery moorland in mottled shades of bronze and green and ochre. From time to time the vista changed, reassuring her that there was life beyond the moors, as green dales, neatly partitioned into strips by straight stone walls, came into view far below. One of the dales had the unlikely name of Great Fryup Dale. She had no idea why. Had Jim and the kids been with her, they'd have amused themselves with landscape likenings to sausages, bacon, mushrooms, tomatoes and fried egg. If Nick had been with them, he'd have known the answer. She wondered if he and Jack were now miles ahead or somewhere not too far behind. She stopped and glanced back but there was nobody in sight.

Since leaving Glaisdale they hadn't passed a house or farm and wouldn't until they reached the isolated inn on Blakey moor. This wasn't the place to be wanting a pee. It was a sunny, summer Sunday and there were walkers of all shapes and sizes: dads with kids, couples with dogs, older folk and family parties. Whenever there was a lull she scouted round for a convenient spot but it would be just her luck that the minute she dropped her drawers, somebody would turn up. There was nothing for it but to press on and hope nothing happened to make her laugh until they reached the Lion Inn.

A determined breeze swished across the tops of the foliage and every now and then a lark would rise and twitter above them. There were occasional sightings of grouse, too, as they scuttled between the clumps, rarely taking to the air.

'I can't think why anybody would want to make a sport of shooting such harmless little creatures,' Linda commented, deliberately steering the conversation away from anything personal.

'Me neither.' It was said in a preoccupied way.

'The awful thing is, that to protect the game birds they're going to shoot for fun, they poison other birds of prey. Did you know that?'

'No. No, I didn't.' Jacquie didn't sound as though she much cared, either.

'It's another example of how illogical humans can be, isn't it?'

'Yeah, I suppose it is.'

Jacquie seemed disinclined to talk and the pace she was setting made it difficult for Linda to find enough puff for words, so she gamely pressed on. She decided that when they reached the Lion Inn she would suggest to Jacquie that she carry on alone. Although Jacquie had great ideas about how much ground could be covered, the logistics of overnight stopping places would dictate the number of miles she could walk in a day. They had already discovered that for much of the first half of the walk they were mostly booked into the same villages, if not the same inns and guest houses, so the chances were that they would meet again.

As it turned out, parting company was not a problem. When they arrived at the higgledy-piggledy collection of buildings that were the Lion Inn, a public house in the middle of nowhere and the highest building in the North Yorkshire Moors National Park, the car park was full and inside it was heaving. It was hardly surprising: it was such a lovely Sunday and the world and his wife were taking advantage of it, either walking, cycling or out for a drive. By the time Linda had paid her much needed call to the loo, Jacquie had become involved with three young men, Linda estimated mid-twenties, who invited them to walk with them.

Linda played the age card and said she needed to take a rest and travel more slowly and wasn't surprised that Jacquie showed not even the tiniest token concern for her travelling on solo. Nevertheless, after Jacquie had gone, leaving her alone with her half litre of mineral water and a salad-filled baguette, she couldn't help worrying if she'd done the right thing. She couldn't shake off the similarities between Jacquie and Fiona, so in a way, she felt like she'd just rejected her own daughter and worse, allowed her to go with three totally unknown men. Had it been Fiona she would have asked 'Do you think it's a good idea? You don't know anything about them.' Fiona would have raised her eyes skywards and sighed exaggeratedly, 'Oh Mother, really!' but at least her conscience would be easy because she'd issued the warning.

She stayed in the busy pub for at least an hour after Jacquie and her admiring trio had gone, not so much as to give them a head start, or because she needed the break to rest and digest her lunch, but because there was no reason to hurry. She had nine miles to walk along a high, undulating ridge, and no meal-time pressure to arrive at her destination, so why hurry? Her thoughts drifted back to Fiona and the last time she had seen her. It seemed a lot longer but it was actually only a week, exactly: the last Sunday in June, the day of the annual Melling Leas cricket match. It had always been a major event in the Challoner family calendar and Fiona had come home for the weekend to lend a hand ...

*

The Melling Leas charity cricket match was a fun affair: a team from the pub against a team from the horticultural society. In a pre-match event at the pub, players from the village cricket team traditionally put themselves up for auction with sponsors for each side bidding charitable donations for the best players. The sides were then topped up with volunteers from the village. Jim, once the star all-rounder for the village team, always played for the horticultural society because Linda was secretary and had been for so long she felt grafted into the post.

When they arrived, the village was in festive mood with the jubilee bunting out for another airing and a local jazz band taking its turn to entertain in the open-sided marquee. The marquee was a precaution because not every year were they blessed with such a perfect summer day. She would normally walk the mile from her home to Melling Leas, but on this occasion, because Jim didn't want to sap his energy before the match, she had taken her car to drop him off at the cricket hut, staying just a while to offer her few words of encouragement to the team.

Despite the exalted height to which he'd climbed, Jim was easy in the company of the men he'd grown up and attended the local primary school with, and they with him, all laughing comfortably at the anecdotes of the older generation who liked to bring him down to size by reminding him that he'd once been a scrumping little urchin with the arse out of his trousers. She found it strange that he still fitted in when his visits to the pub were rare, and it was many years since he'd had any regular involvement in the cricket club, school or any community organisations.

He belonged by proxy: his father still lived in Melling Leas; his youngest daughter lived there with her children and had begun the process of community involvement by doing her bit for the Mother and Toddler Group, and would no doubt progress through Playgroup to PTA at the school; and his wife not only worked in the village but was actively involved in its recreational and welfare activities. Like a good fifty percent of the villagers, she wasn't born and bred local, but she had been brought into it by her mother-in-law, who was third generation, and after nearly thirty years she felt she was carrying the Challoner baton for her generation.

Jim's dark-steel hair and golf-course tan still looked wonderful in cricket whites and she felt a little pang of regret that things weren't as warm as they seemed as she gave him a peck on the cheek and wished him luck, but there was too much to do to stand around feeling sad.

The cricket was played seriously, but the rest of the day was good old-fashioned village entertainment with home-spun side shows for the spectators: Aunt Sally, Toss the Wellie, Lucky Dip and other such games and competitions. As per tradition, the café provided tea for the players and spectators, which included nearly everybody from the village and a good many from outside, too. In the evening a barn dance would be held in the marquee, the pub would host a barbecue and the whole event close with a firework display.

With an hour to go before the start of the match, the road surrounding the green was already nose to tail with parked cars, the owners having arrived early to guarantee the shady places under the trees: a risky thing to do on the western edge as the pitch boundary line was the centre of the road. The road to the north of the green was closed to allow safe access across it from the school, the pub and the Rainbow café. The school was doing a brisk trade selling parking space on the playground, and the café, extended by another open marquee crammed with cloth-covered trestle tables, already had a queue at the two urns where Jenny's son, Leo, in scarecrow fancy dress, at least Linda assumed it was fancy dress, was on duty dispensing pots of tea.

'Ah, Mafeking is relieved!' Jenny, round red face glowing, wiped her hands down her apron then gave Linda and Fiona a hug. 'More hands the better. It's going to be a good turnout. I knew I should have bought in more ice cream!' Her vibrant orange hair was tied back in a ponytail with a huge, bright emerald ribbon that matched her loose-fitting tent of a dress. She was warm and wobbly and wonderful to be with, but there was no time to chatter and catch up with each other's news. They barely had time to say 'Hi' to Jenny's daughter, Lisa, who had been at school with Suzy, and was all frills and ribbons in what might have been a mini-skirted interpretation of Dorothy's costume, but she looked more likely to break into *Good Ship Lollipop* than *Over the Rainbow*, before they were all dashing back and forth to the marquee with trays of sandwiches, pastries and cakes.

By six o'clock they were sold out, which started the natural drift to the pub, and the clearing up could start in earnest. The café's dishwasher was too slow for such volume so it was down to the deep sink with Marigolds and Fairy Liquid to wash the hundreds of hired-in plates, cups, saucers and teaspoons. So that nobody spent too long with one repetitive movement, they had a ten-minute rota: one collecting, one washing, two drying, one stacking back into crates, then they would all move one step along the line

'This is something that I'll miss,' Jenny announced. 'Wherever I am this time next year, I'll think of you all and wish I was here.'

Fiona stopped mid-wipe. 'What's happening? Why won't you be here? You've always been here.'

Jenny looked to Linda with raised brows. 'You haven't mentioned it ... '

Linda shook her head.

'Mentioned what?' Fiona demanded to know.

'I'm moving on,' Jenny told Fiona. 'I've offered your mum first refusal but she's shilly-shallying and if she doesn't make up her mind soon, it's going on the market. I want to be on my way before the winter.'

'What does Dad think?' Fiona asked. It was interesting, and rather irritating, that Fiona had asked what Jim's feelings were before asking whether or not Linda was seriously considering the proposition.

'I haven't discussed it with him yet. I'm going to think about it while I'm away.'

'But you know bloody well what he'll say.' Jenny didn't pull her punches as she vigorously wiped and plonked plates down on the table behind her.

Linda swirled the water in the sink, looking for another pile of saucers beneath the suds. 'Yep. He'll look at the books and deduce it's not profitable enough to warrant the effort.'

'Which is how he'll avoid saying that he doesn't want you to have it because it'll inconvenience his plans.' Jenny said what Linda had thought.

'Jenny!' Fiona sounded shocked at such a blatant attack on her father.

Linda glanced at her daughter's unusually pale face. 'You know it's true, darling. And much as I admire your dad for getting where he has, and truly want him to succeed to chairmanship of the company, I can't say that I'm thrilled at the prospect of a life of small talk at cocktail parties and official functions, however grand the hotels. Sadly, it's beyond his comprehension that I could actually prefer talking to the people who come to The Rainbow. I like cooking and it probably sounds very pathetic and unworldly, but I like being part of the village.'

'And you're so damned good at it,' Jenny added. 'Do you know,' she turned back to Fiona, 'there are some people who only come in on the days that your mum is here, probably because she's the only one with the patience to listen to them burbling on. They might be boring as hell, manic depressives, opinionated or obnoxiously self-important, but however busy we are, your mum'll always stop and listen to them and offer them her tuppence-worth. She makes a difference to their lives.'

'Oooh, Jenny, what a lovely thing to say.' Fiona smiled and turned to Linda. 'She's right, though, you are kind, and you're never judgemental.' Her eyes flicked across her mother's, full of some added meaning that Linda couldn't interpret, but which added to her concern that all was not well with Fiona. She was too pale, but had insisted she was all right, putting her pallor down to the time of the month. 'As Jenny says, however horrid or bad somebody is, you'll always give them time.'

Linda flushed from the slimy inside of her rubber gloves to the damp roots of her hair. 'Come off it, you two, I'm no Mother Theresa!'

'You're the nearest Melling Leas has to it, that's for sure,' Jenny argued. 'Where would the Horticultural Society be without you organising their trips and finding speakers? Where would WI be if you were to give up as hon sec? Who would research new paths for the Walking Group? Who would organise the Over 70s' outing? Not to mention all the other organisers who pop in here to pick your brains.'

'Oh, for heaven's sake! You make me sound like one of Penelope Keith's busy-body characters, Margo in *The Good Life* or whoever she was in *To The Manor Born* ... '

'You're nothing like.' Fiona gave her a spontaneous hug.

'Thank you, darling. However, getting back to the subject. Tempted though I am to take over The Rainbow, I have to ask myself is it worth the fight I shall have to put up? Your father already whinges about the few days I do ... '

'Dad doesn't whinge ... '

'What is he doing about my going away, if he isn't whinging?'

'Manipulating,' Jenny said, crashing a plate down. 'All change.'

'Dad doesn't ... ' Fiona's protest was lost in the hustle of movement as Linda removed the rubber gloves, passed them to Leo who had been collecting, and took a dry tea towel from the pile on top of the dishwasher. Lisa abandoned packing the racks to her mother and skipped through the café to continue gathering from the marquee, although Linda couldn't imagine there could be much more outside as every table in the café seemed to be covered with precariously balanced trays. Leo, who was the same age as, and had been a good friend of Rob, had collected but not stacked very logically.

'Have you heard from Rob lately?' Leo asked once they were all settled into their new tasks.

'Not for a couple of weeks. He's on the move again. Last heard he was heading for New Zealand, South Island.' She sighed. 'My biggest fear is that he'll meet a girl out there and never come back.'

'Don't reckon there's much chance of that,' Leo said.

'Oh? What makes you think that?' Linda wasn't aware that there was much contact between them these days.

He tilted his head and grinned his charming grin. 'Loves his mum too much.'

Fiona spluttered. 'So why's he spent the last four years away from her with only the occasional phone call to let her know he's still alive?'

Leo returned his eyes to the sink and shrugged. 'I dunno.'

Linda was fairly certain that Rob hadn't confided his problem with anybody. It was more likely that Leo shared Jenny's interpretation and believed that Rob had cracked under the pressure to meet his father's expectations. It wasn't a problem Leo could identify with. Linda sometimes wondered what it had been like for Leo to grow up with a mother who could never find a good thing to say about men, but somehow he'd done so without any apparent emotional scars. He had drifted cheerfully through school without straining himself, coasted through university, gained a first class honours in geography and environmental studies and sailed safely into a job with some sort of environmental impact consultancy in Canterbury, which earned him enough to put his foot on the first rung of the property ladder. He was twenty-five and enjoying a bachelor life of sport, holidays and a succession of girlfriends.

Fiona leaned against the dishwasher alongside the draining board, absently wiping the same plate that had been in her hand for ages. 'Why are you thinking of leaving the Rainbow, Jenny?'

'Not just thinking, sweetheart, I'm going. I've made up my mind. I shall be fifty-five in January. I'm single and thanks to my dear departed parents, I have funds. Not a fortune, but enough. I'm gonna get myself a camper van and go on my travels.'

'Where?'

'Initially I'm going to do Great Britain. I know it probably sounds daft to a globe-trotting high-flier like you, but there are places I've never been to. I want to see all the different landscapes, I want to paint them. I want to see the cities and villages. I want to take off and go where the mood suits me. I want to be free.' The last was said with a wide spread of her arms.

Leo smiled lop-sidedly. Clearly he thought his mother was crackers.

Fiona put a highly-polished plate on the table for Jenny to pack. 'How much do you want for it? If Mum's not interested, I might be.'

'Fiona! Why on earth..? ' Linda was staggered that she should even think about it. 'Where will you get the money from?' One thing was certain: Jim would not support such a scheme!

'Depending on the trading figures, I might be able to raise it.' Fiona smiled a little too vengefully for comfort. 'There's a bank manager I know who owes me a favour.'

Jenny's laughter silenced Linda's horrified objection. 'I don't believe it! Suzy, yes, I could see her wanting to take it on and turn it into something veggie and organic, but you? You'd be bored to tears in weeks; the banker in you will be shitting bricks during the lean season.'

'No I wouldn't. I think it has potential.'

'What sort of potential?'

'I don't know, I haven't had time to think about it. But maybe a bistro and wine bar.'

Linda shuddered at the thought of the loss of the café to the community. 'Well, before you get carried away, just remember that *I* have first refusal and have not yet turned down the offer.'

'I'll give you until the end of August,' Jenny said. 'After that it's up for grabs to anybody who wants it. Right?'

Linda nodded then rounded on Fiona. 'And don't you dare discuss this with your father behind my back. I don't want the pair of you conniving while I'm away.'

Fiona stared back at her. 'What do you mean, conniving?'

'You know very well what I mean. He won't want me to have it.'

'I can't see that he'll be thrilled that the golden girl plans to give up a banking career for it, either.' Leo came back into the conversation.

Fiona lifted a shoulder and looked uncomfortable. 'I just think it would be nice to be my own boss, to be doing my own thing, the way I want to do it.'

Both Leo and Jenny glanced questioningly at Linda and then back to Fiona as though expecting further explanation, but Fiona picked up another couple of plates and dried them, her body language saying that the subject was closed. Linda couldn't dismiss it that easily. Fiona's interest wasn't as illogical as Jenny seemed to think. Stimulated by her own interest, all Linda's children were enthusiastic about food and cooking and Fiona had a wide experience of wining and dining. This wasn't the first time she'd fantasised about owning a restaurant, and Linda having stated that it wasn't a money-spinner, Fiona would see it as a challenge.

*

Linda wished now that she'd had the opportunity to talk more to Fiona about it, but the café kitchen in the presence of Leo and Jenny hadn't been the place and time, and then the evening had progressed with the usual barn dance, barbecue and fireworks and on the few occasions she'd seen Fiona, she had been either chatting with or dancing with Leo. It was reassuring that she appeared to be having a good time but her earlier comments were worrying: doubly so because in one minute her worries were maternal concern that all was not well in her daughter's world, and in the next she was seeing her daughter as a rival and wondering what the intense conversation with Leo was about. In a brief moment when they were alone together before Fiona left for London, early the following morning, Fiona did say that she was all right, there was nothing to worry about and most particularly she didn't want Linda to mention to Jim what she'd said. She had laughed and said that it had been a daft idea and he need never know she'd had a wobbly moment. Unusually, they had spoken twice that week on the phone, once when Linda called and was again told there was nothing to worry about, and the last on Thursday evening when Fiona had phoned to wish her luck on her walk.

But of course Linda did worry. She worried that Fiona had a problem she wasn't sharing, perhaps finding her new job tougher than she thought and not wanting to admit to her father that she wasn't up to it. She worried about the nature of the favour owed by the unnamed bank manager: was it personal or business or a messy combination of both? She worried that Fiona had done something that might jeopardise her career, or was about to throw it away, but she also worried that she might stick with it and turn out as cynical and calculating as Jacquie.

CHAPTER 6

REFRESHED AFTER HER LUNCH BREAK she set off at a casual pace beneath a heat-hazy sky, the sun warm and bright enough to necessitate the use of her sunhat to shield her eyes. Her back beneath the rucksack became damp, but the breeze was sufficient to keep things comfortable. The route along a dismantled railway was easy to follow. She walked on, her thoughts wandering all over the place, sometimes thinking about Jim who would now be on the return journey, and Fiona who had probably been for a run in the park before settling down to study for her next set of Institute exams. Suzy would be putting her little ones into the buggy for a stroll to the next village to see Phil's mother, Rob would be fast asleep in New Zealand and Jenny would be flying around her flat above the café with a duster and vacuum cleaner on her one day off in the week.

Her thoughts drifted back to Jacquie's having interpreted her uncertainty about being who she wanted to be as unfulfilled. She wasn't unfulfilled now, but she was very much afraid she would be if the café ceased to be. The café was something of a drop-in centre for the people of Melling Leas and surrounding villages, and being almost next door to the primary school, young mums popped in for sandwiches, cakes, pies or ice creams to keep the kids going until tea time. At Linda's suggestion they had put an area aside to display local arts, crafts and greeting cards, and they had started a charity library whereby people paid twenty pence to borrow a book, all of which attracted extra custom and provided a village amenity, even if it wasn't high profit. And that was her problem. She knew that it wasn't a viable proposition, not when stacked up against the six long days that went into keeping it open. She certainly didn't want to put that sort of time into it and hiring staff would make it even less profitable. And if it went on the open market nobody would take it on as it was. It might change along the lines she feared that Fiona had in mind, but more likely its value was in the property itself: it would sell as a house, idyllically located on a delightful village green with local school and only twenty minutes from main line station, blah, blah, blah. But what would the village be without it? What would she?

Still high on the heathery moors, she had reached a place where a well-trodden path crossed the old railway that she was walking. Although fairly certain that the crossing path was the Cleveland Way, she stopped to refer to her map. As if by magic, Jack appeared, all shiny brown nose, grinning chops and wagging tail. He woofed and danced around her as though he'd found the missing ewe from his flock. She was just as delighted to see him, for his own sake, and also because where he was, Nick was sure to follow. She looked back over the path she'd been walking and there he was, at least she assumed that the solitary figure in soft focus some distance behind her was him because without her glasses anything in the distance was a blur. To prove the point, Jack left her and went bounding over the tufty terrain toward him. She raised her hand and waved. He enthusiastically returned the wave. Jack did a circuit of his master then charged back toward her, his ears flat and long brown and white fur flowing in the slip-stream. It was so Dottie-like that it brought a lump to her throat. Despite the difficulty of bending with a heavy pack on her back, she stooped to fondle Jack's silky ears whilst she waited for Nick to reach her.

'I wasn't sure it was you,' he said, slightly puffed from increasing his pace to catch up with her. 'I thought you were walking with what's-her-name. I saw you set off together.'

'I was, but she sets a brisker pace,' she answered diplomatically.

'Doesn't she just!' He flicked his brows meaningfully. 'Did she go on alone?'

Linda chuckled. 'No, she latched on to a group of men.'

'Now, why aren't I surprised?' he tilted his head, stuck his thumbs into the strap of his pack and started to walk slowly. 'Do you mind if I latch onto you again?'

'Not at all.' She fell into step with his easy stride and Jack trotted on ahead of them, casually investigating the clumps of heather in search of interesting smells, hiding birds or stray sheep.

'I've met a few of her type in my life,' he said. 'Not only in my city days, but since I've been guiding. God knows why they employ a guide when they seem intent on telling me all there is to know. They like to be on top. Have you noticed that?'

'So why do they employ you?'

'I don't know. Maybe it's the ski-instructor or life-guard thing, they expect me to be some hunky young chap they can buy some fun with.' He chuckled as though visualising their disappointment on being met by a rather grizzled grey-haired man. 'Personally I think it's because basically they're not as sure of themselves as they pretend. Setting off on a jaunt like this seems like something to brag about to their friends and colleagues, but in reality they're afraid they'll make a fool of themselves by getting lost or having an accident. I bet they don't admit to their friends that they had a guide.'

'Do you get many like that?'

'Not a lot, but some.'

'Hardly enough, then, to make such a sweeping judgement.'

'Mmm. Maybe. But I saw them in the city, too.'

'Well, as far as Jacquie is concerned, she doesn't pretend to know it all. At least, she doesn't with me. In fact, now I think of it, I did all the map reading this morning, and she hasn't launched off on her own this afternoon, so I expect she'll just let the chaps lead the way. And she's not interested in showing off her knowledge or research ... '

'Just in showing off her expensive gear and all that's under it. And when she gets home she'll be boasting about her achievement and how she did it all on her own, which of course she won't have, because she'll latch onto people all along the way.'

'Maybe she'll learn a lot from the people she walks with. Not, perhaps the sort of historical and topographical things that interest you, but things about people and life.'

'Do you think she's interested in people beyond what they think of her?'

'It's only day two. She has a long way to go,' Linda said. 'And anyway, you can hardly base your opinion on one brief meeting: you have no idea what makes her tick, her background ... '

'You're right. I stand corrected. I just know that life's too short to waste time on people I instinctively dislike.'

'That, if I may say so, is a very narrow view.'

'I wouldn't have thought she was your type of person.'

'How would you know? Just because I'm a housewife doesn't mean that all I want to talk about is dusting and making marmalade.'

He chuckled. 'What I meant was, that you are a listener and a giver. An hour in your company told me that. An hour with Jacquie told me that she likes to do the talking, to be the centre of attention. Her opinions have to be aired and argued but she doesn't listen to anybody else's.'

God! thought Linda, he could be talking about my Fiona. 'Maybe so, but does rejecting her help her?'

'If you pinned her against a wall and told her face-on what you thought, do you think she'd listen? If I've learned anything in my fifty-seven years of existence, it's that there are some people who just do not listen.'

Linda couldn't answer that. She wondered if Jacquie had really listened during their morning's conversation, or had she just been looking for an older woman, a mother figure, to rubber-stamp what she'd already decided she was going to do. She found herself smiling as she projected her thoughts to what might be going on a few miles ahead. Was Jacquie now assessing her three escorts to see which one she would make a play for, which one she thought most suitable to be the father of her child? What criteria might she use? Looks? Personality? Intelligence? Had the mating game really become little more than a livestock market? Were men now only required for sexual gratification and stud purposes? It was scary to realise that some of those futuristic science fiction films she'd seen, where people lived on nutrition capsules and bred hyperdermically, selectively, without emotional or physical involvement, were becoming horribly real.

'I hope I haven't offended you,' Nick's voice interrupted her thoughts.

She smiled at him. 'Not at all. We're all entitled to our opinions, and to air them. I like hearing what people think. I like meeting people. It's why I like my work in the café. We have our regulars, they like to talk about their families.' She wasn't sure why Mr Jenkins came to mind, but he did. 'There's a divorced, retired civil servant who comes in with his newspaper and likes to pontificate on the state of the country.' She chuckled. 'I have some fairly heated discussions with him, but he always comes back, so I guess he likes to have somebody to spat with. It might seem like a rather mundane job, but like most things, it's what you make of it.' She thought for a while about her conversation with Jacquie and how it had related to her fears for Fiona. 'Now I think about it, communicating with people, like them or not, widens one's perspective on life just as effectively as travelling the world, don't you think?'

'Could do.' He didn't sound totally convinced but spent some time thinking about it before he asked, 'What do you do when you're not working, dusting or making marmalade?'

The question led them to a long discussion about books. Both, it turned out, were avid readers. He favoured non-fiction, biographies of people or historical events, travelogues and natural history, peppered with the occasional man's novel of the thriller, crime or adventure type. Her reading was equally wide ranging from Regency romance to crime and spy thrillers, cookery and gardening books and biographies. The conversation lasted until they had descended through a boggy depression and climbed steadily onto Urra Moor, heading for Round Hill, the highest point of the North York Moors. Being a guide, he naturally took her to examine another lump of stone standing like a pillar and explained that it had been put there in the early eighteenth century. It had roughly carved hands and barely readable words.

'This is the way to Stoxla,' he traced the words with his fingers as though marvelling that they had survived three hundred years of wind and rain, 'that's Stokesley to you and me.' And on the other side, 'This is the way to Kirbie. That's Kirkbymoorside.' He gave the stone an affectionate pat, as though congratulating it for its years of service. 'I suppose you did stop to look at the stone crosses on the first leg of today's walk?'

'Some, but we got to the point of seen-one-seen-'em-all.' She didn't think it necessary to say that it wasn't an opinion she shared, but she'd gone along with it anyway. Didn't she always go with the flow?

'Mmm.' Obviously, he didn't agree.

They continued the moorland walk, gradually descending, for which she was grateful because she was beginning to feel tired. After a steep descent that tested the shock-absorbing qualities of the knees and brought them down to a road, Nick asked, 'Is the farm providing you with dinner?'

'No, but I expect they'll make me a sandwich if I ask ever so nicely.' The guide book had said that pub food could be had at an 'inn nearby', but looking at the map, the nearest inn was two miles away. Being an isolated community there'd be no taxi service, and the idea of adding a few extra miles walking to an already long day, just to have dinner, did not appeal. As the farmhouse offered packed lunches, she felt sure they'd have the necessary to make a sandwich supper. If not, she'd just have to survive on her bar of chocolate and the apple she had been going to munch in the afternoon.

'Would it be improper of me to invite you to have a camp-fire supper with me? It won't be rehydrated stuff. Real food. I've the makings of a sort of spaghetti bolognaise.'

'As if you didn't have enough to carry!' The pack attached to his broad shoulders was huge but it hadn't seemed to trouble him.

'Well you know what they say: asses go best well laden!'

She laughed. 'It's very kind of you, Nick. I'd be delighted to accept.'

*

Nick was all set up by the time she joined him. There were other campers in the field, mostly walkers, judging by their lightweight bivouacs and the fact that they were nearly all reclined on their bedrolls or groundsheets beside little camping gas rings the size of a can of beans. The biggest give-away was the boots left to air with their tongues hanging out, and brightly coloured socks drying out on guy ropes. Nick's set-up was little different, except his camping gas kit was a bit bigger and comprised two lightweight pans: the lid doubled as a frying pan and the base a saucepan, with the gas can lodged between them.

'I'm intrigued,' she said after he'd offered her the comfort of his sleeping bag to sit on, 'to see how you manage to prepare spag-bol on that.'

Leaning against her, his tail swishing on the grass behind her, Jack put his head on one side as though he was fascinated, too.

'I cheated. I bought a home made ready meal for two before I left Glaisdale, and some pasta.'

'For two?' she queried.

'I'm a big bloke. I get hungry.'

'Now I feel I'm denying you … '

'Not at all. There's plenty of pasta, and I scrounged some biscuits and cheese from Mrs,' he paused, 'Thingey. I'm sorry, I'm dreadful with names, the farmer's wife.'

At the mention of cheese, Jack lifted one ear.

123

'All that's missing is a bottle of red wine!' she laughed and hugged the dog.

'Tarrah!' Nick flourished a bottle of Rioja from his rucksack, and two glasses.

Jack joined in with a triumphant bark. The other campers, who all seemed to know each other, looked across to see what the excitement was about and raised their beer cans in salute. She recognised three of them as Jacquie's escorts and wondered if she had proved too high-powered for them, too. Having read so much about travelling light, she was amazed at what men considered to be necessities worth the extra weight. In the case of some of the guys in the field, the cans appeared to have supplanted shaving tackle as they were sporting facial hair that had grown well beyond the designer-stubble stage. From that she deduced that that group were walking west to east and therefore close to the end of their journey.

'The glasses are also borrowed from the farm,' he explained. 'The wine is at least room temperature,' he gesticulated to show that the ambience of the evening served the purpose, 'if a little shaken by its travels.'

'I'm sure it'll be wonderful.'

They clinked their glasses to his toast, 'To good company.'

During their hours walking together, within the context of the conversation, she had mentioned her husband, his job, her children and what they were doing, but he had not mentioned a wife, nor children.

'Do you have a family?' she asked, sipping her wine and watching him sitting beside his primus stirring the bolognaise.

'I have a brother, sister-in-law, a niece and two nephews. About the same ages as your lot. My wife couldn't have children.' He sat back, his arms around his knees, and sipped his wine. 'Cheryl was diagnosed as having MS shortly after we were married. She died six years ago.' His voice dropped for the last few words.

'I'm sorry,' she said, knowing she should say something but feeling that whatever she said would be inadequate.

He accepted the condolence with a nod. 'That's when I moved back to Cumbria. We'd been living in Brighton, it's where she came from. We'd met in London, at work, in the bank. She bravely coped with the illness for fifteen years or so. I think we both tried to pretend it wasn't there, but when it became more debilitating I gave up work to be with her. After she died ... ' he lifted his shoulders, 'there didn't seem much point trying to get back into city life. Things had changed. I'd lost my footing on the ladder and, really, I didn't want it any more. There seemed no point. Although I got on okay with Cheryl's family, and I'd made lots of friends, I didn't feel right there, so I came home.' He stirred the pot which had started to bubble. 'My parents farmed near Shap. They're gone now. My brother works the farm and lives in a bungalow he built for himself.' He smiled. 'Ponderosa, I call it. Rambling great place. I live in the old farmhouse.'

'How did a Cumbrian lad from a farming background end up working in a city bank?' She watched him put a plate for a lid on the bolognaise pan and wrap it in his jumper to keep it warm while he cooked the spaghetti, which wasn't spaghetti but macaroni because it fitted more easily in the pan. Jack, warm and faintly doggy-smelling by her side, was equally fascinated, he tilted his head again, one ear forward.

'There's none for you, my lad,' Nick said. 'You've had your rations.'

Jack looked at his master and wagged his tail hopefully. The guys across the field were laughing. She wondered if they were amused by what they were seeing. It must look odd, a woman old enough to be their mother being entertained to supper by a grey-haired man.

Nick went back to her question. 'I was one of those odd kids who actually enjoyed school. I was good at maths and loved geography. I suppose, if I'd had the opportunity, I would have gone to university and done some sort of geography or history degree and ended up doing something completely different. But in my day kids left school and went to work. Because I was bright I got a job in the bank, and because I was good at it I got offered promotion, and when the opportunity came to leave the branch and go for management training in London, I was off like a shot.'

'Did you enjoy it? Living and working in the city?'

'It was different. I was young. I was away from the eyes of my parents, free! You bet I enjoyed it. My horizons were expanded. I even thought about taking my banking career abroad. But then I met Cheryl so I tempered my plans and thought instead about wife and family and a head office career.' He smiled. 'I've no regrets on that score. It was a different dream.'

But it was another dream unrealised, she thought. 'Do you enjoy guiding?'

'Ye-es,' he said, with some reservation. 'But I don't see me doing it for very much longer. I think I started it because I needed to be doing something that was more than just physical. I help my brother on the farm for a bit, which is certainly physical, but I needed something more. It sort of evolved from my interest in history, really.' He stopped talking to concentrate on his cooking.

The sun was low, making long fingers of yellow that pointed between the trees and across the dried grass of the camping field. Sunset was officially not until after nine, but the surrounding high moor was about to take it from view. When it went, it was as though a light had been switched off. The sky was still a cloudless opalescent blue, but without the golden warmth there was a feeling of the coming night. She felt vaguely naughty, like she had as a child when she'd stayed out beyond her curfew.

When she'd first met him, she hadn't gained the impression that Nick was a lonely man: more self-contained, a loner, but now she realised that there was a big vacuum in his life. He hadn't needed to say that he had loved his wife: the fact that he'd given up his career to spend her last years together showed that he had. The way his voice had dropped when speaking of her, showed that he still did.

'Hell-o-oh?' his voice interrupted her thoughts. 'Have you fallen asleep?'

'God! No. Sorry. I was miles away.'

'Dinner is served.' He presented her with a metal plate piled with pasta and a sauce smelling richly of tomato and herbs. 'You have a choice of cutlery: spoon or fork?'

Laughing, she selected the fork leaving him the spoon, which was probably more appropriate as his meal was in the larger of the billycans.

'So,' he said, after they'd both tasted and approved. 'Enough of me. I have to ask, because I'm rudely curious, why isn't your husband walking with you?'

'Jim has long ago outgrown this sort of thing. I was always the late developer! He's gone on a Rotary trip, which isn't my scene.' She smiled and hoped that she was conveying an image of a couple who were happy to go their separate ways and that there was nothing at all amiss with her marriage, then she suddenly realised that she hadn't telephoned Jim from the farmhouse. He would be home by now and she'd been having so much fun that she hadn't given him a second's thought.

'No contest, really.' Nick returned her smile.

'Maybe I need a bit of discomfort and hardship to make me realise how lucky I am.'

'Do you think this is hardship?'

'Actually, no. So far I'm enjoying it. Hugely.' She grinned and tucked into her meal, watched by Jack who eyed every forkful.

'Lie down,' Nick growled.

'What, now?' she said, without thinking. Then blushed furiously.

Nick also coloured. 'I meant the dog.'

'Sorry … that wasn't … it's just … well, my silly sense of humour.' It was the sort of banter she'd once enjoyed with Jim.

An owl hooted in the trees quite near them. Nick looked around and, spotting it, pointed it out to her. For a while it stayed on its branch, its unblinking stare fixed onto the neighbouring field which had just been cut for hay: there would be many a vulnerable field mouse out there tonight. Then it opened its big mottled brown wings and glided silently away. The awkward moment over, they turned their attention to the biscuits and cheese. Jack's patience was rewarded with two cream crackers topped with a thick slice of cheddar. They finished the wine and Nick brewed some water for a couple of mugs of instant coffee. Bright little stars began to appear in the darkening blue above them. The lads in the other tents had trooped off some time ago, she assumed to trek the two miles to the pub. She wondered at their energy because now that she had wined and dined, she was whacked.

'I think it'll be another fine day tomorrow,' Nick said, surveying the sky, 'but the forecast for Tuesday isn't so good. I hope you've got waterproofs with you.'

'Of course. But we'll be off the moors by then.'

'Aye. We've had the best of it up here. What are your plans for tomorrow?'

'A shorter walk. To Ingelby Cross. It's only eleven or twelve miles but reads like quite a strenuous pull up some hills. Hopefully I'll have time to take a look at Mount Grace Priory.'

'I was hoping you'd want to. I always find it very thought-provoking.' He smiled at her. 'Would you mind walking together, tomorrow? I won't be offended if you prefer to be alone.'

'No, I don't mind.' But would Jim, she wondered? 'I'd be happy to walk with you.' She stopped herself qualifying it with 'until we get to the point of boring the pants off each other.' Immediately she was unnerved by the feeling that the time could be a long time coming. There was nothing underlying his request. He was lonely and it was simple companionship that he wanted, and, she realised, so did she. So where was the harm?

*

Day three, Monday, started hot and the route was uphill and down dale all the way, hard work but interesting and enjoyable. Her shirt was sticking to her back, her hair felt damp and limp and her toes were slippery with sweat inside her boots. Like her, Nick didn't see the point in rushing things and they'd sauntered most of the way, stopping now and then at viewpoints and enjoying a cool paddle in the various streams they'd come across. The shade of the latter woodland sections had been more than welcome and despite her weariness and looking forward to a deep relaxing bath, she stuck to the planned diversion to the Mount Grace Priory.

As Nick had said, it was thought provoking, although the thoughts that came to her mind were probably very different from his. It was a monastic ruin of soft, peachy-grey sandstone surrounded by a carpet of close-cut grass. The tower of the church-sized chapel still stood, albeit with no glass in the windows, no floors or doors, and only odd bits of the chapel walls remained. Some walls, in places reduced to foundation level, indicated the outline of the compound and living quarters of the monks. She found it hard to believe that it had survived thus for over four hundred years since the dissolution of the monasteries, without all the stones being purloined for farm buildings or walls, or the ground cleared for grazing.

The grounds were peaceful with colourful flowerbeds, trees, and all sorts of birds. For the most part the tourists strolled around, talking in hushed voices, duly affected by the air of tranquillity, so a raised voice drew attention from everybody within earshot.

'But this is so boring.' It was spoken deliberately loudly by a girl aged about thirteen. She was wearing hipster jeans and a skimpy white top that stopped at her waistline. It was a fashion that didn't suit her puppy fat, nor the fairness of her exposed skin which was reddened by the sun. The girl's father, embarrassed by the attention his daughter had drawn, hissed something urgently.

'No, I won't effing shut up. You can look at a load of bloody stones if you have to, but I'm going back to the car.' Making a point of sticking the headphones of her walkman into her ears, the girl turned her back on her parents and strode off. Like everybody else within earshot, Linda watched until the parents, after a moment's dithering, continued their circuit. To a small chorus of muttering, other visitors returned to their stroll around the ruins. She wondered how the parents would handle the outburst. Would they lecture their daughter on thinking of others, telling her that she'd spoiled their day, embarrassed them? Might they reason with her, as she and Jim would have done, although they would have set the scene before they arrived to encourage the children to see the pile of old stones as a place where people had lived, and to imagine themselves in the lives of those people. Or would they ignore it and pretend it had never happened, which is probably what her parents would have done had she ever been on holiday with them. Her parents didn't do holidays, both too busy with parochial duties, which, now she thought about it was fine, because she'd enjoyed her camping holidays with the Girl Guides or Church Youth Club much more than she would have enjoyed being trailed around churchyards and cathedrals.

Nick interrupted her thoughts. 'Carthusian monks lived as hermits,' he told her, although she already knew because she'd read about it. 'There were twenty-three cells, fifteen around this cloister.' He pointed to the stones in the grass which gave some idea of the layout. 'They lived in their cells and tended their personal high-walled gardens, never speaking to each other, their lives devoted to prayer.'

One of the cells had been reconstructed. It was stark with only a bare wooden desk in one room, a bed in the one above. It was hard to imagine such a life, spent cloaked in a heavy hooded cowl, effectively blinkered, seeing no evil, hearing no evil and speaking no evil; not sharing their thoughts, their joys, their anxieties; not commenting on the purity of a day, the birdsong, the flowers, the warmth of the sun or exchanging ideas, opinions, recommendations. The only time they would have opened their mouths was to chant their psalms. She wondered, why? What good could such an existence do for the man or mankind? She wondered if they were doing penance for some dreadful crime and this was effective self-imprisonment, or were they hiding from the realities of life? And what about their parents, brothers, sisters, what did they think about a man who excommunicated himself from society and withdrew his service from his family, his liege lord or whatever? And what sort of God would be impressed by such a waste of a life? Temporary retreat was one thing, but total exclusion from life, for life, was beyond her comprehension. The austerity and coolness of the cell made her think of her parents. It seemed to her that they were doing the same thing but in twentieth century style. Again she wondered, why? Why had they chosen to live the way they did?

Ambling around the ruins, her thoughts became centred on her relationship with her parents. She had often marvelled that she had ever been conceived. Her parents had never been demonstrative. They never held hands, they never spontaneously kissed or hugged, at least not that she could remember; they never took a sudden fancy to dance around the kitchen as she and Jim did, or used to. Their affection for her was constant, but cool. Her father used to pat her shoulder and smile approval when she'd pleased him. Her mother was responsible for discipline but it had never been extreme, it hadn't needed to be because until her mid-teens Linda had been a biddable child.

Looking back, she realised that from her mid-teens they had allowed her freedom of choice. They may not have approved some of her choices and advised a different course, they may have been hurt by her ignoring their advice, but nevertheless they had respected her right to choose her own way in life, or, more likely, they hadn't known how to handle her adolescent change of persona and hoped that by ignoring it, it would go away. She had grown up and away from them, despairing of their lifestyle rather than despising it, but never really understanding it. She was little better than the girl they'd seen earlier: she had shut her ears to them and stalked off to do her own thing.

She knew little about her father beyond the fact that he had grown up in Halifax, the second son of a middle-class family destined to go into his father's accountancy practice. But war intervened and he had served in the Green Howards and been amongst the first wave of troops to land on D-Day. She had seen films and read books about that day, but her father had never spoken of his personal experience, except a brief reference to it once in a Remembrance Day sermon. The fact that the annual Remembrance Day service was as important to him as other holy days of obligation said a lot to her about the awfulness of his wartime experience, and always in his sermon he included thoughts for the innocent victims of war; people, she supposed, like her mother whose entire family had been wiped out by the blitz. It was hard to imagine how it must have been for a girl in her late teens to lose everybody she cared for in one night, and to live every day thereafter without them there to go home to, without them there to give support and advice.

'You're very thoughtful.' Nick spoke softly.

'Like you said, it's a thought-provoking place.'

CHAPTER 7

AFTER A SHOWER AND CHANGE OF CLOTHING at the Inn in Ingleby Cross, she sat on the double bed with her legs stretched, guidebook and postcards on her lap, pen tapping her teeth, trying to work out what to write. For Jim's card she eventually settled for 'Having a lovely time. Wish you were here.' But did she really wish he was there? She wondered if she would be enjoying herself so much if he had been with her. It was a long time since he'd done any serious walking and the accommodation she'd chosen would not have been up to his standard. There was nothing wrong with any of the places she'd stayed; they were clean, comfortable and friendly and the food good, but in recent years Jim had become more used to five-star establishments with haute cuisine, expensive wine lists, room service and all the trimmings. She couldn't help feeling that he'd be grumbling about the smallness or basic nature of some of her bookings. Heaving a sigh, she stuck a stamp on the card.

The card for her parents was even more difficult. Usually she would say something bland, but this time she felt she wanted to say something, or, feeling she had utterly failed when she saw them just before she came away, find some way of getting through to them that she really did care about them. Sitting on her bed, her pen still tapping her teeth, recalling the visit, she was not surprised that the hermit's enclosed spaces at Mount Grace had brought her parents to mind. Their retirement home was a small, two-bedroom bungalow, a square box with a patch of grass in front, small vegetable garden behind and just enough width for a high privet hedge between it and it and its identical neighbours ...

*

Her parents had been expecting her. They didn't like surprise visits. They liked appointments that their day could be planned around; not that they did a lot to plan around these days. When visiting her in-laws, she had always gone to the back door, let herself into the kitchen and likely as not been the one to put on the kettle and make a pot of tea: but at her own parents' house, she rang the front doorbell and waited to be let in like any other visitor.

She watched the almost hairless, tall, thin, stooped shape of her father coming slowly toward the rippled-glass door. He fumbled with the chain and lock. She had noticed over the last few months that his movements had become slow and careful in an effort to control the shaking of his hands. Her parents had always been old, but now they seemed ancient.

'Hi, Dad.' She greeted him with a smile and leaned forward to touch his thin, cold cheek with hers.

He peered over the specs which had slipped down his long nose, then the corners of his thin lips lifted slightly.

'Come in, my dear.' He pointed her toward the door to the sitting-room as though she were a stranger to the house. On such a lovely day the windows and doors should have been open to the fresh air, but they weren't and the house was stuffy with the smells of disinfectant, old books and ancient carpet. Their previous two homes had been large vicarages in which their few pieces of furniture had looked stranded, but the dark oak bookcases which lined the walls of this tiny room, floor to ceiling, left only the patch of wall above the fifties-style tiled fireplace for a picture, a gift from grateful parishioners. It was a rather lovely watercolour of the Sussex village where she had grown up. She often wondered if her parents ever really looked at it, and if they did, what memories it prompted.

For her there was some laughter in the picture: there were the fields where she had played with Linda Anderson; the manor house the Andersons had rented and made cheerful with colourful wallpaper and pretty drapes and where she had spent most of her time; the big oak tree the village kids had their camp in; the primary school and church they had all attended; and beside it, all wings and gables and warm red brick was the Vicarage. The painting didn't show that three-quarters of it was shuttered and unoccupied nor that the rest was merely a place to live, not a home.

The bungalow had the same quality. It was a place to read, study, contemplate or pray. There was no television in the sitting-room, only two wing chairs, which had been retirement gifts from her and Jim, and a pair of Windsor-backed chairs either side of a gate-legged table beneath the net-curtained window.

The rattling of cups in saucers heralded the arrival of her mother with the tea tray. When the tray had been safely placed on the table, she kissed her mother's deeply lined cheek and gave her the cake she had baked and a tin of home-made biscuits which, rationed to two a day, should last her father the whole month until she visited again.

Apart from the facial lines, Edith Ramsey hadn't changed much in the fifty years that Linda had known her. She was of medium height and painfully thin, and looked more than ever like a scarecrow in the mismatched grey twin-set and shapeless brown skirt that had probably been purchased for pence in jumble sales way back in the sixties. Her short, straight-cut, fine grey hair had probably been fair but Linda couldn't remember it as such. She had interesting eyes, blue like Linda's, eyes that saw and watched, but any observations were not readily commented upon. Mrs Ramsey had been a model vicar's wife, organising the cleaning of the church, the flower rota, sitting on the committee for the annual Church fete, teaching in Sunday school, committee member of Mother's Union, arranger of collections for Church-sponsored charities. Linda had never heard her complain. It had always been a case of Mrs Ramsey being asked and Mrs Ramsey saying that if nobody else wanted to, then of course she would do her best to serve.

While tea was being poured they exchanged the usual 'how are you' questions and received the usual 'very well, thank you' answers, regardless of how any of them really felt. It was obvious that her father's health was failing, but when she had remarked on it in the past, he had simply put it down to old age; there was nothing for her to worry about.

'How is the family, mmm?' her mother asked with a hint of a smile.

When the children had been younger it had been easy to talk about their progress through school, their sporting and social activities, but since they'd become adults it had become more difficult. What could she comfortably say about Suzy who was living in sin with two bastard children, or of drop-out Rob, or high-flying materialistic Fiona, that they would really want to hear? But she told them anyway and went on to tell them about the weekend's charity cricket match. They dutifully listened as they would to any parishioner talking about a family whose way of life was alien to their ideals.

Unlike Nan and Fred's house, there were no family photographs on display, there never had been. Somewhere, no doubt, after they had departed this life, she would find a drawer or box with her old school photographs, a wedding picture, and all the snaps she'd given them over the years of her children. As she sipped her tea she wondered what else she might find. The thought made her feel suddenly quite vulnerable: they were old and not in the best of health. Time was slipping by, every second of it being counted by the old, wooden-framed clock, the sole occupant of the dusty mantelshelf. Every tick was a wasted opportunity for her to try to understand what had made them the people they had become. But how to broach it?

She started a little uncertainly. 'The cricket match is a village tradition. It started just after the first war, to raise funds for the memorial hall. Jim's great-grandfathers were founder members. Fred's got masses of photographs. It made me realise that I know very little about my family history.'

Her mother lifted her cup from the saucer to her lips as though she hadn't heard, although her hearing was still as sharp as a cat's. Her father adjusted the position of his cup in its saucer.

'I'm not sure that I understand, my dear.'

'I know you're from Yorkshire and that you served in the army in the war, but what made you want to become a vicar? How and when did you meet each other?'

Her father smiled benignly. 'I joined the Church because I found God. The war was a terrible time for everybody. My faith in God saw me through it. After that, I wanted to serve Him.' So simply put but with no elaboration, no explanation of a defining moment, no particular horror or fear or close encounter with the grim reaper. She wanted to know because she wanted to understand, but if he wasn't going to volunteer the information after such a prompt, how could she push him?

He went on, 'I met your mother just after the war. In London. In the Church where I was curate. I thought we had told you that.' They had, but not the details, nothing of the emotions they had felt, their courtship or where her mother had been living, or how she had supported herself. She knew nothing of her mother's family and teetered on the edge of probing further, but as neither seemed to want to enlarge on the basic information, like it or not she had to respect that they didn't want to talk about it, either because it was too painful or too shameful. All sorts of fanciful ideas floated through her mind: her father had committed some act of vengeance or cowardice in the face of the enemy; her mother had been a prostitute and her father had rescued her from a life of degradation; her mother had been depressed by the loss of her family and attempted suicide and her father had saved her immortal soul. Any number of explanations came to mind, but the idea of them having a 'zing' moment and falling in love wasn't one of them. Whatever it was, it was obvious that they were going to leave her outside the knowledge and she had to accept their right to do so.

She sipped her tea for a while, listening to the ticking of the clock, more time ticking by when important things could be said. There was something she wanted to say, before it was too late, but it was so incredibly difficult. 'I … know that I'm not the daughter you hoped I'd be. I er … just want you to know, though, that I do appreciate all you've done for me and that I do love you.' Had she made such a declaration to somebody like Nan, it would have rung great clanging cathedral bells that something was amiss: the instant response would be an enquiry as to whether she was all right. Not so with her own parents. Again, her mother stared into her cup and it was her father who responded with an embarrassed little cough.

'Thank you, my dear.' He paused, realising that such an unusual statement required more but apparently not sure what to add. 'Nobody has the right to expect a child to be anything. Our duty was to guide and educate until you were old enough to make your own decisions.' He smiled his vicar smile. 'I think our only regret is that you have moved away from the Church, but we hope that one day you will find it again.'

She had no answer to that.

'Would you like another cup of tea, mmm?' her mother asked.

'Thank you, yes.' She passed her cup over, not because she wanted another cup of slightly coloured, vaguely milky, warm water, but it was something to do and say.

*

She had stayed for another half hour by which time the ticking clock had more to say than anybody else. She had tried to reach them, but it was too late: they were as set in their ways as prehistoric flies in amber, and just as inaccessible. She returned to the problem of the postcard and considered, 'Visited here today and thought of you.' It was true, but could appear cynical, or she could be referring to the name they'd given her that she'd rejected, along with everything else they held dear. How about, 'Visited here today and thought kind thoughts of you'? Too sentimental, not their style. But in the end, that was the best she could come up with and it was sincere, her thoughts were kind, if confused.

Nick camped in the field behind the pub but joined her for supper in the busy bar. For the last bit of their walk he had been aware of her distraction and offered a penny for her thoughts. It had led to a general discussion about their relationships with their respective parents. His folk had been struggling farmers with not a lot of cash to spare, and he had been required to do his bit around the farm before and after school and during holidays, but he had enjoyed it. He hadn't always seen eye to eye with his father, who was old-fashioned and set in his ways, but he felt they'd got on okay. He had the feeling that his parents had been proud of his achievements.

They had died, within two years of each other, while still in their seventies. In many ways, Nick was very like Jim: they came from farming backgrounds, both felt comfortable with their parents and both had banking careers. Both were easy conversationalists and well-informed. In the old days, when her children had been small, Jim would have prepared himself for answering any questions the kids might ask about the places they visited on holiday. He was also, she recalled, very good at fudging it when necessary.

They didn't sit long after they'd finished their meal because she wanted to make her phone call to Jim. They said goodnight and arranged to meet at eight the next morning for breakfast. It was taken as read that they would walk on together.

Back in her room she checked her mobile to see if anybody had called. They hadn't. She pressed the key for her home number, it rang and rang but there was no reply. It was nine-thirty in the evening, Jim should be home from work by now. She pressed the number for Suzy.

'Hi, Mum,' Suzy answered.

'Hello, darling, how are you all doing? Missing me?'

'Lots. Danny keeps asking for his Ganna.'

'Bless him. Give him a kiss from me.'

'I went to see Grandpa Fred today, he was having a good grumble, so no change there. I sorted something out of the freezer for him, he ate it all and went to the pub for a pint so I guess he's okay really. How are you getting on?'

'I'm really enjoying it.' The phone crackled. 'Hello?'

'I'm still here but you keep disappearing.'

'The signal's not good. I'll tell you all about it when I get home. I'm keeping a journal so I won't forget the details.'

'Hello? You disappeared again.'

She moved over to the window and twisted until the signal improved. 'Have you seen your dad since he came home from Holland?'

'He's here.' Suzy giggled. 'It takes you to abandon him for him to pay us a visit. He called in on his way home from work so joined us for supper. Here he is.'

She heard Jim's denial and a rustling sound as the phone was handed over.

'Hello, darling,' his voice sounded strong.

'Hi. How are you doing?'

'Fine. It was a good trip. Everybody enjoyed it. You don't know what you missed.'

'I think I do. I'm having a good time, too. Do you remember me telling you about the man and his dog that I walked a bit with on Saturday?'

'Vaguely.'

'I met them again yesterday and we walked all day together. He's handy to know because he's a professional guide.'

'Isn't that cheating?' He sounded amused, a bit as though he'd scored a point.

'It would be if I'd set out to prove something or do the walk solo, but I didn't. I wanted you to come with me.'

'Lindy ... '

'I know. Anyway, he's good company and very informed.'

'Good. At least I needn't worry that you're going to get lost or fall off a crag in the middle of nowhere.'

'Are you worried?'

'Of course I am.' But not, it seemed, in the least bit concerned that she had teamed up with a man. It came as quite a shock to realise that he probably considered her past sexual attraction. It couldn't be denied that their sex life was not as active as it had been, but whose fault was that? She felt a dull ache churn deep inside her, and a yearning for things to be as they once had been.

'Lindy? Are you still there?'

'Yes. The signal's not good.' The understatement of the year: the signal between them had become very disjointed over the last few years.

'We'll talk again when you can get a better signal, or a landline.'

'Okay. Take care of yourself.'

'And you, nutcase.' She wondered if the humour was genuinely felt, or was it for Suzy's benefit, maintaining the pretence that all was well between them?

*

The following day, Tuesday, she set out with Nick for a peaceful, easy ramble across the Vale of Mowbray. Nick was not convinced that doing the full twenty-three miles in one day was a good idea, but that was the way she had planned it and she didn't want to mess about with her overnight accommodation plans, and she had set a target to reach Kirkby Stephen on the Friday night, when she hoped that Jim would make the effort to join her. There was no reason why he shouldn't. As far as she was aware he had no plans other than the usual golf which could easily be cancelled. Kirkby Stephen was reachable by train, albeit not conveniently, and anyway, he preferred driving, and who wouldn't if they had a big powerful car with all the gismos.

As predicted, the sun didn't come out to play, but the showers were light and in no way spoiled the day. The route was a wonderful combination of hedgerow-lined country lanes and footpaths across green pastures and golden harvested fields. It was almost entirely level and liberally interspersed with watercourses for Jack to splash in and places offering morning coffee, lunch, afternoon tea and comfort stops. It amused them when in the pub at Danby Wiske, where they'd stopped for lunch, the barman referred to her as Nick's wife. Nick had smiled warmly at her. 'I rather like the idea. Will your husband mind if I borrow you for a while?'

It was said in jest, of course, because he knew that she was married and she'd made much in their conversations about how happy her family life was. She hadn't gone over the top with declarations of love and devotion to her husband, one didn't with strangers, but she had been conscious, deliberate even, in making sure he knew that she was not available. As they walked on in easy silence, she found herself thinking that Nick would be a comfortable man to be married to and was surprised to realise that she was attracted to him. That he liked her was obvious by the very fact that he chose to walk with her and, now she thought about it, all the little considerations like extending his hand to help her over stiles or stepping stones across rivers. He talked about his wife from time to time, which gave her to believe that his grieving was over, that he'd reached a turning point in his life and was ready to move on. She couldn't remember his exact words, but it had been sort of inferred when he'd said that he didn't intend to go on guiding for much longer. There was also something about the way he smiled when they got together again in the mornings, or even after short separations, that gave an inkling that it wouldn't take much encouragement from her for him to take the first steps toward forming another relationship.

The passage of her thoughts shocked her. She had never had unfaithful thoughts, at least, nothing vaguely realistic: like most women she'd drooled over Piers Brosnan and Robert Redford, to name but two, but to actually contemplate replacing Jim, she had never, not even in her darkest moments, considered that.

The King's Head Hotel in Richmond had been booked with Jim in mind. It was more his sort of place and would, had he joined her, have been an island of luxury in her sea of cosy inns and B&Bs. On arrival in the carpeted foyer she realised that the clothes packed in their rucksacks for evening wear would not have conformed to the restaurant dress code. She assumed there was one because the place was very smart. It would have annoyed Jim not to be able to enjoy it properly. She sighed and wished she wasn't going to spend the night here alone. Nick had been lucky enough to find a guest house that would accept dogs, so he was looking forward to a bath and a night in a real bed. Thinking that spending quite so much time with him was not a good thing, she had turned down his invitation to join him for dinner and was already regretting it. She had said she was going to have a long wallow in a bath, a quick supper, a landline phone call to her husband and then an early night. Nick had nodded acceptance but she had the feeling he was disappointed.

'What about tomorrow?' he had asked, his grey eyes holding hers hopefully.

'If you're game, so am I, but before we leave I'd like to make a quick visit to the church.' She had considered visiting the Green Howard's regimental museum, too, to see if there was anything there to satisfy her curiosity about her father, but as her father had put his army involvement firmly into his history she felt it would be intrusive to do so, and there really wasn't time to do everything on this trip.

*

Jim wasn't at home when she phoned, which didn't surprise her: he wouldn't want to be at home on his own. Almost certainly one of their friends had taken pity on him, or he might even have stayed in town and maybe dined with Fiona. She left a message on the answerphone and went to bed.

She slept well and woke early to a day that was grey, drizzling and, according to the forecast, likely to remain so for the rest of the day. It didn't augur well for the ten-mile walk through the Yorkshire Dales which was to include some fairly steep climbs and, on a good day, would have given some spectacular views. One might ask what was the point of making the effort if there was nothing to see when she got there, but, as she'd often said to the children, you don't know what adventures you might have on the way, and making the effort had its own reward. She had already covered over sixty miles in four days and was feeling remarkably fit. Her thighs and calves ached a bit but her feet were fine and she had no problems with the weight of her pack. So far, all her accommodation had been comfortable and she had been well rested and well fed between walks. She had to concede that with the plethora of guide books, the planning had been easy and even if she hadn't met Nick, there were plenty of other walkers going in both directions that she could have walked or conferred with, so the chances of her being hopelessly lost were really quite minimal.

After a good breakfast, she left her backpack in the safe keeping of the hotel while she visited the church. Despite being the daughter of a vicar, or maybe because of it, she wasn't usually a visitor of churches on holiday, but the guidebook references to the effect that the church in Richmond had a chapel dedicated to the Green Howards attracted her.

The church, in the middle of the town, was large and solid and very Victorian but, according to the literature, many of the features went back to the twelfth century. Inside, the Victorian atmosphere persisted but there was also an ambience of an older cathedral: it was masculine, monkish and cool. There had been a wedding within the last few days, quite a fancy one judging by the abundance of floral sprays and garlands of white and cream flowers in the area of the altar and along the aisle. She sat in one of the pews and imagined the vicar in gold-threaded vestments in front of the altar, the bride and groom kneeling before him, their vows witnessed by a vast congregation in fancy hats and morning suits. The picture was a far cry from her own wedding which had been simple in the extreme. One of her father's colleagues, in simple black cassock and white surplice, had performed the ceremony in the Whit Bay church. Her dress, and that of her bridesmaid, Jim's niece, had been inexpensively made by a friend of Jim's mother. There had been a floral arrangement on a pedestal alongside the altar, but that was all, and the congregation of fifty invited guests had been swollen by a few parish faithful who had come to see their vicar's daughter wed.

She hadn't felt short-changed: it was the way things were in those days. It had been their special day, looked forward to and entered into in all seriousness. She remembered them making their vows, 'until death do us part', and the vicar intoning the words of warning 'those whom God hath joined together, let no man put asunder'. Their kiss at the altar had been chaste compared with those previously experienced in his car. She had been embarrassed, but could still recall the look in Jim's eyes, the sparkle, the love and the anticipation.

She leaned forward and bowed her head onto the back of the pew in front. How, she asked herself, had it all gone so wrong? They had been so happy with their family, doing things together, supporting each other, working together to improve their lot. How had they fallen so out of step? Why was she here on her own, walking with a stranger instead of

Jim? Where was this walk taking her? Why had she done it? She knew why, and here she couldn't hide from it.

Reluctantly, like being forced to sit through a film she'd not enjoyed first time around and vowed never to revisit, her mind went back to the events of four years ago. It had been a difficult time. Suzy was stressed out with her A-levels, Jim had problems at work, Nan was terminally ill with cancer and Fred was finding it hard to cope. She somehow managed to keep all the balls in the air, scheduling in daily visits to the hospital, feeding the family, keeping house for Fred and making time to help Suzy with her revision. It hadn't been easy, but supporting each other was what she believed family life was about. And if all that hadn't been enough to contend with, when Rob had come home from university for the Easter holidays, it was obvious something was wrong ...

*

There had been several times when she had thought Rob was on the point of confiding his problem, but then he'd drawn back. She didn't know what to do. He hadn't been particularly stressed about exams in the past, so she found it hard to believe that he was worried about his work. Obviously he was concerned about his grandmother, they all were, she had been very close to them all. He had come home to see Nan rather than go travelling with his friends and, she supposed, to be with his family, part of them during this difficult period of impending bereavement. He had been very good, offering to drive and spend time with Fred, sitting for hours in the hospital with Nan. She appreciated his help, but when at home he spent most of his time either in his room, or out on his own, and he didn't seem able to look at her. He was usually so enthusiastic, warm and communicative: something was definitely bothering him, but what? Was it drugs, or a girl in trouble? Had he still been a child, she would have cornered him in the kitchen and gently talked to him, eased the problem from him, but now that he was twenty and living a good three-quarters of his time away from home, it wasn't so easy.

It had been going on for a week. Knowing he was in the kitchen, she went to join him, hoping to find a way to talk to him. She had just said, 'Hi,' when the telephone rang. She was nearest, so she picked it up. Rob watched her.

'Lindy?' It was Jim.

'Oh, hello, darling.' She glanced at the clock. It was six o'clock.

'I'm sorry, love, I'm going to be late again. There's a board meeting tomorrow. I haven't had a chance to prepare for it.' He was talking quickly and sounded stressed.

Disappointed and overcome with tiredness, she sank onto one of the chairs at the table. 'So what time will you be home?'

'I don't know. Probably the last train. Don't wait up.'

'Okay. I'll see you later.'

They said goodbye and she put the phone down. Rob was still by the kitchen sink looking into the garden with his back to her. She noticed that his hands were tightly gripping the edge of the sink.

'He's working late again,' she said, unnecessarily.

He didn't turn round. 'I note he didn't ask after Nanna or Grandpa. Doesn't he care?' His voice was hard.

'He's got a lot on his mind,' she defended. 'When he gets home … '

'Wouldn't you think that at a time like this he could put his family first?' Rob said, already on his way out of the room. A few moments later the front door shut with a decisive clunk.

In a way, she shared the same feeling, but on the other hand things were pretty critical at the office, too. The merger was going ahead and Jim still didn't know which of the two chief executives was going to head the combined company. She couldn't blame him for wanting to do everything in his power to ensure that it was him. As if sensing that something was wrong, Dottie came to her side and put her head on her thigh. She stroked the dog's head, caressing the tan eyebrows with her thumb. Dottie swept the stone tiles with a few wags of her long-haired, white-tipped tail.

She did wait up, not just for Jim but for Rob. She hoped that after an evening out, probably at the pub, he would be less inhibited about his problem. When the phone rang, just after eleven, she was afraid it was the hospital with news of Nan. Nothing had been said, but it was obvious that the end was not far away: there was no more that could be done other than keep her comfortable.

'Hello?'

'Hi, Lindy. I'm not going to make the last train. I'll have to stay at the club.' He spoke urgently, rather loudly, in the way he did when he'd had rather too much to drink.

'Oh, right … ' This was the second occasion within the last two weeks that Jim had found it necessary to work so late that it wasn't worth coming home. On the last occasion she'd asked what he'd do about clean undies and shirt. He had laughed, making her feel horribly house-wifey, and said that a steward at the club would sort it for him. Stupidly, it was her first thought again. 'How's it going, the work you had to get done?'

'Nearly there. Should be ready for tomorrow. I'll see you tomorrow evening.' He seemed to be in a rush to go.

'I went to the hospital today,' she said, a little annoyed that he was going to terminate the call without asking about his mother or how her day had been.

'How are things?' He had the grace to sound concerned.

'She's comfortable, most of the time. When she's awake she worries about your dad.'

'I'll pop in on her tomorrow on my way from the station.' The quieter, lower tone of his voice was more sober, as though her silent reprimand had hit home. She softened.

'She always asks after you. She's very proud of you. We all are.' She didn't know why she had added that last bit. It was true, but for some reason she felt he needed to be reminded that even if he didn't get the top job, it didn't mean he'd failed or let anybody down.

'Oh … Right. I'll see her tomorrow. Goodnight, then.'

'Goodnight, sleep well.'

She replaced the receiver slowly. Jim had been drinking. Other people might not notice it, but she knew the signs. She could hardly blame him, he had a lot on his plate. So had she.

Maybe a nightcap would help her sleep. She went through to the sitting-room and poured herself a Scotch, rather a large one, then returned to the kitchen for some sparkling mineral water. She switched off the kitchen lights and took her drink to the open-plan family room where she sank onto the cushioned windowseat. The only illumination was that which shone in from the outside light she'd left on for the late arrivals. Dot jumped up beside her and stretched out with her head in her lap. She sipped her drink, absently stroked the dog's warm silky fur and gazed out at the spring flowers coming into bloom in the patio tubs. Spring, the season of hope, but all she felt was despondence.

Rob came home a little before midnight. He had also been drinking. A lot. He lurched into the kitchen and fumbled for the light.

'Don't switch it on,' she called, quietly.

'Christ!' he staggered to support himself on the kitchen table. 'You scared the shit ... What you doin' in the dark?'

'Having a nightcap. I'd ask you to join me, but it seems you're a few ahead of me.'

He stayed by the table, swaying slightly. All she could see of his face was that it was pale.

'Come and join me, anyway.'

Under normal circumstances, he would have joined her automatically, without being asked. Now, he hesitated.

'Come on, Rob, please. I need some company.'

It was the right card to play. He came towards her, carefully navigating the step down from the kitchen. He pulled one of the pine chairs from the table and sat astride it, as if it were a horse, resting his elbows on the back so that he could support his chin. 'What time's Dad due in?'

'He's staying in town.'

Rob sank his head into his arms on the back of the chair. One of his long legs was jiggling, a sure sign that he was either impatient, irritated or stressed.

'What is it, darling?' she coaxed. 'I can tell something's wrong.'

He pushed his head harder into his folded arms. His leg jiggling increased. 'I don't know what to do ... '

'I can't help if you don't tell me what it's about.'

Rob looked up suddenly. His eyes were bright, tearfully bright. 'It's about Dad.' His eyes met hers now. 'He's a lying, cheating, selfish bastard!'

Shocked, she stared at her son. Selfish, yes, she had to agree, to a degree, but lying, cheating? 'What makes you..?'

Rob's anger was boiling over now. His hands were gripping the back of the chair, his knuckles white. 'I saw him. Last week. I stopped over with a friend in London on my way home. I saw him, my own father, get out of a taxi with a woman and go into the house opposite. They were ... ' He shook his head as though not wanting to recall what he'd seen. 'It was late in the evening. I didn't want to believe it was him. I phoned home and asked for him. You said he was working late, staying in town. I phoned his direct office line but there was no reply.'

He looked at his mother, tears shining on his cheeks. 'If I'd any doubts, I wouldn't be ... I always thought he ... and you ... ' He threw his arms forward. 'What was I supposed to

157

do? Ignore it? Pretend I hadn't seen the father I've always admired cheating on my mother? If I told him what I'd seen, would he deny it? Would he beg me not to tell you? And whatever he said, could I look you in the eye and pretend I hadn't seen what I saw?'

She didn't know how to reply.

'Oh, Christ,' Rob mumbled and buried his head deeply into his arms again. 'I shouldn't have told you.'

She eased the dog's head from her lap and went over to her son. 'Yes, Rob, you should.' She squatted beside him and wrapped her arms around his bony shoulders to give him a hug. 'You shouldn't have to bottle those sort of feelings. Don't feel guilty. I'm glad you told me.'

'I should have confronted him.' His clenched fist hit the back of the chair.

'I ... I think that maybe you were right. It might not have helped. You would still have felt bad holding the secret from me.'

'Nothing will ever be the same again ... ' Rob sank his head into his arms and his shoulders heaved. Tears came to her eyes, too, not for herself, but for her son. He was right, nothing would ever be the same again.

CHAPTER 8

SHE COULDN'T RECALL IN DETAIL what happened after that. They had talked well into the night and at some stage he had told her that the friend with whom he had been staying had told him that the woman was a high flier in the fashion business called Wendy Longden. All she remembered was the feeling that she couldn't deal with it, not with so much else going on. She had advised Rob not to say anything to anybody, particularly not Jim. Rob had bitterly regretted telling her and wasn't comfortable with her decision not to bring the whole thing into the open but she told him that they had to put Nan and Fred first. The only way he could handle it was to return to Oxford, which he did that same afternoon. She remembered, too, that when Jim came back the following evening, after calling in to see his mother, he looked haggard. It had given her little pleasure to know that his conscience was probably giving him hell.

So as not to add to the family's problems, she kept her knowledge of Jim's infidelity to herself. Over the next few weeks it became apparent that his conscience had won. There were no more late nights, he brought her flowers as a token of his gratitude for all she was doing for his parents, he even tried to make love but, pleading tiredness, she turned away from him. Then his mother died and they were all overcome with grief. At the time she had thought her inability to weep was because she needed to be strong for the rest of the family.

The truth came out several months later. She remembered that it was a hot and humid summer evening. She had called in to see Fred on her way home from work. He was tearful and lonely and, as she had promised Nan that she would look after him, she had stayed with him until it was time for *Emmerdale* and his attention was diverted.

She was tired when she got home, so she made herself a cup of tea and sat at the family room table to drink it. It was the first opportunity she'd had to look at *The Times*, but with only a few minutes to spare before she had to prepare dinner in time for Jim's return, she just flipped over the pages snatching headlines and looking at the pictures. A photograph of a strikingly attractive woman caught her eye, probably because she could see that, given a few years, Fiona would be just such a woman. The woman was straight-backed, confident, slim and wearing a tailored, dark business suit and crisp, striped shirt open to cleavage level. The accompanying article was about a mail order fashion business that was to be floated on the stock exchange, and the photograph was that of its founder, the forty-two-year-old Ms Wendy Longden.

Linda studied the other woman. Her blonde hair was shoulder-length, glossy, not a strand out of place. She had high cheekbones, arched brows, long lashes and light eyes. The clothes spoke of a determined woman, a professional, but the fine chain around her neck with a single diamond teardrop was a delicate feminine touch. The cut of the blouse was an indicator that she knew how to use her femininity. That woman was clever and would, no doubt, have a string of relationships to add polish to her bedtime performance. Linda, who had never aspired to a career, had only ever slept with the one man, felt overcome by a feeling of utter inadequacy and anger. At that moment, she knew she could not let Jim get away with it. Whatever the consequences, she had to tell him. And the time was right. Suzy was away for the week with friends, celebrating the end of school for ever, Fiona living in London, and Rob, having finished the university term, had gone travelling around Europe for the summer. She and Jim would be alone.

When he came home at eight, she was still sitting at the table, the newspaper open in front of her.

'It's quiet around here,' he remarked, pecking her on the cheek, hovering behind her with his hand on her shoulder.

'Just as well, really,' she said, deciding to dive straight in with no pussy-footing. She pointed to the picture. Up to then she had been contained, determined not to be hysterical, but suddenly the emotion shot up like some sort of internal volcano. Tears filled her eyes so that when she looked up his handsome features were swimming. Any thought he might have had about denial were washed away. He violently swept the paper off the table.

Her tears, having started, wouldn't stop. This wasn't how she had wanted to handle it, but they just kept coming. She buried her head in her arms to hide them, but her stomach kept heaving. She felt sick and swallowed, time and again, but still the convulsive sobbing wouldn't stop. She felt Jim's hand on her back. She shook her shoulder to shrug it off, but he dropped to his knees beside her and taking both her shoulders, pulled her firmly against him, folding his arms tightly around her.

'I'm sorry.' He buried the whispered words into her neck. 'So very, very sorry.'

She still couldn't speak. She sobbed onto his shoulder because she hadn't the energy to pull away and nowhere else to release her feelings. He stroked her hair, every now and then hugging her a little more tightly. Eventually the eruption eased to a slow, smouldering trickle. Forcing herself to sit upright, she fished up her sleeve for a tissue. Jim left her side to fetch the box, appropriately man-sized. He took a couple himself and blew his nose loudly. Her arms and neck were soaked. She dabbed them with tissues until she felt able to trust her voice to ask the one-word question.

'Why?' It came out as a croaky whisper.

He reached for her hand and grasped it tightly in his. 'I don't know. Believe me, Lindy, it was nothing to do with you. I couldn't ask for a better wife. You are everything … '

She shook her head. 'Then why..?'

'However I try to explain it, it sounds … ' He talked hesitantly, his fingers twining and untwining around hers. 'It just happened. I was at a function. You were supposed to be there but,' he hesitated and folded his hand tightly around hers, 'you had to stay here … something to do with Suzy.' He swallowed hard, his grip on her hand hurt her fingers. 'It … it just started as banter … and got out of control.'

She couldn't find words. Instinctively she tried to understand. He had been under pressure, his wife had been preoccupied. A psychiatrist might say he was subconsciously

162

wanting to reassure himself that he was in control, except that he wasn't. He was weak. In all their years together, despite his faults, she had always thought of him as dependable. He'd always been flattered by the way other women flirted with him, and had flirted back, but that was always as far as it went.

'But it wasn't just that one night, was it?'

He met her eyes, surprised that she knew. 'A couple, then … I came to my senses. It was only ever a fling. It wasn't serious … '

'Not to her, or you, maybe. It means a lot to me.'

He gripped her hand hard again. 'It didn't and doesn't affect my love for you.'

Finding that impossible to believe, she met his eyes. 'But it does affect mine for you.'

For a while he said nothing. He just sat there, staring at her with something going on behind his eyes that registered disbelief that she could cease to love him, horror that he might not be able keep the whole business secret. 'I … I hoped you'd never know.'

'I've known for weeks … '

'How did you find out?' His bewildered chestnut eyes searched hers, making her heart ache and bringing fresh tears.

She had already decided that telling him that Rob had told her would serve no useful purpose, and until she had decided what she was going to do about it, she didn't want to risk the rest of the family becoming aware. 'Does it make a difference? It happened and I know it happened. My problem now is how can I live with it?'

'What do you mean?'

'How can I stay with you when everything I thought I was working for has been tainted?'

*

She had stayed, of course, for the sake of the family and most particularly for Fred, and having decided she had to stay, she had done her best to forgive Jim, but she could not forget. Love-making had never been the same. It became something she did to show that she shared his desire for things to be normal but she couldn't respond with the same warmth and joy as she had. She felt he sensed it, too, but he never made a comment. He probably accepted it as the price he had to pay, but had it ever occurred to him that she was paying it, too?

She had told Rob that the issue had been discussed, that his father had been very contrite and promised it wouldn't happen again, and that she was going to forgive and forget. She wanted him to do the same and most particularly she didn't want him to tell the girls. More than anything, she wanted to keep her family together. On the whole it had worked but Rob's admiration of his father had been severely knocked. Everything that had motivated Jim became suspect in Rob's eyes, so much so that he didn't bother to return to university, he just kept travelling, largely on foot, from France, Spain, Italy through eastern Europe, Africa and now Australasia. His wandering, she had believed, was his search for something worth striving for.

She wondered now if her own walk had been a subconscious test of Jim's sincerity. It was difficult to identify exactly what had motivated her. She was just aware that she wanted to feel that he valued her as a person with feelings and preferences. She wanted something more than the passionless relationship that now existed. And now she realised that more than anything, what she had wanted was for them to be as they used to be.

Outside the church she sat on a bench and dialled Jim's office number on her mobile. It was his direct line and he answered the phone himself.

'Hi,' he said, obviously recognising her mobile number on his console.

'Hi,' she replied, 'I just thought I'd give you a quick call as I didn't catch you at home last night.'

'I wasn't there. With nobody to go home to, I worked late and stayed at the club. How are you getting on?'

Worked late and stayed at the club. She wondered but determinedly put the suspicion from her mind. 'I'm doing fine. I'm sitting outside the church in Richmond.'

'It's all right for some.'

'There's been a wedding. It's all flowers and confetti.'

There was a thoughtful pause. 'Er … how nice. I'm just off to a meeting. In fact, you only just caught me.'

'Just think, you could have been here with me, enjoying the tranquillity.' She lifted her face to the cool drizzle.

'I'm glad you're enjoying it.' He sounded more rattled than glad.

'I'll be walking with Nick again today. Ten miles to Reeth.'

'I'm happier knowing you've got somebody to walk with.'

His apparent lack of jealousy was really quite hurtful. Didn't he care that she might be attracted to Nick? Or was it simply that as she hadn't abandoned him when she'd had good cause, the chances were she never would? Or was there another reason: that he didn't care?

'Come in,' he spoke to somebody else. 'I'm sorry, darling, I'm going to have to go.'

'And so do I. Have a good day.' She certainly planned to. She was going to put the blue feelings to the back of her mind and just enjoy herself because that's what she'd set out to do.

'And you. Love you.'

Did he, really, or were they words said out of habit?

*

She had arranged to meet Nick by the stone cross in the cobbled market square. His smile as she walked toward him brought an unexpected girlish flush to her cheeks. He looked so happy to see her, so eager to spend another day in her company. Jack was also pleased to see her, circling around her and lifting his front feet in a half jump.

She ploughed her fingers into the thick damp hair around his shoulders. 'Hello, handsome.'

'Is that me or the dog?' Nick laughed.

'Mmm,' she grinned at him. 'Tough contest, but … '

'But no contest. I know when I'm beaten.'

As Wainwright had written in his book, Richmond was a town too interesting to be simply passed through. They spent a couple of hours wandering around the narrow streets of higgledy-piggledy buildings, mostly Georgian, up to the ruins of the castle which should have had a commanding view, but the river snaked mysteriously from and into the mist. After a light lunch, they set off to follow its course westwards for the ten-mile walk to Reeth.

The persistent misty rain didn't dampen her enthusiasm. It was an exciting moment, another very different stage in her journey. She was now heading into the Yorkshire Dales and Pennines. The going would be harder, more challenging. The landscape was becoming more dramatic, hillier, with limestone escarpments and long lines of walls dividing green pastures, and the river, which remained in view below for much of the way, rushed through the valley like a great stream of frothy coffee.

This was her fourth day walking with Nick and they had become easy company. They could stride on for ages in silence, and just as easily chat about whatever came to mind. Her diversion to Mount Grace Priory and visit to the church in Richmond had prompted quite a lengthy discussion about religious belief, or, in his case, lack of it, which then occupied her thoughts for several miles. After her marriage she had stopped regular church attendance, not because she ceased to believe, but because she couldn't fit it into her busy life. When the kids had been born she'd had them christened, more to please her parents than any real belief that their little souls would be condemned if they weren't. She'd also sent them to Sunday school because she felt that she should not deny them the opportunity to make up their own minds, and on the whole, she believed in the basics. The ten commandments and Christ's teachings of humility and honesty were good rules to live by, but she had always struggled with the concept of life after death, and still did. As far as she was concerned, this life was the only one she would have, in which case, did it make sense for her to devote the rest of her life to somebody to whom she felt unimportant?

They arrived at the village of Reeth in the early evening. It reminded her strongly of Melling Leas in that its houses surrounded a large area of green, but whereas Melling was largely enclosed by woodland and fertile agricultural land, Reeth had a more open aspect of grey-walled pastures and rising heather moors. The King's Arms, where she had booked a room, turned out to be a three-storey Georgian building sandwiched in a terrace of houses and shops and facing the village green.

'It's all right for some,' Nick grimaced when they arrived at the door. They were covered head to foot in dripping waterproofs, his face was rosy-cheeked and damp, little droplets of water clung to his beard.

'Come in and at least have a drink in comfort,' she suggested, reluctant to part company.

He looked down at Jack whose coat was dark and dripping. Jack wagged his tail, sending a little shower of droplets into the air.

'I'll find out if he's welcome,' she said. He was and the chap in the bar very obligingly found an old towel for Nick to give the dog a quick rub down to get the worst of the wet off. To Jack it was a game, he danced away as Nick tried to catch his feet to wipe them, and then he grabbed the towel in his teeth for a tugging match.

When they were divested of their waterproofs and muddy boots and sat at a table with their pints of Black Sheep, the thought came into her mind that he didn't have to trudge off to spend the night in a tent with a soggy dog. She had booked a double room. The thought brought a hot flush to her face.

'Warming up?' he asked, his grey eyes fond and smiling as though he had read her mind.

'It's my age,' she said. It could be, but she hadn't been troubled much with hot flushes for at least a year. That thought brought her back to her senses. She was fifty-one, for heaven's sake! How could she, who had only ever slept with one man in her life, expose her cellulite and wrinkles to another!

When he went to recharge their glasses, Nick came back smiling.

'I'm in luck. They have a room.'

'Oh, good!' she beamed back at him, relieved that she wouldn't be spending another evening on her own. 'We can have dinner together.'

It was a super evening. Considering how much time they'd spent together it was amazing how much they still found to talk about. Nick made her laugh with his anecdotes about his work and life on his brother's farm. She liked the sound of his family who came across as easy-going but caring and close. She told him about the Rainbow and her dilemma about whether or not to take it on and he then told her about the village of Hesket Newmarket in Cumbria where the villagers had formed a consortium to buy their local pub and brewery, rather than see them close or absorbed into a larger business and lose their unique identity. It was certainly an option worth thinking on.

Over coffee they discussed the route for the following day. The weather forecast, which she'd seen on the television while getting ready for dinner, was good with just an outside chance of a shower. She had planned to take the low-level route which stayed with the river Swale and meandered along footpaths and lanes which, she imagined, would offer plenty of flora and fauna to interest her. Nick favoured the high-level route across the moors.

'You can do riverside walks at any time,' he said, 'but up there is one of the most interesting sections of the walk. You'll be walking in the footsteps of Romans, Vikings, Saxons. There are the ruins of the old lead mines which once employed hundreds of people. It has atmosphere. Real history.'

They tossed a coin: he won. It didn't cross her mind that they could go their separate ways.

Sleep did not come easily that night. Her mind was all over the place. She was having a lovely time and enjoying the undivided attention of her companion, but he should have been Jim. Had Jim joined her, the evening's meal would have been a romantic affair, they would have left the table and gone to bed and made love, tenderly and unreservedly. They might, after five days of walking together, have found what they'd lost and, perhaps, spent time planning their post-family future. But he wasn't with her and the future wasn't clear. During the dark days that had followed her discovery of Jim's infidelity, divorce had not been discussed, but she had certainly thought about it, long and hard. In the end, she had realised that her pain was only part of the equation. Her parents, her father-in-law and her children would all have been deeply affected and she couldn't bring herself to hurt them. But now? And why now? The answer was there in her head and making her body tingle. Nick. Before there had been no reason to put her family through the torment, beyond salvaging her dignity and punishing Jim, but now?

Before leaving Reeth, she checked her mobile and discovered that Jim had called the previous evening.

'Hi, darling. Sorry I had to rush off this morning. I hope you had a good day. Call me when you can. Love you.'

She returned the call straight away, hoping to catch him having his usual coffee and toast breakfast before leaving for work.

'Hello,' his voice snapped irritably.

'Good morning.' She resisted the temptation to make a crack about getting out of the wrong side of the bed.

'It's not good. I've overslept. I'm not yet dressed and won't have time for breakfast.'

'Catch a later train,' she suggested, feeling very relaxed.

'I've got appointments.'

'Oh, that's a shame. So, apart from over-sleeping this morning, how are you getting on?'

'Lindy, I haven't got time for this. I'm in a hurry.'

'No change there, then.' She used Suzy's oft-repeated phrase.

'I'll call you tonight, okay?'

'Okay. Have a good day.'

'Humph.' The phone clicked.

'And you have a nice day, too,' she said the words she would have liked to have heard and then answered herself. 'I will, thank you. I know I will.'

*

True to his word, Jim phoned that evening and she told him about her wonderful day, which had begun with a heart-pumping mountain climb onto heather-covered moors for a lesson in industrial archaeology and history. She tried to describe the endless, magnificent views over the moors and down the dales and how exhilarated she'd felt when, at the end of the day, she dropped down to Keld, a small village in the heart of the Pennines, and the official halfway mark of the Coast to Coast walk. She told him that as it had been mid-afternoon when they had arrived, she and Nick had taken a couple of hours to relax and scramble alongside foaming waterfalls and refresh their feet in ice-cool water of crystal clarity. She made a point of telling him that it had reminded her so much of when the children had been small and the fun they'd all had building dams and splashing about.

His mood had been considerably improved and he responded with remarks like 'How interesting,' and 'Sounds marvellous,' and 'Those were the days.' He made no comment about the fact that she was still walking with Nick, which either meant he trusted her completely, or not in his wildest imagination did he think another man would fancy her now that she was middle-aged. Just a little suggestion of jealousy would have made her feel that she meant something to him. He told her that he had called to see his father the previous evening and they'd had a pretty average supper together at the pub. That really surprised her. He didn't usually see his father during the week, so she hoped the diversion from the norm was a hint that he was planning to be away at the weekend, possibly even in Kirkby Stephen, paying her a surprise visit, or even that he had taken the whole week off to join her for the second half of the walk.

*

By the time she descended from the Pennines the following day, heading for Kirkby Stephen, she was beginning to feel nervous. She should be feeling excited at the prospect of seeing her husband after a week's separation, but she wasn't. She wasn't even sure that he would be there. He used to like planning pleasant surprises, so it was possible that he had taken the hint. She had to acknowledge that what she was hoping for was the old Jim, the man he used to be, the man she had loved. Had loved? Past tense? Had it really come to that?

'Well, here we are, then,' Nick's voice broke into her thoughts as they entered the town. She had already told him that she was expecting to meet her husband here and might not be completing the walk, at least, not this trip; she was absolutely determined that she would do the rest of it, one day, and hoped that, inspired by her enjoyment of the first half, Jim would be motivated to join her for the second.

'Will you come to the hotel and meet Jim?' She was being polite but wasn't really sure that she wanted them to meet.

He smiled, a little sadly, 'No, you're all right.'

She smiled at his Cumbrian way of saying 'No thank you'.

'If you decide to go on, and want company, here's my number.' He gave her a card which had his address, home and mobile phone numbers.

'Thank you. But I think you'll be a couple of days ahead of me by Monday.'

'I'll walk on to Shap tomorrow, but plan to take Sunday off.' He grinned. 'If I'm lucky I'll get a proper roast dinner at my brother's house. You can either catch me up or I'll come back for you.'

'You're very kind. It's been really lovely walking with you. I shall miss you.'

'Aye, and I you, lass.' He leaned forward, kissed her cheek and squeezed her arm. 'Until we meet again, then.'

She nodded, then bent to stroke Jack. 'Goodbye, Jack. It's been nice knowing you, too.' She could feel that she was about to get emotional, so she straightened and took a deep breath. Lingering would only make it worse. 'Right. I can find my own way to the hotel from here.'

'Call me tomorrow and let me know what you've decided to do.'

She nodded again. 'Okay.' With another goodbye nod, she turned and left him to walk in the other direction. Before rounding the corner, she turned back. He was walking slowly away, Jack at his heels. The dog kept turning his head back to see if she would follow.

*

The first person she saw when she went into the hotel was Jacquie hobbling along the red carpeted corridor toward the lounge. An avid reader with a lively imagination, Linda could create all sorts scenarios as to what might have happened in the few days since they parted company. None of them put Jacquie as a victim or heroine. Hoping that Jacquie wouldn't notice her, she rang the bell on the reception desk. The hotel was not what the brochure had led her to expect. The carpet was worn, the paintwork chipped, the large-patterned wallpaper unchanged in forty years. A smell lingered of stale cigarettes and chips. A young man came across from the bar. His crumpled white shirt and baggy black trousers made a mockery of the attempt at hotel uniform.

'Hi,' he said, cheerfully. 'What can I do for you?'

'I'm Mrs Challoner. I have a room booked.'

The lad checked the book. 'Aye. There you are. Room six.' He handed her the key. 'Up the stairs, along the landing, last on the right.'

Oh, dear, she thought, Jim isn't going to like this. 'Has my husband arrived?'

'Can't 'ave, if the key's still here.'

Picking up her rucksack, she headed up the stairs. Her feelings about Jim joining her became whisked rather than

175

mixed. She wanted to see him, if he was going to be like he used to be, jolly and seeing the funny side of things that weren't right, but if he was going to grumble about the long journey and be picky about the poor standard of the hotel when they could now afford something better, then she didn't want the hassle. He didn't often get picky, but in his current mood she couldn't be certain that he would make the event a pleasurable one.

Liberal use of polish and lemony bath cleaner had left the room smelling fresh, and a quick inspection of bed linen and bathroom confirmed that it was perfectly clean. She had no idea what time Jim would arrive, if he did at all, but guessed, based on previous experience, that he wouldn't have left London any later than three, so she estimated it would be seven at the latest. That gave her plenty of time for a bath and to get herself as tidy as was possible in clothes that had spent seven days packed in a rucksack.

She spent half an hour in the bath and at least the same again drying and styling her hair and applying lipstick and mascara, none of which she'd done since she left home. She sat on the bed and watched the six o'clock news. Her stomach felt as though it hadn't seen food for a week, when in fact she'd had a very hearty sandwich at lunchtime, but that had long since been converted to necessary energy. To pass the time, she telephoned Jenny to tell her the story so far.

'So tell me about the bloke you're walking with.'

'He's tall, dark and handsome. The spit of Piers B.'

'I get the picture. Short, fat, bald … '

'Tallish, greying, but then aren't we all, bearded, chunky but fit. He's an outdoor person, incredibly well informed.' She could have added warm, old-fashioned, gentle, but that could well be misinterpreted by somebody who thrived on gossip.

'I don't suppose you could bring him home with you, could you? As a present from your holiday? So much more interesting that a stick of St Bees rock.'

'He's not your type. You don't like walking.'

'Is he yours?' The voice on the phone acquired a serious, concerned edge.

She kept it light. 'For the purpose in hand, he's just the job.'

'Hey! Do I detect a holiday romance?'

'Oh come off it, Jen, I'm way past holiday romances!'

'I'm a year or two older than you and I'm certainly not past it. Just give me the chance! I tell you, when I've off-loaded this business, I shall have the time of my life!'

A holiday romance would be all it was for Jenny. No way, under any circumstance, was she ever going to let another man into her life. Twice bitten forever shy had become her mantra, but that didn't preclude the occasional excursion with like-minded males.

When the call was concluded, half an hour later, and Jim had still not shown she knew he wasn't going to. If he had been coming, she was sure he'd have organised it to arrive early. It was now nearly eight. In a way she was not surprised, almost relieved, but, to be contrary, she was also hurt. She rang her home number but there was no reply. All she heard of Jim was his voice on the answerphone asking her to leave a message, so she did.

'Hi, it's me to report safe arrival at Kirkby Stephen. Will phone in the morning.'

Before going down to dinner, to be sure that she wasn't giving up hope prematurely, she telephoned Suzy who reminded her that Friday was Rotary night.

'How could I forget that?' She was amazed but the week had been so different that all the routine stuff had been completely forgotten.

'It's old age!' Suzy chuckled.

'Thank you, darling. How are things?'

'Fine. Dan misses you. He loved the postcard with the lambs. Dad's missing you, too.'

Not enough, she thought, but didn't say it. 'You mean he's missing coming home to a cooked meal and someone to clean up the bathroom after him,' she laughed.

'He's not finding it easy, that's for sure.'

'It's a challenge. He's always liked challenges.'

'Are you okay, Mum, you sound as though you've been drinking?'

'I'm fine, and I haven't, yet. But I'm about to go down for dinner.'

'Are you still walking with the guide? Is he there, too?' The question was asked uncertainly, as if Suzy felt she had to tip-toe around her fears. It did something for her ego that at least Suzy seemed to recognise that her mother might be attractive to another man, enough to be worried that the family boat could be rocked.

'He's gone on alone. I plan to take a couple of days rest here.' It was the truth but she felt she was deceiving her daughter because she was already missing Nick.

'Are you going on?'

'I see no reason not to. I'm feeling really well.' And now she thought about it, she wasn't feeling a great urge to go home, which was unusual for her.

'I don't know whether to be pleased or disappointed. I do miss you.'

'Thank you, darling. Be pleased for me. I'm taking just two weeks out of your life, your dad's life, everybody's, to do something I particularly wanted to do. It's not too much to ask after a lifetime of service, is it?'

'Put like that, no. You go on then, and enjoy it.' For the first time Linda heard a maternal tone in her daughter. It was quite weird; she quite expected to hear the follow on, 'and be careful', in the way that mothers do when they're allowing their kids to go out to play.

'Thank you. And now, I simply must go and get something to eat before I die of hunger.'

*

When she went down to the restaurant, Jacquie was at a table on her own. As with the bedrooms, an effort had been made to make something of the large room: the cloths on the square tables were crisp and white, the linen napkins folded into mitres, the cutlery and glasses shining, but the carpet was stained and the red-flocked wallpaper not only dated but scuffed and peeling at some of the joins. Once, perhaps, the hotel had lived up to the pretensions still promoted in their brochure.

'Hi!' Jacquie waved and called, 'Come and join me?'

Being in a tea room or coffee shop on one's own was never a problem but in a restaurant it was different, somehow more lonely, so she readily accepted the invitation. They studied the menu which, they both agreed, was uninspired and both opted for poached salmon.

Having committed herself, she did her best to be pleasant. 'I thought you'd be at the finishing line by now.'

'I've had to take a couple of days' break. Blisters, would you believe it?'

'I thought yours were top of the range boots?'

'They cost a fortune, but I was caught in the rain.'

'Don't you have over-trousers?'

'I didn't think I'd need them, my trousers are waterproof, but I tucked them into my socks.'

Linda had to laugh. 'That wasn't very bright.'

Jacquie agreed. 'I just didn't think. Now if I'd been with that guy we met in ... hell, where were we?'

'Glaisdale.'

'Seems ages ago, doesn't it?'

Linda nodded agreement. In some ways it seemed a lifetime.

'Anyway, he'd have put me right. He was a strange chap, wasn't he?'

'How strange?'

'I don't know. Sort of obsessed with history and stuff. Didn't seem to notice people, sort of hiding from reality.'

Linda laughed. 'He caught up with me again after you strode off with the three musketeers. We've walked together since then. He's very nice, very interesting and more involved with today's reality than anybody I know.'

'Oh!' Jacquie sounded almost offended. Her observation that Nick didn't notice people was probably how she interpreted his not being attracted to her.

'How long were you with your three admirers?' she asked, somewhat exaggerating the situation to boost Jacquie's bruised ego.

The girl tossed her hair and sipped her wine. 'They were sweet, weren't they, but so immature. It was like walking with a crowd of puppies. I left them to camp at Clay Top and walked on to my hotel.' She smiled widely and looked well pleased with herself. 'There I met a group from a southern Round Table. They were doing it as a fund-raising exercise. I walked on with them and had a lot of fun, but then there was a bit of grumbling from some of them, you know: man's club, wives wouldn't like it, that sort of thing, so I took the hint. Just as well because then I met this gorgeous man.' She rolled her eyes and sipped her wine. 'Talk about having it all. Good-looking, everything well set up. I crossed the Vale of Mowbray with him. He spent the night with me. I tell you, I would have travelled to the end of the world with him for another night like that, but next morning, he said he wanted to be alone and off he went. He never even offered to pay his half of the bill!' She shrugged, but a hard glitter in her eyes told that she hadn't taken too kindly to being used and dumped. 'Anyway, having done twenty-three miles in a day, and none the worse for it, I reckoned I could manage it again and walked from Richmond to Keld in one day.' She tilted her head back, jutting her chin. 'I set out to do the whole walk on my own, you know. I don't need someone to hold my hand, but company's nice when you find it, isn't it?'

'It is.' Linda had the feeling that Jacquie's long walk in the wet had been an angry one. 'Wednesday was a wet day, I remember.'

'Awful. Everywhere was muddy like the Somme and you couldn't see more than a few yards ahead for mist.'

'It was wet, but not unpleasant. Rain changes things, makes them shiny, makes rivers rush, wonderful waterfalls and big splashy puddles. I like walking in the rain when I'm dressed for it. When you have a dog you have to, so you might as well take the positive view.' Walking in the rain without a dog, however, seemed somehow pointless, although, of course, it wasn't: she did it for the fresh air and exercise, but she did still miss Dottie.

'Well, that day created the blisters. The next day I stuck a couple of plasters on and pushed on, but by the time I got here I was bloody nearly crippled. They'd burst and bled and were really sore.' She took a sip of her wine. 'Now I'm losing time, kicking my heels in this place while they heal.'

'Oh dear. How frustrating.' Linda felt genuinely sorry for her, but not enough to want to walk with her again. A young waitress in a tight black skirt and white shirt, both at least two sizes too small, plonked their meals in front of them. The food was better presented than served and the vegetables looked wholesome.

After helping herself to one small potato and most of the broccoli and courgette, Jacquie said, 'Joe, the barman, said that you thought your husband was joining you.'

'How very unprofessional of him, to discuss another guest's arrangements. Unfortunately my husband can't make it. Business.'

Jacquie flicked her eyes in an infuriating way that suggested mice playing while cats away. Linda didn't really believe that Jim would ever be tempted again, but then she had never believed he would be tempted at all.

'So, where's ... the guide bloke?'

'Nick. He's camping.'

Jacquie smiled knowingly. 'Maintaining a low profile in case hubby turned up?'

'Don't be daft. At my age I'm quite happy to walk with a guy without feeling the need to score.'

'You might be, but he's definitely interested. I could tell.'

'We are friends, that's all.'

'Pretty good friends after nearly a week, I should think.'

'Yes, but as they say, just good friends.'

'Will you be walking with him tomorrow?'

'Probably.' Now that Jim hadn't shown up, there didn't seem to be any point in hanging around. Had Jim been here, she might have abandoned the walk, but as he wasn't, well, it rather demonstrated that he couldn't be bothered or didn't want to make the big show of surprising her, so having started it she might just as well go the rest of the way.

'The forecast for tomorrow isn't too good. I might just give my heels another day and see what Sunday brings.'

That more or less confirmed for Linda that if she was going to avoid twenty-odd miles of Jacquie's company, she had to go on the next day.

*

She had another turbulent night. Her conversations with Jenny, Suzy and Jacquie kept turning over in her mind. They all seemed to feel there was something going on between her and Nick. Jenny was a great believer in the 'you only have one life' maxim, and that it was to be used to the full and not wasted on slime-balls like her philandering ex-husband. Flirtation was par for the course on Jenny's holidays, but even though Linda allowed herself, briefly, to fantasise having Nick in her bed, she knew that a holiday romance was not for her, and, as much to the point, she couldn't imagine that it was Nick's way, either. Even so, it couldn't be denied that there was some electricity between them, a spark that, given the opportunity, could develop into something deeper and longer-lasting. She could easily imagine that he would be just as easy wherever they were and whatever they were doing. She couldn't imagine him criticising her friends, belittling her job or being embarrassed to have to admit that Suzy and Phil were anything to do with him, and she didn't suppose he would expect her to fall in with his plans if they weren't her scene. As it happened, from what he'd told her about himself, he didn't belong to any organisation or get involved in any group activities, so it was unlikely to be an issue. He spent his time either guiding walkers, walking alone for pleasure, helping on his brother's farm or visiting places of historical interest. It all sounded good to her.

But it was just a fantasy. She knew that. She might feel justification in leaving Jim, but what about her family? Only a few days before her father had spoken of his sadness that she had left the church. Divorcing Jim to take up with another man would be just about the worst possible thing she could do to them. And her children, what about them? Rob might understand, but it could just as easily add to his guilt problem. Fiona, who was very close to her father, would probably never speak to her again, and poor Suzy would be heartbroken. Christmas would never be the same again: the kids would have to decide which parent they were going to spend it with. That thought brought a wry little laugh. How daft that she should even consider those three days out of three-hundred-and-sixty-five as significant, but they were, or had been, the highlight of her year. In a way the annual family gathering had symbolised her achievement. For just a few days they were all together, or they used to be. Rob had been missing for the past three Christmases but he always sent a video of himself with a Christmas message, just for her. She was touched by that because it meant that the family tradition was still important to him, but she was also pained that he didn't feel he could be there in person. Throughout the recent troubled years, the family had remained the focal point of her life and was the main reason she had suppressed her pain and stayed with Jim. She had, she supposed, always hoped that one day things might gel again, but it was beginning to look highly unlikely that they would. That being the case, she had some very uncomfortable decisions to make, because she didn't think she could spend the rest of her life with the status quo.

CHAPTER 9

S HE DID EVENTUALLY GO TO SLEEP and woke up still weighing up the pros and cons of her life as it was. Her life with Jim wasn't bad. She liked her home and, on the whole, she had always enjoyed the social life that spun off from his golf, Rotary and business, albeit of late there'd been rather too much of it. She had her own set of friends: the mothers of kids who had been at school with hers; the women she'd met on the catering course; village people she'd met through her mother-in-law, WI, and Horticultural society, and the regular café customers, all of whom she was involved with on a daily basis, so she was never bored or lonely and felt very much part of the village community. She didn't even mind keeping an eye on Fred, it was the fact that Jim saw it as her duty that sometimes got up her nose. She particularly liked having Suzy and the kids within fifteen minutes' walk. So why did she feel so ... it was difficult to say what she did feel. She wouldn't say she was unhappy, nor even dissatisfied, it was more sort of unsettled, a kind of frustration.

Jim returned her call soon after she had finished an unsatisfactory breakfast of tinned grapefruit segments, solid scrambled egg and soggy toast, but at least they'd managed a decent pot of tea.

'It seems really strange here on a Saturday without you,' he said after the initial hello and how are yous.

'It's pretty strange here without you, too.' On the spur of the moment, she decided to be straight with him. 'I thought you'd join me as I'd booked a break here.'

'You didn't really think I'd drive all that way, did you?'

'Mmm. Silly of me, wasn't it?'

'You didn't make it very clear that that's what you expected.'

'I thought you'd want to.'

'I know you said something about a break, and possibly not doing the whole thing, but as you seemed to be making good progress, with no problems and hadn't mentioned coming home, I assumed you were going for gold. Mind you, having seen the abysmal forecast for the next week, I think you might want to reconsider.'

'The forecast's not that bad. Sunshine and showers. I can cope with that. I've never minded walking in the rain.'

'I heard there's going to be storms. Anyway, I couldn't have taken the time off yesterday. I had meetings to attend.'

'Had you really wanted to see me, you could have driven up after the meeting, or even set off early this morning. You used to do mad things like that.'

'For crying out loud, Linda, it's difficult to know what you want these days. My understanding was that you wanted to do this thing on your own. You said you were quite happy for us to go our separate ways. Dammit, it was you that suggested it, remember?'

'You have very selective recall, Jim. Originally, I said I wanted us to do the walk together. I only suggested going our own ways because you weren't keen and I didn't want to go on yet another Rotary weekend or golfing holiday.' The thought suddenly occurred to her that perhaps he preferred group holidays because he felt uncomfortable alone with her. These days they seemed to spend very little time alone together, and when they were, they were often preoccupied with preparations for some event or other.

He heaved a long sigh. 'I'm sorry. Really. I obviously misunderstood. I miss you.'

'I miss you, too. I miss the man you used to be.'

'What does that mean?'

'You've changed. Our life has changed.'

'Of course it's changed.' Adding, after a brief pause, 'for the better. We have a lot going for us and a comfortable retirement to look forward to.'

'Are you looking forward to it? Retirement, I mean.'

'It's still a long way off, but yes, of course I am.'

'How do you see it?'

He sighed. 'Like a load of Saturdays and Sundays all linked together. Golf, days out, entertaining, time to read, see a bit more of the world, travel, that sort of thing.'

'Walking holidays?'

'That, too, while we're able.'

'And time with the children and grandchildren?'

'Of course.'

She noted that neither walking nor family had rated in his first list of retirement activity.

'Linda?'

'Yes, I'm still here.'

'I worry about you, you know. You say that I'm not the man I used to be, which might not be a bad thing.' It was a weak attempt at humour. 'But you're the one that's acting pretty strangely these days. I wonder, do you really know what you want?'

'I want to feel valued.'

'Darling, you are.'

'Then why don't I feel it?'

'I don't know, it's not for want of my trying. I buy you flowers, chocolates, take you out to dinner.' He certainly did, but it was no longer done spontaneously, not fired by a sudden desire to surprise and please, and it would, she supposed, be churlish to point out that he took her to the restaurants he liked, and that he ate far more of the chocolates than she ever did.

When she didn't answer him, he changed the subject. 'So, what have you decided to do? Are you walking on?'

'I've started, so I'll finish.'

'What about your companion, is he still with you?'

'As I was planning a break, he was going on.'

'Come home, Lindy. You've had a good week.'

The feeling of not being ready to go home hit her again. 'I think that as I've made it this far, I'll go on. I might never have the opportunity again.'

'Not alone?'

'Maybe, some of the time. It depends who I meet.'

'Listen, if you're going to go on, contact Nick. I don't want you going alone. You're moving into mountainous territory. You might fall.'

'Aren't you in the least bit concerned about me being constantly in the company of another man?'

'He's a professional guide. It's more than his job's worth to seduce his clients.'

'I'm not his client.'

'No,' he sighed heavily. 'I suppose, technically, I am.'

'I beg your pardon?' A cold, almost ghostly feeling crept around her shoulders.

'I hired him. I wanted you to feel you were doing this thing your own way … it's what I thought you wanted, but I was worried about you.'

A sudden hot flush seared through her whole body. Anger, frustration, humiliation twisted round her mind so that words couldn't form to express the fury that boiled inside her.

'For God's sake, Lindy, I just want you to be safe.'

'So … ' she had to control her breathing carefully. 'So you hired somebody to do what you couldn't be bothered to do yourself!'

'It's not a question of being bothered – '

'It bloody is! What is boils down to, Jim, is that I am not your top priority. That being the case, I see no reason for feeling guilty for taking another week to do my own thing. And by my own thing, I mean MY OWN THING.' She shouted the last words and immediately flicked off the phone, effectively shutting him out, slamming the door in his face.

Her breakfast fought the tautness of her diaphragm, threatening to go into reverse. She swallowed hard and took a series of deep breaths, forcing herself to calm down. Her anger was more easily conquered than the embarrassment regarding her feelings about Nick. She had so nearly made a real fool of herself. She had made a fool of herself: just fantasising about him the way she had, had been foolish, and even though she was the only person who knew, it was utterly humiliating. Had his chat been simply to keep her interested so that he could fulfil his commission? And she, poor fool, had thought he was attracted to her, had even been flattered by the thought! What a sad, sad person she was. A shivery feeling passed across her back as she wondered what Jim had told Nick about her? What reason had he given? Had he told Nick that his poor wife was having some sort of menopausal mid-life crisis? How utterly, utterly humiliating.

After a while she got up, washed her face and phoned down to the reception desk.

'Could you prepare my bill, please. I'm leaving this morning.'

'You're booked in for tonight.' The voice was that of the lad in the crumpled shirt.

'I know, but my husband isn't after all able to join me so I'm leaving today.'

'There'll be a fifty quid cancellation charge.'

'Fine.' Good. All the rest of her holiday had been financed by her own earnings, but this one would be put onto Jim's credit card.

She carefully repacked her rucksack, ensuring that her waterproofs were ready to hand, then sat on the bed to study the map. The next stage of the walk looked fairly level: it was the plain between the Pennines and the Lake District mountains, but unlike the Vale of Mowbray, this was not going to be a pastoral valley stroll. She would be walking for twenty miles, most of it along a high, uncultivated, limestone plateau with very little in the way of habitation, although there would be evidence, according to the book, of ancient settlements. No doubt Nick would have given her chapter and verse as to how human beings had eked out an existence in such inhospitable terrain, and why. She was going to miss his company but had no intention of contacting him. It would be too embarrassing. And besides, he had deceived her just as surely had Jim had. She put her shoulders back, recalling that she had set out from Robin Hood's Bay expecting to do much of the walk on her own, and she still felt she was capable of doing so, in fact she was now bloody determined to do so. She did not need Nick or any man to guide her. Her mind did a quick flash to Jenny who would be saying something like 'Go girl! Who needs a man anyway!'

'You're bloody right,' she replied.

She sent a text message to her children and Jenny, '9 a.m. Leaving KS for Shap. e.t.a 5 p.m. Love you.'

*

As it happened, she didn't leave Kirby Stephen immediately, but went in search of a bakery to provide her with a packed lunch, a greengrocer for some apples, and was then enticed into a clothes shop by a 'Sale' sign and a rather pretty crepe skirt that wouldn't suffer from being stuffed into a rucksack, which, feeling a rebellious need to treat herself, she bought, complete with a top to go with it. It was nearly eleven before she left the market square.

To start with the going was easy, the track mostly distinct with directional waymarkers across the moors. She set out with a determined stride and enjoyed the sensation of being alone in the landscape. There was just her, and for all the notice the shorn sheep took of her, she might have been invisible. Only the birds reacted to her presence, making her jump as they rose suddenly from the wind-blown grass, squawking or tweeting their protest at her intrusion. Occasionally she exchanged a few words with groups of people walking the west to east route. Most remarked that the weather was better than forecast, but at mid-day the cloud descended, shrouding the landscape in a fine soaking mist, reducing visibility to just a few yards. A stop to don waterproof jacket and trousers seemed prudent. Fortunately, she had just reached a point on the walk where she had to walk for nearly three miles along an unfenced road so she didn't feel threatened, in fact she rather enjoyed the sensation of the cool mist on her face and the total silence that surrounded her. The road seemed to go nowhere because she neither saw nor heard a vehicle. It reminded her of a time-slip novel she'd read as a child, in which the young hero had set out on a causeway to an old Abbey, only to get caught in a mist and emerge at the Abbey in Norman times. Where, she wondered, might she emerge from this mist, this mist of her life?

She was, she realised, experiencing some sort of crisis, but she strongly refuted that it was a mid-life crisis, at least not one in a menopausal sense. True, her nest was now empty, but she was still very involved in her children's lives and had no feeling of having outlived her usefulness. To be honest, and she had said as much to Jim, she didn't actually miss them being at home. It was nice to come home and find the place still tidy and not to have to go around their rooms in search of mugs and plates. It was even nicer to be able to listen to the radio without them talking over it as though she'd only got it on for background sound. Meal planning was easier, too, with no fads, fancies or varied timescales to be considered. Her books, her sewing things, her clothes didn't disappear, her newspaper remained intact, the crossword not magically completed before she'd had a chance to look at it.

So, she contemplated, if not the children, what was this big vacuum she felt in her life? One answer came quickly. Nan. She and Nan had been on the same wavelength, shared the same ideals, loved the same people. Nan had helped her throughout her early days of motherhood, rarely interfering but always available when she needed help or advice and, having taught Linda basic cookery, she'd been really interested and enthusiastic when she had taken it up professionally. They had been good friends.

The other more recent vacuum had been created by Dottie. Somehow, the dog's passing had brought everything to a head. She couldn't think why, except that without Dottie she felt so alone. It was ridiculous because she was surrounded by friends and family but, she now realised, she hadn't had support from the one person who should have understood. When Nan had died, her own grief had been expressed in caring for the people that shared the loss; or had it in reality been suppressed, confused by everything else that had been happening then? At the time she had realised that Jim's grief had been combined with guilt; he had even said that he felt he had let his mother down. She thought she knew what he meant. Nan had approved of Linda from almost the day they were introduced; she had told her son that Linda was good wife material and that he'd be a fool not to look after her.

It begged the question: had he married her because he loved her or to please his mother? It was a silly question, quickly dismissed, because they had been happy, and she was sure it wasn't just her blindly thinking they were happy. They had been absolutely, passionately happy, but then something changed. He changed, and now he had the gall to suggest that *she* was the one having a mid-life crisis!

The waymarker she had been looking for appeared out of the mist. She had a decision to make. The route pulled away from the road back onto the moor. According to the map, much of it followed the line of the lichen-covered walls, but there were areas where in the mist she might not see where she was aiming for. She had experienced this before, one morning walking with Dottie across fields that she knew well, but in thick fog she hadn't been able to see the corner of the field and was amazed to find that she had walked in an arc and ended up in a totally different spot. However, if she stayed on the road, she could walk to a village called Orton which, she had read in one of her many books during the plotting stage, had the added attraction of a chocolate factory, and probably accommodation if she decided that she didn't fancy more moorland walking in poor visibility.

A little voice in her brain accused her of making excuses to take the easier option. The little voice was right. However, she argued, launching into unknown territory in thick mist was hardly the behaviour of a mature, sensible person, was it? In the end, she opted to head for Orton and was pleased she did because it was, even on such a dreary day, a delightful little town of old farmhouses, terraced cottages, little streams and greens, tall trees and some rather fine residences. See, she told her inner voice, if I'd headed over the moors, I'd have missed this.

The chocolate factory wasn't a factory in the accepted sense, more a large craft kitchen with a café. Inside it smelled familiar, warm, sweet and comforting. She purchased a few items in the shop to stow in her rucksack, in case of emergency, and arranged for luxury boxes to be sent to Jenny and her daughters and a chocolate rabbit for Daniel. The café was not over-busy and she was able to find a table to herself where she could spread her map. She looked again at the plotted route and decided that to head onto the fells would be both foolish and pointless. There appeared to be several lanes leading toward Shap: the more direct would take her quite close to the motorway and onto an A-road, which she didn't much fancy; the alternative was to head northward along a road which ran more or less parallel to the official route, then turn west along a track to pick up the route on an obvious farm road. This seemed a sensible compromise.

Sensible compromises, she recognised, were the tenet of her life.

Again, this was one she didn't regret. At least she could enjoy the environment without concern about getting lost or having an accident, and she wasn't too bothered about missing the excitements of a few disused quarries, ancient settlements and tumuli. Once out of Orton, the road climbed quite steadily and on a fair day she imagined there'd have been a good view of the surrounding fells and farmland. She passed a few old farms but mostly the aspect was open, rough grassland, inhabited only by sheep. It was a summer Saturday afternoon but hardly any traffic passed her. She wondered if there was a big test match or golf tournament on TV to keep people entertained indoors. On such an afternoon she could hardly blame them. The rain was now persistent, plastering her hair to her head and finding its way down her neck. If she was sensible she would pull up her hood, but she hated wearing a hood because it obstructed her side vision and shooshed around her ears so that she couldn't hear approaching cars, and it wasn't as though the rain was cold, just a little uncomfortable.

To start with she was fine, striding along the lane, enjoying her solitude, taking pleasure in the things she saw. Things like the chunky lambs, now several months old and quite capable of fending for themselves but who still wanted the comfort of mother's milk: they buffeted the poor ewe so hard that her legs left the ground. There were wild flowers, too, in the grass by the roads, and the beginnings of fruit in the brambles and blackthorn which reminded her of Nan, blackberry jam and sloe gin.

By the time she reached the pretty riverside village of Crosby Ravensworth, the persistent rain had become a hefty downpour driven by a freshening westerly wind. When she turned west onto the track that should join the Coast to Coast route, she walked straight into it. It stung her face and even though she gave in and pulled up her hood, it found its way in. Walking head down into the wind was no fun. Her waterproof trousers couldn't cope with the force of the rain being thrust at them and streaming off her jacket, they began to leak at the thighs and she could feel the water penetrating her trousers and running down her legs into her boots. She trudged on towards a slate-grey sky along a deeply puddled, stony track alongside a beck which tumbled and foamed over and around boulders and rocks.

Taking the rough with the smooth was part and parcel of the adventure, she told herself in an effort to dismiss her discomfort and think positively about the nice warm bath and hot meal that was awaiting her somewhere in Shap. She hadn't anything booked. Her thought on leaving Kirkby Stephen had been that Shap was a sizeable community on a busy road and therefore bound to have a good choice of accommodation. Her guidebook listed several, although she had no idea where they were in relation to the walk, but they had telephone numbers which she would try when she approached her destination. Head down, she pressed on, fantasising about a warm cosy farmhouse with huge kitchen warmed by an old fashioned range; she could almost smell the delicious casserole that would be simmering in the oven behind the steaming socks and trousers on the clothes horse.

In theory, the track was not quite two miles but it seemed much longer before she came to a small cluster of farmhouses where she rejoined the Coast to Coast path. It was already gone six, she was wet and tired and contemplated seeing if there was accommodation to be had at these houses, but decided to press on for Shap. The next day's walking, according to the book, was a long one with a high climb, so she really didn't need to add a couple of miles to the beginning of it, and besides, stopping short of her stated destination smacked of weakness.

The rain was now lashing down in wind-driven swathes and the going underfoot was heavy. Her boots were sodden and it seemed that every item of clothing beneath her waterproofs was soaked. For the first time since she'd set out, her pack felt heavy. This was no longer fun, but it was still a challenge and the brief thought of calling it a day at Shap was quickly dismissed. At the very most, she might just consider taking the day off that she had planned at the last stop at Shap instead. That made sense: it would give her time to dry out and rest before she tackled the steeper Lake District terrain.

The path emerged into Shap conveniently opposite the King's Arms Hotel. It was twenty past seven and all thought of cosy farmhouses were abandoned. She had to wait for a while for a few cars to swish past and then hurried across the road, but before she reached the door a man's voice called out.

'Linda!'

She turned and saw Nick slam the door of a car and jog towards her. There could only be one reason for his being there: Jim had contacted him. The thought revived the anger of the morning. She turned away but he was too quick and had hold of her arm before she made the door to the hotel.

'Linda, wait, please. Let me explain.'

'Thank you, but it's not necessary and right now I'm not in the mood.'

He gripped her arm to prevent her escape. 'I've been looking for you all day.'

'So now you can tell your client that you've found me. I'm sure you'll be adequately recompensed.' She pulled her arm from his grip. A man making for the door of the hotel hesitated then stopped and turned back.

'Are you all right, lass?' He looked from her to Nick and back to her.

'Yes, it's okay. Thank you.' She forced a bit of a smile.

The man frowned at Nick, still uncertain, but then headed for the shelter of the hotel.

'Look, I can understand how you feel, what you must be thinking, but I promise you … '

'You don't have to explain. It's not your fault, but whatever Jim may think, I don't need a shepherd.'

'Are you staying here tonight?' He indicated the hotel with a flick of his shoulder.

'I will if they have room.'

'You're not booked?'

'No, but I'm sure that if they haven't got a room, I'll find somewhere else.'

'I have a spare room. You're welcome to it.'

'Is this your idea or Jim's?'

'Mine. Okay, Jim called me this morning, since when I've been trying to second guess your movements. You'd left the hotel before ... ' He raised his hands palm up to the rain. 'Look, do we have to stand out here discussing this?'

'No. I told you, there's no need to explain anything.'

'Please accept my offer. No strings. I need to talk to you.'

All she wanted was a hot bath and dry clothing, something to eat, a comfortable bed and a long, long sleep. So what if Jim had set it up. Did it matter? Too tired to argue she capitulated with a sigh. 'All right. Thank you. I'll come to your place.'

'Come on.' He led the way to the old estate car. She didn't note the make, just that it was green. Jack was in the back looking very woolly as though he'd been very wet and had a good towelling down. He wagged his tail and did a little dance as Nick helped her remove her rucksack. He tried the tailgate door but it wouldn't open. He went to the driver's door and pulled on the door handle but the car was locked. He put his hand in his pocket for the key, frowned and tried several more pockets, then bent to look into the car. 'Bugger!' he said with feeling.

She followed his line of sight and saw the key in the ignition. 'Oh bugger, indeed,' she groaned.

'I don't suppose you have a wire coat hanger in your rucksack, do you?'

She shook her head. 'Nothing remotely like.'

'Don't go away.' He left her standing in the rain by the car while he dashed into the hotel. Five minutes later he emerged, already unwinding the hanger.

Being a responsible dog owner, he'd left the windows on both the driver and passenger sides open by about an inch, just enough to get the extended wire through. It wasn't easy to control but after about ten minutes he managed to get the hook through the key-ring. Despite the rain, several people, huddled under umbrellas, had stopped to watch his progress. She held her breath as he tugged and twisted. He concentrated in silence, gripping his words of frustration between tightly pursed lips until he had the keys removed from the ignition and dangling precariously at the end of the wire. Carefully, he started to withdraw the wobbling hanger but just as he brought the keys to the window, they slipped off the hook and rattled to the floor. The crowd groaned in united frustration. Nick drummed the roof of the car with his fingers then bent a little to talk through the open window.

'Jack,' he commanded. Jack's ears pricked. 'Over.'

Jack put his head on one side, his thoughts transparent. 'Er ... you want me to jump onto the back seat? I don't think so. It's not allowed.'

Nick tapped the window alongside the back passenger seat. 'Come on Jack. Over.'

Jack seemed to frown, then cautiously put one leg over the back of the seat. When his master didn't object, he slithered over from the tailgate section onto the seat, where he sat wagging his tail nervously, his eyes fixed on his master.

'Good boy.' Nick praised the dog then tapped the window by the driver's seat. 'Over.'

Again Jack looked uncertain, his head on one side as if to say, 'You know this is breaking all the rules?'

'Over, Jack. Come on,' Nick urged.

The gathering crowd waited in hushed anticipation.

'Come on, Jack. Over.'

Jack eased himself between the two front seats and settled in the passenger footwell, his golden eyes still on Nick.

'Good boy.' Nick dangled the wire coat hanger in the general direction of where the keys had fallen. 'Fetch it, Jack. Fetch it.'

Jack crept across to the driver's side well and searched for whatever it was he was supposed to fetch. He found a Twix wrapper and lifted it to his master's waggling fingers. The gathered crowd laughed.

'Good boy.' Nick took the paper. 'And the other one,' he urged. 'Fetch it.'

Jack went down to find something else. Finding only the keys alongside the seat, he twisted his head and used his paw to pull them towards him.

'That's it,' Nick said. 'Fetch it here.'

The keys were difficult for Jack to grasp in his mouth. He dropped them a couple of times but on the third attempt he was able to lift his head without them escaping.

'Good boy. Good boy.' Nick encouraged. 'Fetch it here.' He waggled his fingers through the small gap. Jack put his front paws on the seat and lifted his head to his master's fingers but let go too soon and the keys fell onto the seat. Everybody sighed. 'Come on, Jack. Fetch it.' Nick urged again. Jack retrieved the keys and again brought them to the waiting fingers. This time Nick managed to hook a finger through the ring and brought them out. The crowd of half a dozen or more people burst into applause. Nick unlocked the door and Jack jumped out to receive the adulation of his audience.

'What a dog!' they said, eventually dispersing into the rain, eager to tell their family and friends the tale.

Linda took her turn to pay homage to Jack's brilliance, giving him a good rub around his ears and sinking her fingers into the depths of his damp coat. 'What a hero!' She looked up to Nick. 'How on earth do you train a dog to do something like that?'

He bent to give the dog a congratulatory bash on the shoulders. 'He's a working dog, intelligent, good stock, but also a playmate. He learns through play.' He went to the back of the car to let the dog in, giving him another affectionate rumble around the ears. She had previously observed that Nick's relationship with his dog was exceptional, born, she supposed, out of his loneliness, but now she saw the total trust that Jack had in his master. Nick was a kind man, a man to be trusted. She felt ashamed that her earlier thoughts about him had been so uncharitable. He smiled at her, more relaxed now. They both were. 'Come on.' He picked up her rucksack and put it in with the dog.

CHAPTER 10

'I 'D GIVEN UP HOPE OF FINDING YOU,' he said, once the car was on the move.

'How did you know where I'd be?' She stared ahead, trying to see where she was going through the rain on the windscreen.

'Luck. You were seen passing Oddendale. I have a friend there and asked him to call me if he saw you.'

The windscreen wipers were going full time but even so, it was difficult for her to see much of the surroundings beyond the fact that he had driven out of the town on the main road, then turned off into a stone-walled country lane. They passed a couple of isolated houses, but otherwise it was all open country with occasional copses. He turned down a track and through an open gate into a large farmyard. It was still raining heavily and Nick didn't hang around long enough to give her time to take stock of where she was. All she noted was that the stone house was part of a sizeable complex of barns and buildings. Hood up and head bent against the rain, he led the way around the side, through a tall gate into an overgrown, small back garden. A path along the back of the house ended at a door into a small barn extension. He opened it then stood aside to let her pass.

'Welcome to Gill Head.'

She crossed the threshold into a large room where she stood dripping onto a stone-flagged floor while Nick and Jack followed her in.

'Sit!' Nick commanded Jack, who promptly obeyed, swishing his wet tail in an arc across the floor. The utility room had an old deep sink and wooden draining board, modern washing machine and tumble drier; a whole assortment of coats hung on hooks and boots and shoes on a rack. A dog bed and bowls were in one corner. Nick's dripping walking clothes were suspended from the ceiling on an old-fashioned drying rack.

'Let's get you warm and dry and then we'll talk, okay?'

Feeling muscle-weary and emotionally exhausted, she acquiesced with a nod. 'Thank you.'

While she took off her waterproofs and boots, he took a towel to the dog. It was a job that Jim and the kids had always hated but she and Dot had made a game of it, just as Nick and Jack did. She waited for them to finish, her t-shirt and trousers sticking to her body, her thick socks making puddles on the floor.

'Grief,' he said. 'You're soaked through. We'll have to look at those before you go on.' He indicated her discarded things.

'They're not new.' She stated the obvious. 'But they weren't cheap and coped with southern rain well enough.' Old habits die hard and she'd baulked at spending a lot of money on new gear that might only be used once.

'I bet you didn't test them in ten hours of it!' His brows raised teasingly but then he smiled. 'They'll be all right. I've got some water-proofing stuff.' He opened the cupboard beneath the draining board and extracted a blue plastic bin bag. 'Empty your rucksack into this. Let's hope everything's dry inside.'

She nodded her gratitude, did as bid and then followed him, barefoot, from the utility room into a huge, Aga-warmed kitchen that ran from the front to the back of the house. The long dresser and dining furniture were rustic, old and dark; a high-backed wooden chair with indented cushion stood beside the Aga. He crossed the room into a short hall and led the way up the narrow stairs to one of the rooms at the front. It probably hadn't been re-furbished in three generations but the big old-fashioned, wooden-headed bed, draped with a patchworked quilt, looked divinely comfortable.

'It's all much as my parents left it,' Nick apologised. 'I don't have visitors so haven't got around to changing anything. Bathroom's down the hall.' He dropped the bag full of her things, which were mostly dry, onto the bed. 'The water's good and hot. Take your time. I'll bring you a cup of tea to take with you.'

He left the room but came back very quickly. 'You might need this.' He handed her a paisley dressing gown. Obviously one of his, it would go around her twice if not three times. He was right that she'd need it: to minimise what she had to carry, she had not packed dressing gown or nightdress, sleeping in just a t-shirt and knickers, so she appreciated its decorous cover for the walk to and from the bathroom.

When alone, she looked at her watch. It was gone eight. She knew she ought to phone Jim but was still too angry. She wondered if Nick was now calling him to let him know the missing ewe had been found, but somehow she thought not. Not wanting to get drawn into conversation with any of her family, she sent a text message to Fiona, Rob, Suzy and Jenny, letting them know of her safe arrival in Shap.

*

Feeling clean and feminine in her new skirt and top, she returned to the kitchen after a good, deep soak in an old-fashioned tub.

'That's pretty. I haven't seen it before,' Nick remarked, picking up a bottle of red wine.

'I bought it this morning,' she said, giving him a twirl.

'In Kirkby Stephen?' he asked.

She nodded.

'So you didn't leave at nine?'

'No. I went shopping.'

He looked skyward. 'I was told you'd left at nine. I went like the clappers to catch up with you!'

The telephone rang.

'That could well be Jim.' Nick paused in the process of pouring her a glass of wine. 'Shall I let the answerphone take it?'

She nodded and sat down, leaning against the high back of the chair at the kitchen table, her aching legs extended, bare feet supported on the rail of the refectory table. 'Do you know Jim?'

He stayed at the kitchen end of the room, leaning against the sink, nursing his jug of beer. 'Not directly. He contacted me through a former banking colleague. As I understand it, he was telling her about your planned walk and she told him about me and what I did.'

She. At one time mention of female colleagues hadn't worried her, but ever since Jim's affair she'd reacted with a twinge of suspicion which she'd had to work hard at hiding. 'What did he tell you about me and what I was doing?'

'Not a lot. Just that your son had done the C to C and that you wanted to do it, too, but he was concerned for your safety. He hoped you'd change your mind and wait for a time convenient for him, but as you didn't ... ' he lifted his shoulders. 'He did say that as you wanted to do it alone I wasn't to tell you that he'd sent me. It seemed somewhat unusual.' He grinned. 'I told him that I wasn't a private detective and wasn't going to report back every move or person you met up with.'

The mental picture of him ducking and diving behind bushes and boulders to avoid being seen made her smile. 'Supposing, having met you, I'd decided I didn't want to walk with you?'

'I asked that. He said that it wasn't necessary for me to walk with you, just to keep an eye on you.' He lifted his shoulders again. 'I said that given the terrain and route options, that would be nigh impossible. He was pretty laid back about it, gave me your itinerary, and said to just do my best and that it was worth a try. As I didn't have anything else on I thought I might as well.' He smiled softly. 'I have to say, I'm glad I did.'

A warm glow crept up her face.

'Look,' he said, leaving the support of the sink, coming toward the table and taking the chair opposite hers, his elbows on the table. 'It's none of my business, but it's pretty obvious to me that your walk isn't simply a matter of following your son's footsteps.' He twisted his mouth from side to side as though uncertain about saying what he thought. 'You're making a statement, right?'

'Huh! If I am, I'm not getting my message across.' She felt he deserved some explanation. 'I wanted Jim to do the walk with me. He's a busy man and I've always supported him. All I wanted was two weeks for me. But,' she shrugged, 'he couldn't, so I took the time for myself.'

He kept his lips tightly closed as he nodded, his interpretation, his thoughts, kept securely to himself. He drained the rest of his beer and she sipped thoughtfully on her wine.

'Well,' he said, getting up from the table. 'Now we both know where we stand. What are your plans now?'

'I'm going on.'

'Would you like me to accompany you?'

She twiddled the stem of her wineglass. Yes was the instinctive answer, but was it wise? Was it fair to him?

'You don't have to answer now. Think about it. I'll just say this, though. If I came with you it would be as a friend. I'll not charge a fee to your husband.'

She nodded acceptance of the gesture, unsure, but at the same time excited. Jim had said that Nick wouldn't risk his reputation by seducing his client's wife, but if Jim was no longer the client..? She had to bite back a little smile: Jim

210

obviously didn't know Nick very well because she had a feeling that Nick wasn't too bothered about his job, and although seduction might not be his style, he was capable of, and ready for, something more lasting.

Nick topped up her wineglass. 'May I make another suggestion?'

She nodded.

'The next stage of the walk is a high climb with spectacular views, but the forecast for tomorrow is appalling. Heavy rain all day. You won't see a thing. So why don't you take the day off, stay here? It'll give me the chance to re-proof your jacket and trousers, and for your boots to dry out.'

Put like that, she didn't see there was much option, and was glad of it. She smiled at him. 'Thank you. I should like that.'

'Good. Now, let's get some food.'

They spent the next couple of hours at the kitchen table, talking about the day's walk. She told him about the decision she had made to take the lanes rather than the moors.

'I should have known,' he laughed, 'that you'd take the easy option. I've been all over the bloody moors looking for you!'

'I don't always take the *easy* option. There's nothing cowardly about being sensible.'

'Absolutely. I should have known, but then I also knew that you were angry. Maybe not thinking clearly. As you didn't call me, I guessed you were angry with me, too. Perhaps feeling I deceived you.' His voice dropped. 'I didn't want our friendship to end like that.'

She put her hand over his which had been repositioning the salt and pepper pots in the centre of the table. 'I was angry, but not for long. I can see it must have been difficult for you.'

He turned his hand to grip hers. 'Very. I didn't expect to find somebody like you.'

She laughed. 'What did you expect?'

'I don't know, really. I just didn't expect to … ' He released her hand and scraped his chair on the flags as he pulled away. 'I somehow imagined somebody more strident, not so … soft.'

'Soft?'

He smiled back at her from the kitchen sink where he placed their plates. 'It's meant as a compliment. You are soft. You don't like offending people. You even spent several evenings with that awful woman, and agreed to walk with her, though it was plain she wasn't at all your type.'

'She's not awful. Just,' she struggled to find the right word, 'lost. I think she's lost her way.' As often happened when thinking of Jacquie, Fiona came to mind. 'I can't just ignore her, she reminds me too much of my elder daughter. I worry that she'll end up at the top of her mountain, only to find herself stranded there because nobody else can climb that high.'

He smiled. 'I expect you'll keep her feet on the ground.'

She wished she had his confidence. Nan had said that she would keep Jim's feet on the ground but she'd totally failed to do so. She leaned back in her chair, stretched and returned the subject to the walk. 'I'm looking forward to the mountains. It's years since I've been to the Lake District and even then I didn't often get the opportunity to do the big climbs because Suzy wasn't up to it.'

'Like I said,' he smiled, 'you're soft. You surrender to the wishes of others.'

'Not this time. This is my time.'

'Good on you. I suspect you deserve it.'

*

All night, wind and rain clattered across the window, the tiles rattled as if doing a Mexican wave above her, but beneath the blankets she was cosy and warm. The bed had a stretched mesh base with horsehair mattress and candy-striped flannelette sheets which reminded her of her childhood, and of long cold nights spent fantasising about the life she wanted to make for herself. Her fantasies had always included a man whose arms would be around her, loving her, protecting her, needing her. For years, Jim had satisfied that need.

The earlier call had not been Jim. It was becoming painfully obvious that despite the morning's altercation, she wasn't his number one priority. No doubt he thought that by contacting Nick he'd done all he had to.

She thought a lot about Nick during the night. It seemed odd that he'd had the house for several years and still hadn't changed things; she wondered if that indicated that he wasn't yet sure that he was going to stay. She felt that perhaps he was another lost soul, wandering the moors and fells looking for something to make his life feel worthwhile. There was little doubt in her mind now that he was attracted to her, and although she tried very hard to understate the discord between her and Jim, Nick, it seemed, was beginning to put his own interpretation on things. It presented her with an awful dilemma. He had asked if she'd like him to do the rest of the walk with her, which she did, but it seemed a risky thing to do because the further she walked with him, the further she was walking away from Jim.

The question was not resolved when she was woken in the morning by the closing of a door downstairs. She looked at her watch. It was gone ten o'clock. How long was it since she'd slept in so late? She stretched and felt her muscles protest. A day of rest was a good idea. Getting out of bed she pulled on the paisley dressing gown that Nick had loaned her and went to the window to open the floral curtains. Sheets of monsoon-style rain swept across the fields that sloped down to the Eden valley, obliterating the view of the Pennines which, Nick had assured her, were there. Sodden sheep were huddled against the dry-stone walls in one field, black cows crowded beneath an old oak tree in another, slapping each other's faces with their dripping tails. Another field had been cut for hay but not gathered, probably ruined.

This was Nick's environment, his background; the world that he had left when he was young, to which he had returned when his hopes had turned to ashes. He had been quite blasé when he'd spoken of giving up his career to care for his wife, but she wondered if the choice had been that easy, and if the necessity had affected their relationship. If something like that had happened to her, what would Jim have done? Without a shadow of a doubt, he'd have brought in somebody else to care for her. As much to the point, she would not have expected him, or even wanted him, to give up his career, particularly if her condition was terminal, because she would have known he would need something to keep him going after she'd gone.

She wondered what it had been like for Nick, day in, day out, for several years, being constantly with somebody who was slowly deteriorating, knowing that he was going to have to re-think his plans for the future, and that when that day came, his previous career would not be there to go back to. He didn't give the impression of feeling that he had nothing to live for: on the contrary, he seemed quite content plodding along with his dog, doing a bit of this and that. Making money didn't seem to be an issue either, he seemed to make enough for his needs, which were simple. She wondered if there really was a hole in his life, or was it her wishful imagination?

The day that followed was another that she would never have imagined when planning her journey. They lunched with Nick's brother's family in the sprawling bungalow that had been built to one side of the farm. Nick introduced her as the wife of a friend of a friend, so that there would be no misunderstanding about their relationship. Even so, the novelty of Nick bringing a friend to their house was sufficient to create curiosity. It became immediately obvious that she need have no worries that Nick might end up a lonely old man: he was very much part of the family and the farm. From the conversation across the table it became apparent that he'd taken responsibility for the business side of the farm and was not, as he'd previously suggested, just lending a hand now and then.

The rain eased off in the afternoon so, in borrowed rainwear and wellies, she went with Nick and Jack on a tour of the farm. It was a brief glimpse into a world very different from her own, but one where she felt comfortable, and as on their walks to date, he was happy to talk about it for as long as she was interested in listening. They returned to his house, jointly knocked up a pizza of sorts for their supper and spent the evening in the kitchen playing Scrabble. It reminded her of the days when the children were young and she and Jim had hired the holiday cottage near Keswick. They'd had their fair share of wet days, and yes, the kids had grumbled, but on the whole they'd been fun and were remembered with fondness by them all. When Nick got up to make the hot chocolate and she packed the Scrabble things back into the box, he said, quietly, cautiously,

'You haven't said yet whether you'd like me to come with you tomorrow?'

'I do,' she replied with equal caution, 'but … ' How could she say what she meant without it sounding presumptuous, or creating awkwardness between them? She didn't want him thinking her acceptance inferred she was game to move the relationship on, tempted though she might be.

'As a friend,' he said, squeezing her shoulder as he placed a mug of steaming sweetness in front of her. He might have added, that's all, but it remained almost hopefully unsaid.

'Okay,' she agreed, still uncertain as to the wisdom of it. 'But you're on your word of honour that you'll not be contacting Jim.'

He flicked his mouth sideways as though to say that contact with Jim was the very last thing he wanted.

*

She phoned home early the next morning to catch Jim before he left for work. There was no reply which could mean one of several things: he had left early, he was in the shower, he was running behind schedule and didn't have time, or he knew it was her and didn't want to speak to her. The answerphone clicked in with his cheerful voice.

'Good morning,' she said after the tone, forcing herself to be bright and breezy. 'It is up here in sunny Cumbria. I'm about to leave Shap for Patterdale. I'm walking with Nick, so I'll be quite safe. I'll text you when I get there.'

The weather forecast for the day was for a bright start, turning humid with the threat of storms later in the afternoon, so they planned an early start. Nick's brother dropped them at Shap. They strode off with Jack happily sniffing ahead of them, first down lanes, then across rough open grazing land to arrive at the first of the lakes. For a couple of miles Haweswater twinkled in the sunlight to one side of the path, the bracken-covered fells rose at the other. Water was everywhere, trickling down crevices, tumbling down waterfalls, puddling across the path. Nick had told her that England's only nesting pair of golden eagles lived here, but they weren't around, leaving the clear blue skies to the skylarks, crows and buzzards.

Turning away from the lake they braced themselves for the two-mile climb up Kidsty Howes, the steepest, if not the highest, that they would encounter on the walk. It was hard, sweaty work, involving many stops to mop brows and admire the view. Every stop was worth it. The Pennines behind them were blue and distant. It was hard to imagine that she had walked from there to this spot and for many miles before them, every step on her own two feet. At the top they diverted slightly to a point where, through Nick's binoculars, she could just make out Blackpool tower to the south west, and the Scottish power station across the Solway to the north. Somewhere between them, hidden by range upon range of mountains was St Bees. There were just over fifty miles to go in five days and then it would all be over. Nick pointed out the various mountains, including Helvellyn, which they'd be tackling the following day. It looked benign, easy, nothing like as challenging as the one they'd just climbed, but she knew from what she'd heard and read that it was one of the most dangerous, at least it was when approached via Striding Edge. It was a challenge that this time she was determined not to shy away from. But that was tomorrow and tomorrow she might think differently and opt to bypass it altogether, and settle instead for the valley walk through Grisedale, which was, in fact, the recommended route.

She had read somewhere that life was a journey and that the destination was less important than the journey itself. It was a maxim she had always liked but doubted that Jim would agree. He set his sights, plotted his course and let very little divert him unless it offered a shortcut to his goal. She, on the other hand, was far more likely to take a meandering path, stopping to investigate things along the way. Originally she had thought she and Jim were headed in the same direction, albeit on different paths, but now it seemed that their objectives were different, and possibly had been all along. Jim's career was the single most important thing in his life and not, as she'd always thought, the means by which he provided for his family. The family no longer needed his financial support, the roof over his head was secure, his pension fund adequate, but that didn't lessen his drive for the top. And what, she wondered, would he find when he got there? Would he realise that he was there on his own, and that his wife and family were still miles behind him enjoying the view from a lower level? She began to see that their drift apart had started long before his affair.

Such thoughts were not to be dwelt upon. Now was not the time for thinking too much about the future, it was all too complicated and she wanted to enjoy the journey.

They arrived at a pile of stones heaped upon rugged, lichen-covered granite. A young man was there, alone. He was tall and thin, reminiscent of Rob, and much the same age.

'Hi,' he said. 'Great day.'

'Isn't it,' Nick agreed.

The lad's rucksack was huge with bedroll tucked in the top.

'Are you doing the Coast to Coast?' Linda asked.

'Yeah. You?'

'Yes.'

Nick and the lad chatted for a while about the pros and cons of various routes and then, as they were about to part company the lad asked, 'Would you mind taking a photo of me on my camera?'

'Not at all.' Nick took the proffered camera and the lad posed by the cairn with his pack on his back, one foot on a rock as though he'd just conquered Everest.

'Brill. Thanks. Would you like me to take one of you two?'

'Yes, if you don't mind.' Linda quickly extricated her camera from the side pocket of her rucksack and handed it to the lad. Nick drew her to his side and put his arm across her shoulder. 'C'mon, Jack,' she said. 'You, too.' The dog obligingly sat at their feet and when the lad mentioned the word 'cheese' he looked hopefully at the camera.

After that, the lad strode away, intent on reaching Orton before the forecast storm arrived.

Nick looked to the west where the distant view had disappeared into a dark grey haze.

'I think he'll be lucky to get to Shap before that lot reaches us. We'd better get a move on, too.'

For a while, as she and Nick progressed along a well-defined path, a Roman road which was basically a high grassy plain, she thought about Rob. Whilst she understood his reason for leaving, she didn't understand the aimlessness of his wanderings. It wasn't as though he claimed to be broadening his horizons or gaining life experience, he was just constantly moving on, stopping long enough to earn a bit of money to see him through the next stage of his journey.

She felt sure it had nothing, or very little, to do with his future plans, but was a statement about how he felt about his father.

Like Fiona, he had always worked hard to make the grades at school because he wanted his father's praise. It was hard to imagine how he had felt when he discovered that his father was not the role model he'd wanted to emulate. It must, in his mind, have made a mockery of all that praise. It had certainly made it very difficult for Rob to stay at home and pretend that he didn't know what had gone on. She wasn't sure that Rob had properly understood why she hadn't wanted him to tell his sisters: in his opinion they had a right to know. Keeping the knowledge to himself had been too big a thing for him and now she began to wonder whether she had been wrong. She hated him being so far away where she wasn't able to talk to him properly, to see his face, to read in his expression things that his words didn't tell her.

The route was full of ups and downs and twists and turns around placid little basins of water and craggy outcrops, with many paths criss-crossing, requiring frequent references to the map. That was one of the things she really liked about Nick: although he knew the way, he gave her the opportunity to develop her map-reading skills and follow the route she had planned. Just before they began the steep part of the descent to the Ullswater valley, they stopped to look across to Helvellyn.

'Tomorrow's challenge,' she said.

'Mmm,' he commented. 'We'll worry about tomorrow, tomorrow. Our next and most immediate challenge is to find shelter for the night.'

'Aha,' she teased. 'It was you that said not to book in advance.'

'For good reasons, still held.'

His reason had been that too much forward planning could take away spontaneity and put a timescale pressure on things. They might, he had said, want to dally somewhere. She, who traditionally planned everything, had found the suggestion rather daring: it added a sense of freedom to this last part of the expedition.

The first big spots of rain fell just as they reached the Patterdale valley. Her guide book listed two farmhouses, two guest houses, a large hotel and an inn.

'The inn's good,' Nick said. 'Good beer.'

'We'll go there first, then. At least we can shelter there until the storm passes.'

She could immediately see why the old pub appealed to Nick. It was a walkers' and drinkers' sort of place, clean and recently up-dated but unpretentious. They were not alone in thinking it a good place to shelter, there was almost a crush at the door.

Nick went first to the reception desk to enquire about a couple of rooms.

'Sorry, mate,' the Australian lad shook his head. 'Only one room left. It's twin bedded, though.'

'I'll take it, if you don't,' a man behind him said.

'I'll take it. Thanks.' Nick turned to her. 'That's you sorted. I'll have to look elsewhere.'

She thought about it for just a moment. 'Don't get the wrong idea, but, heck, we spent two nights in your house together, so is a twin bedded room so different?' She could feel her colour rising. 'What I mean is ... I know I can trust you ... and ... '

His eyes held hers. 'If you're sure.'

A hot flush chose that moment to completely suffuse her. As if interpreting it as extreme awkwardness to be discussing it in front of the guy at the desk, Nick touched her arm in a soothing gesture.

'We'll take it,' he said to the young Aussie.

CHAPTER 11

I T WAS ACTUALLY QUITE FUNNY. Having been shown to their room, Nick left her there and returned to the bar with Jack so that she could use the facilities and sort herself out, and then she vacated the room to give him the same privacy. When it came to bedtime, after a splendid steak dinner and convivial evening in the bar comparing notes with other walkers, she went up first so that she was safely tucked up in her bed before he and Jack came up. Diplomatically she turned her back and closed her eyes while he undressed, visited the small en suite bathroom, got into his bed and turned out the light. She couldn't help giggling. Jack's tail softly thumped the floor in the dark.

'You peeped,' he said.

'No, I didn't. It just seems so ... funny.' The word she'd first thought of was naughty: naughty like children doing something a bit daring that grown-ups wouldn't approve of.

'It's certainly an unusual situation.' His voice sounded deeper in the dark.

Her eyes acclimatised to the gloom of external lights glowing through the rain-streaked window and casting a weird, watery image on the ceiling. He was right, the situation was completely weird. She had expected to do the walk very largely on her own, perhaps, as Rob had said, joining others for bits and pieces along the way. She had expected to make new friends, if only in passing, but never in her wildest imaginings had she anticipated that she would meet a man who would stir feelings in her that she hadn't felt for a very long time. She turned her head on the pillow and looked across the three-foot gap between the beds. He was lying on his back, his hands behind his head, eyes open, apparently watching the progress of the raindrop image on the ceiling. She felt a huge urge to cross the gap and snuggle in beside him. Would he be surprised if she did? She didn't think so. He would welcome her, wrap his big arms around her and hold her close. Love-making would be tentative. They would be strangers getting to know each other, careful not to embarrass or cause discomfort. It would be lovely.

Jack let out a long sigh in the dark as he relaxed into his doggy world of dreams. Nick grunted as though envying the easiness with which the dog was able to switch off the day. She was tired, but her mind was still too active for sleep, her body ached, not just from physical activity but with a need for which satisfaction was just an arm's length away. It would be so easy, but wrong. That Jim had transgressed first wouldn't make it right. That Jim had let her down and failed to see how much she needed reassurance from him, didn't justify her having an affair. And it wouldn't be an affair, it would be the beginning of something bigger, instinctively she knew that.

'I've made up my mind. I'm going to give up the guiding business.' His voice intruded on her thoughts. 'I think I'm ready to move on.'

'Move on to what?' She felt there was something underlying the statement.

'I've often thought I'd like to run a bookshop. Second-hand books. Something specialised: walking books, guides, history, geography, all the things that interest me. I've got the capital. I've got my pension from the bank so it won't have to be hugely profitable.' After a short pause, he added, 'It would be nice to have a little coffee-shop, too, where people can sit and browse the books.'

'Sounds lovely.' Even to her, her voice sounded husky. A nervous, excited warmth spread over her body: was he letting her know that he was daring to dream that they could have a future together? She could imagine it. She could see herself living in his farmhouse and the two of them setting off daily to a little shop, or maybe they would find a shop with living accommodation, somewhere in the heart of the Lake District. He would potter among the bookshelves, happily passing on his knowledge to anybody interested, she would run the café; they would take Jack for long walks on the fells and her children and grandchildren would come up for holidays.

But would they? Rob, yes; Suzy, probably; Fiona? No, Fiona would stand by her father. But her loyalty would be misplaced. That, she realised, was what was still bugging Rob. Nick's plan for the future appealed to her far more than the future Jim had outlined: it was warmer, more peaceful and, most importantly, together. But could she do it? Could she live with her conscience if she left her family? Even if they accepted the situation, they would never be a family again in quite the same way. And what about Fred and her parents?

And how would Jim feel? How would he feel having been the one that had introduced Nick into her life? He would be amazed, truly amazed, because he didn't think for one minute that she would ever contemplate straying from his side. That, she realised, was partly her own fault. She had given him to believe that he was forgiven and, because she'd always gone along with his plans, he'd assumed that she was happy with them. When she'd finally said she wasn't, he'd been surprised, so surprised that he didn't believe it. He really did think this was a temporary blip, the change-of-life, empty-nest thing that she would recover from and resume life as normal. He will have gone to work this morning, frustrated that she was continuing the walk, but reassured that he'd done what he could to ensure her safety. He'd have grunted when he received this evening's text message advising of her safe arrival in Patterdale, but never in a million years would he imagine that she would be sharing a room with the man he'd commissioned to look after her. Was that complacency or trust?

'Are you still awake?' Nick said, very softly.

'Mmm. Just,' she lied because she was afraid to talk. It would be too easy to drift along with his line of conversation, and where might that lead?

'Goodnight, then.'

'Goodnight.' She heard the rustle of sheets as he rolled over.

She rolled over, too, and reverted to her childhood habit of fantasising about warm arms surrounding her. In tonight's fantasy they were Nick's arms: it was as far as she dare go.

*

Jack putting his chin on her pillow woke her. He wagged his tail enthusiastically. The room was bathed in sunshine. Nick was already out of bed, dressed and making tea.

'Good morning,' he smiled warmly. 'You were sleeping well.' His eyes were gentle, her lack of response to his statements of the previous night clearly understood. He wasn't going to push or rush but must have felt the need to hint at his feelings. Perhaps he'd been testing the water, letting her know that he was game if she was. The next move was hers, when she was ready.

'What time is it?'

'Seven.' They had agreed that they would make an early start to avoid the seasonal crowd that trailed up Helvellyn. She pulled herself up in the bed, sitting back against the pillows and pulling the sheet up to cover the fact that she was obviously bra-less beneath her t-shirt.

He passed her a cup of tea, his smile conveying several messages: amusement, disappointment, patience, affection. 'It's a lovely morning.'

'Will it last?'

'Who knows?' The forecast had suggested another day with a fine start but deteriorating into storms later. He sat on his bed facing her. 'Are you sure you want to do Striding Edge?'

'Yes. I've got no excuses this time, no child holding me back.' If she wanted to use it, she did have a very valid excuse, and that was that Helvellyn wasn't strictly on the Coast to Coast route. All the guide books inferred that the Grisedale valley route was the more direct and that Helvellyn was a diversion. It wasn't as though she had a driving ambition to put herself in danger or climb great heights, but she felt driven by an uneasy feeling that she was seen as somebody who always opted for the easy route and she wanted to prove that she wasn't afraid of a challenge. 'You don't have to come with me. I don't want Jack put at risk.'

Nick laughed and gave the dog a roughing up around the shoulders. 'He'll be all right. He's sensible and does as he's told.'

'I'd hate anything to happen to him because of me.'

'It won't, but if you want to use him as an excuse, or if you want to go on your own, then that's fine by me.'

'That's not what I meant.'

'That's settled, then. Personally I'm glad, because I think you'd be forever kicking yourself if you didn't do it.'

She wondered if there was more to his statement than appeared at face value, and that he was aware that the ascent of Helvellyn wasn't the only diversion challenging her courage.

*

They set off a little before nine and were not alone. Several pairs of walkers were visible ahead of them, and they even met two people coming down who had been on the top before five o'clock to watch the sunrise. It sounded so wonderful that she put it on her mental list of things to do, but it didn't have to be Helvellyn, any big mountain would do.

The going underfoot was boggy but started gently uphill until they crossed a bridge over the Grisedale Beck, an exciting, deep foaming torrent of red-brown water, constantly being fed by lots of little white watercourses that streaked down from the high mountains on either side. After that they started a long steady climb along a boot-eroded path that pulled away from the bracken and grassy fells into an inhospitable landscape of mottled, deeply fissured crags that had been thrust out of the ground by volcanic forces millions of years before. They had been walking, one behind the other with Jack in the lead, for about an hour when they reached a point on the map that was called 'the hole in the wall', for obvious reasons, and a path veered steeply away to the right, down to a small lake in a basin.

'This is your last chance to change your mind,' Nick said, taking his water bottle from its holder at his waist. 'We could turn off here, go down to the tarn and along Swirral Edge instead.' The exposed part of his face was red and shining from exertion and exposure to the sun. Guessing hers was also unattractively glowing, she wiped her brow on her t-shirt sleeve and looked at the path ahead. The ridge didn't look as narrow as she'd feared, but the drops either side were steep and stony with nasty jagged crags, and this was not yet the infamous Striding Edge. The ridge extended in front of them, curving a little to the right around the Red Tarn basin. Seen from this distance, it looked a bit like the hackled blades on the rising neck of some sort of huge dinosaur: at the moment she was still on its comparatively broad back.

'Are you sure about taking Jack along there?' she asked, fearful that he should lose such a wonderful dog.

'He'll be all right.'

It was his dog, his decision, but she knew if it were hers she wouldn't risk it.

' 'Scuse me,' a voice piped behind her. She looked around to face the child, a boy who would be about nine or ten. He was as brown as a berry with almost white-blond hair.

'Sorry,' she stood aside to let him pass. He was striding with determination, obviously keen to get to the exciting part of the walk. He was well ahead of the rest of his party, presumably mother and sister. The girl, in pink t-shirt and cut-off jeans, was a little older, possibly about twelve or thirteen.

'Come on, Gem,' the mother stopped within earshot to wait for her flagging daughter. 'Tim,' she called. 'Wait.' Tim apparently didn't hear but kept going.

Linda sympathised with the woman's difficulty: she had one child that was keen and wanted to get on, and another who obviously hadn't wanted to be party to the expedition in the first place. They had probably struck some sort of compromise: the daughter's choice of activity would have been the day before, or was scheduled for the day after. It's what she and Jim would have done.

The woman nodded a quick greeting and flicked her eyes skyward as she passed them, hurrying towards her son, leaving the girl to catch up in her own good time. Linda approved the tactic. The girl didn't appear to be frightened, but was making a statement that this wasn't her idea of a fun day out.

'There are times,' Nick said in a quiet voice, 'when one really has to stop oneself from interfering. I could have shouted to make him hear.'

'I know, but some mothers can be very touchy at any suggestion they can't handle their kids.'

The mother called again, more sharply, and this time Tim could not pretend he hadn't heard. He stopped and turned, putting one hand on his hip to make his frustration obvious. The mother caught up and made him wait until his sister finally joined them. An argument ensued, loud enough for Linda to hear the girl's whine and the boy's defensiveness, but not the words. The mother stopped them with a firm brief lecture, then the party moved on, the boy in the lead, but obviously he had been told to slow down, the hands in his pockets said that he wasn't happy about it.

'Take your hands out of your pockets,' the mother instructed.

Without turning, Tim did as he was told, exaggerating the move by extending his arms as if walking a tightrope.

'The joy of kids on holidays,' Nick commented, putting his water bottle back in place and preparing for the off. Jack, ever ready, took up the advance position.

'It must be hard for a parent on her own. At least my slowcoach always had me to walk with when the others strode on with their Dad.'

'Didn't it spoil it for you, though?'

'I never thought of it that way. As long as they were all happy, I was.'

He smiled but made no further comment.

They arrived at a tall, forbidding upshot of rock which marked the beginning of Striding Edge; fortunately there was a well-trodden path around it. The sight at the other side made her heart thump even harder. The ridge was narrow, spiked rock, about a third of a mile long and rising. Either side the ground dropped precipitously with nothing to break a fall other than crags and sharp shale. The distance between them and the family in front narrowed to within easy earshot as the way became more difficult, in places necessitating a scramble over stones that offered very little in the way of foot and handhold. Left to his own devices, Tim would no doubt have bounded along, but the girl was making a big performance about breaking her nails and her legs being scratched and the worried mother did well not to lose patience with her. Jack managed it as sure-footedly as a mountain goat but didn't go too far ahead, and although Linda found the weight of her pack unbalancing, overall it wasn't as terrifying as she'd expected it to be.

The family had reached the last craggy bit of the Edge with Linda then Nick close behind. She wasn't sure exactly what happened, only that it happened suddenly. Tim was in front, beyond the crag, the mother in the middle with the girl still making a fuss at the rear.

'Tim! Wait for us.' The mother called, then suddenly flung up her arms, cried out and disappeared in a great

233

rumble of tumbling stones. The girl screamed in genuine terror as her mother rolled like a rag doll, bouncing haphazardly from crag to crag, down and down the steep slope toward the watery basin. It seemed she would never stop. Linda turned cold, then hot and cold again, every nerve ending stinging on the backs of her hands.

'Christ!' Nick gripped her arm tightly to steady her.

'Mum!' shrieked the girl, 'Mum!'

'I'm okay,' Linda said, moving away from Nick toward the girl who looked as though she were about to jump over the edge.

'Muuuum,' wailed another voice from the other side of the rock.

Nick moved carefully past her to grab the boy. 'Okay,' he said with calm authority. 'You're okay.'

Linda held the shaking girl close to her. The mother had come to rest, motionless, some distance short of the tarn, possibly three hundred feet below.

'Phone, Linda.' Nick waved his free hand in her direction. The other still held the hysterical boy.

Her hands shaking, Linda took her mobile phone from the side pocket of her rucksack, handed it to him and watched him punch 999.

'Cumbria Police, for mountain rescue.' He was put through almost instantly and calmly explained what had happened and where. When the call was over he handed back the phone. 'It'll take them about an hour.'

'An hour?' wailed the girl, her sharp-nailed fingers digging into Linda's arm.

'Right, kids,' Nick said authoritatively, 'we're going to move on, just a little way so that people can get by, okay?'

Neither child seemed able to move.

'Come on,' Linda coaxed. 'You'll still be able to see your mum.'

Hesitantly the children moved, following Nick. Her legs felt stiff but she forced them on. It wasn't far to go before the path widened to where other walkers could pass. Nick then unhooked the boy's hand from his and passed it to Linda. 'I'm going down.'

'How ... ' she went cold again.

'On my backside. I'll be okay. You look after the children, and Jack.'

'I want to come with you,' the boy cried, clutching again at Nick's arm.

'No, lad. You stay here with Linda. She'll see you safely down.' He shrugged off his rucksack, undid the straps of a side pocket and took out a small pack, which she assumed was a first aid kit in something like a bum bag, which he strapped around his waist.

'I want to go to my mum,' Tim insisted, clinging to Nick's arm, tears streaming down his face.

'This is all your fault,' the girl said, hiccupping. 'If you hadn't ... '

'Not now, Gem.' Linda squeezed the girl to her. 'Not now.'

Trembling, she looked down the steep slope. The woman hadn't moved. It was very possible that she was dead. Nick was right, the children shouldn't go down there. But an hour? What was she to do with them?

'Right, I suggest you find somewhere to sit until I get back.' He smiled reassuringly at her. 'I may be gone some time, but I will be back. Look after Jack and my pack.'

She nodded.

He leaned forward to kiss her cheek and squeeze her arm. 'While I'm gone, find out what you can from the kids: names, home address and where they're staying. Someone to contact.'

She nodded again.

'I'm not sure if the mobile will work down there.' He was thinking fast. 'The safest and most comfortable way down will be to go to Wythburn, so unless you hear otherwise, that's where we'll take the kids. I'll come back via Swirral. It'll take me an hour or so.'

Again she nodded.

He turned to Jack and spoke firmly, 'Jack. Sit. Stay.' He pointed to the dog who was already sitting. 'Stay.' Jack looked intently at his master and blinked as though moving was the last thing on his mind.

A middle-aged couple caught up with them. 'What's going on?'

'A woman has fallen. We've called mountain rescue. I'm going down.' Nick explained.

'D'you think that's a good idea?' the man asked, obviously doubtful.

'I'm an experienced climber. I'll be okay.'

They all stood, looking over the edge as Nick sat down and started a controlled descent, moving his feet first to a secure foothold, then moving his bottom, practically lying against the steep side of the mountain, stretching his legs again, and following on, picking his way, slowly, carefully going down. Her heart was thumping, hands prickling: one unbalanced moved and there'd be no stopping the momentum. Once or twice he slithered a bit faster than he intended and her breathing stopped. Another two couples joined them. Linda stayed rooted to the spot, her arms tightly around the children whose eyes were glued to Nick. Jack watched his master, his ears forward, tail still.

It seemed to take a very long time, time enough for quite a crowd to gather and cause obstruction, but eventually Nick made it to the woman. She expected him to wave some sort of signal but the ground was still too steep for him to safely stand. He seemed to be doing something. Taking off the bum bag, getting something from it. An emergency body wrap, she guessed. That was a good sign: the woman must be alive. Then he just sat and waited. She wondered if the woman was conscious and if he was able to reassure her that help was on its way and that her children were being cared for.

She squeezed the children close again. 'Now, you have to tell me your names and where you're from so that I can get somebody to collect you. Okay?'

The girl's face was waxy white, her eyes fixed on her mother below. 'I'm Gemma Beckett,' she whispered shakily, 'he's my brother, Tim. Mum's Gillian. We're from Chester.

We're staying with Mum's sister, in Grasmere.' Fresh tears coursed down her already blotched cheeks.

Linda frowned. 'In Grasmere? But you were walking from Patterdale?'

Gemma nodded. 'Auntie Pauline brought us there this morning, on her way to work. We were walking back.' They hadn't mentioned their father so it seemed tactless to bring him into it.

'Do you know her mobile number?'

'M ... mum has it.' More tears filled Gemma's eyes.

Linda hugged her again. 'Where does your Auntie Pauline work?'

'All over the place. She's a rep.'

'Do you know what company she works for?'

Gemma shrugged. 'Something to do with things for hotels. Coffee and tea and stuff.'

She didn't think she'd get anywhere with that one: there must be hundreds of catering supply companies serving the Lake District. 'Is there anybody at your home, in Cheshire, who might have the number?'

'Grandma,' Tim suggested.

'Do you know your Grandma's number?'

'It's in my mobile.' He sniffed and fished in his pocket. He pressed a button and the number came up in the window.

'Before you dial it, tell me, is your Grandma fit and well?' She had visions of some poor frail soul being given a heart attack.

'She's all right,' Gemma wiped a tear from her face with her lacquer-tipped fingers. 'She'll be at the shop, though.'

'Do you have that number?'

Tim nodded and pressed another button.

'Do you mind if I speak to her on your phone?'

'Her name's Mrs Roebuck,' Gemma said as Tim handed it over. It rang for quite a long time then a strong woman's voice answered.

Linda explained what had happened, reassured her that the children were okay and that she needed to contact their Auntie to make arrangements for them. Mrs Roebuck gave her Pauline's home, work and mobile numbers and said that she would shut up the shop and motor up to Grasmere as soon as she could. She spoke to both the children, adding her reassurance and telling them to stay calm.

The people that had gathered on the top had mostly dispersed as there was nothing they could do. Only the original couple, John and Sandra, remained, standing by in case there was something that they could do and doing a good job of keeping people moving on.

She dialled the mobile number. It rang a few times before it was answered.

'Hi, Pauline Roebuck,' she answered brightly as if expecting a client to place a big order.

Linda again explained who she was and what had happened and that the plan was to take the children down to Wythburn.

'I'm in Cockermouth. I can be there in an hour.'

'I think it'll be two or three hours before we get there.'

'Whenever. I'll be waiting for you. Can I speak to the kids?'

She handed the phone to Gemma who exchanged a few tearful sentences before passing it to Tim who immediately started crying again.

'Here come the rescue team,' John pointed and they all looked down into the valley at the four heavily back-packed people making good progress along the track by the beck. They still had quite a way to walk but for the sake of the children, she decided to stay put so that they could be reassured that their mother was receiving attention.

They sat, mostly in silence, watching what was happening below. The team had barely reached the victim when she heard the distant drumming of a helicopter. The sound became louder and deeper as it arrived and circled above them, reverberating, disturbing the air, drowning all other sounds, coming lower and lower with every circuit until its draught whisked their hair, going lower, and then they were looking down on it as it hovered close to the cliffs. All along the ridge, people stopped to watch as a man was lowered. There was a lot of purposeful activity on the ground. No time was wasted and within minutes the helicopter man and what looked like a stretcher began to leave the ground. Gemma's knuckles were pushed hard in her mouth, her eyes glazed and staring. Tim had his arm around Jack as though gaining comfort from a huge cuddly toy, his unstoppable tears still rolling down his cheeks. The stretcher disappeared into the helicopter. Almost immediately it began to lift in a half circle to clear the rising cliffs around it, then it was away.

'There, she'll be all right now. She'll be in hospital before we get down.' She watched Nick and the guys from the mountain rescue team carefully negotiate the lower slope to the tarn. They stopped to confer and suddenly her mobile phone bleeped, making them all jump.

'Hi Linda, it's me. Tell the kids that their Mum's alive and in good hands. It's as much as we can say, really. She's in a bad way. Were you able to find out anything?'

She relayed the information, which he repeated, she assumed so that one of the team could take note, and told him of the arrangements she'd made with the children's aunt.

'Well done. I'm on my way. If you want to start without me ... '

'I can't carry two packs.' She could, she supposed, ask somebody else to take it but John and Sandra were both already carrying day packs. She smiled at tearful Tim. 'And I think Tim's got a bit of growing to do before he can manage it.'

'Okay. I'll be as quick as I can.'

'Be careful.'

She saw him hand the phone back to one of the team, exchange a few words, then he waved to where he knew she was standing and set off around the tarn.

'I'd offer to take the children,' John said, 'but we were planning to return to Patterdale via St Sunday Crag. It's the wrong way ... '

'That's okay. It was kind of you to stay. We'll be okay, won't we kids?'

Both nodded.

John and Sandra were obviously a little uncomfortable about leaving them, but after she reassured them that there was no more that they could do, they prepared to go.

'You've done a wonderful job, you and your brave husband. Look after each other and God bless you.' John shook her hand, Sandra awkwardly hugged the children, wished them well and off they went.

After that there was little that she could do. Neither of the children wanted anything to eat but she did persuade them to drink some water. As Tim seemed to attach himself to Jack, she passed the time telling them about the incident of the keys and then went on to tell them some amusing stories about Dottie and her own children to keep them calm and entertained until Nick rejoined them, which he did, much sooner than she expected.

Jack became aware of his nearness first, suddenly getting to his feet, ears pricked and tail swinging. He barked. Afraid that he might run too enthusiastically, she ordered him to stay. He did but he barked again. And then Nick appeared, red-faced and sweaty and breathing heavily. Without thinking she jumped up to greet him and found his hot arms around her, holding her tightly. It didn't last long because their first consideration had to be the children.

'How's Mum?' Gemma asked.

'She's on her way to Newcastle. As you can imagine, she's pretty knocked about. I told her you were in safe hands. She wants us to take you to your aunt, so how about we get going, eh?'

Both children nodded.

After Nick had had a good drink of water, he heaved his pack onto his back and set off in the lead with Tim behind, then Gemma and Linda bringing up the rear. They were a silent little procession intent only on reaching the bottom. Other walkers came up the hill, passing them, with no idea of the drama that had taken place, no concept of the trauma being experienced by the children. She couldn't help thinking about the future for Gemma and Tim. Their mother was seriously injured, possibly disabled for life. What did that mean for the children? What did it mean for Pauline and Mrs Roebuck? Somebody was going to have to make major adjustments to their lifestyle, working pattern, social life, in order to look after the children. One short moment of carelessness or distraction, and the lives of the whole family had been irrevocably changed.

The one short moment of distraction played on her mind as she trudged on. Jim's moment of distraction had changed her life, and Rob's: family life had never been the same.

They had been descending steadily when they rounded a craggy point and came to a bit where the steep path zig-zagged to lessen the strain on the knees. Heading toward them was a single lady walker in a white shirt and black trousers.

'It's Auntie Pauline,' yelled Tim, showing the first sign of life since his mother's fall. He shot past Nick and ran toward her.

'Tim! Slow down,' Linda and Nick shouted in unison, but it was no good. The boy had seen somebody familiar, a refuge, and charged headlong down the rocky path towards her. Gemma's pace didn't alter, she was less sure-footed, less reckless, or maybe less sure of her aunt's reception. Poor child, thought Linda. She had been quick to blame her brother, but in her heart she must know that had she not been making such an unnecessary fuss, her mother's attention might not have been divided: she might not have missed her footing, might not have fallen. She quickened her pace to catch up with the girl and put her arm around her.

'It wasn't your fault, Gemma. I was there. I know. It was an accident. It could happen to anybody.'

'If Tim hadn't … '

'It's not Tim's fault either. I'm sure your mum won't be blaming either of you, and neither must you.' She didn't know if her words got through, but it was the best she could do.

Pauline, looking somewhat incongruous in her business clothes on the mountain path, greeted her nephew with a tight hug, and when Gemma reached her, she too was given a serious hugging. It was difficult to talk on the narrow path so they simply exchanged introductions and waited until the children had been shepherded safely to the car park before Nick and Linda recounted what had happened. The children stood quietly either side of their aunt until they had finished.

'It was Tim's fault,' Gemma interjected. 'He kept going too far ahead.'

'It wasn't,' insisted Tim, tearfully, 'it was you 'cos you kept lagging behind.'

'It was neither,' Linda said patiently, and then to Pauline. 'You know what it's like. No two kids are the same and mums have to have eyes all over the place. It wasn't anybody's fault.' She didn't really believe it but couldn't bear the thought of Gemma going through life feeling responsible.

The priority was then to get the children home. After Nick and Linda had hugged them both, and they were prompted to thank them for their help, Pauline took them to the car and shut the door. Nick was then able to tell her that her sister's injuries were serious. He handed Pauline one of his cards. 'If you can, call us to let us know how things go.'

'I will. And thank you again.' Pauline gave them both a quick, grateful hug then got into her car and drove away.

For a moment they both just stood there, readjusting, then Nick put his arm around her shoulders and pulled her close.

CHAPTER 12

H IS EMBRACE WAS STRONG AND HARD and spoke volumes about his feelings and, perhaps, his fears. When she looked up his lips found hers in a firm unhurried kiss. It was unexpected, but welcome and returned with deep affection. He put his hands either side of her face and stared with eyes that were bold and determined into hers.

'You're a lovely lady, Linda. I know your life isn't your own, and this may be all I'll ever have of it, but I just want you to know how very glad I am that we met.'

She felt like jelly. 'Oh Nick,' she pushed her head against his chest.

His hand caressed her neck. 'I know. I understand. It's just ... well, you don't know what's going to happen, do you? I couldn't help thinking about that poor woman whose last moments, or what could have been, might still be, her last moments, were in conflict with her kids. They've probably never really told her what she means to them. I just wanted to tell you.'

She pressed her head against his sweat-dampened shirt. 'I'm glad we met, too. You're kind and brave, but ... ' She didn't know how to say what she felt. Half of her wanted to surrender to the temptation: it would be so easy, so immediately satisfying, but beyond that, what? 'I won't pretend I haven't thought about it but it's not my way to have affairs. It has to be all or nothing and at the moment I can't see my way through. It … it would alter my relationship with all my family. Not just Jim, but all of them.'

'I understand, really I do,' he said again, giving her another quick hug before letting her go. 'I don't know about you, but I'm starving.'

They settled on a grassy bank in the shade of a mountain ash tree to consume the packed lunch they should have eaten two hours ago. By unspoken mutual consent they changed the subject and talked about the experience of the morning.

Having ended up three miles north of where they had intended to be, they had to walk into Grasmere, mostly beside a busy main road. After one or two disappointments, they were lucky to find a hotel that had two rooms and allowed dogs. She appreciated that although he had made his feelings clear, he didn't take it for granted that having shared a room once, she was willing to do so again. It just made her admire him more.

Before going down to dinner she sat on the chintz-covered bed of a rather over-frilled room to telephone Suzy. Even the phone was a rather fancy affair in ivory and brass and weighed a ton in her hand as she told her daughter of her ascent of Helvellyn and the mountain rescue.

'Oh, Mum, how awful. You must have been terrified.'

'I was too preoccupied to be frightened, but I don't think I'd want to do it again. Fortunately there isn't anything like it for the rest of the walk.'

'Thank goodness. Have you spoken to Dad or Fiona?'

'Not yet. Dad won't be home yet and he doesn't like being interrupted at work for trivia, you know that. Fiona was next on my list. Why? Has something happened?'

'No.' There was a slight extension on the 'o' which suggested lack of conviction. 'Fi was down for the weekend. She stayed with Dad but spent Saturday afternoon here. Right through to kids' tea! She even made the effort to be interested in her nephew and niece.'

'Gosh, that's amazing! Dad, I suppose, was playing golf.' She could imagine that Fiona had nobly decided to go home to look after her poor old dad in her mother's absence, and then been a bit miffed that he'd carried on with business as usual and left her to entertain herself, and cook his dinner, and probably iron his shirts into the bargain.

'Actually, Fi was a bit odd altogether. She was asking a lot of questions about you and Dad. She thought you'd had a row on the phone. You didn't call on Sunday.'

'Not a row exactly. He's just not used to me not being there. Doing my own thing.'

'No ... ' Suzy sounded unconvinced.

She wanted to say that, really, there was nothing to worry about, but could she, in all honesty? 'How's Grandpa?'

Suzy seemed to hesitate just a moment before answering. 'Grumpy. Fi spent Saturday morning with him, and Dad went to see him on Sunday.'

She wondered if that was supposed to make her feel guilty that she wasn't there looking after him, but emotional blackmail wasn't Suzy's style: Jim's and Fiona's, yes, but not Suzy. Nevertheless, she did feel just a brief moment of concern that perhaps all was not well with Fred, but then Suzy went on to talk about Ruthie's new tooth and Danny's new words and the poundage of soft fruit that she had picked from her garden before eventually running out of news and saying goodbye.

As always concerned that there should not appear to be any favouritism, she immediately dialled Fiona's number but with some trepidation, fearing there might be awkward questions about the state of things between her and Jim.

'Hi, Mum,' she sounded bright and breezy but with a nervy edge.

'Hello, darling. I thought I'd take a few minutes to update you on my adventures. Have you got time?'

'Plenty. What have you been up to?'

She told her all about the Helvellyn incident.

'Oh, how awful. Those poor children, to see it happen. I can't imagine it if it had happened to us.'

'I can't help thinking about the repercussions: how that one moment will change all their lives.'

There was a pause. 'Yes, yes, I know what you mean.' Her tone had changed to something lower, more pensive and she was reminded of Fiona's odd comments on the day of the cricket match.

'I understand you went home for the weekend.'

'Yes. Have you spoken to Dad?'

'Not yet. Suzy told me. I gather you spent some time with her. That was nice of you.'

'Yes. I think she was surprised, too.' There was another little pause as though Fiona either couldn't think what to say, or wanted to say something but didn't know how to broach it. 'I thought you were coming home. I wanted to chat ... Still, it was nice to chat with Sooz. I felt we sort of touched base.'

'I'm pleased.' Linda bit the bullet. 'How was Dad?'

'Oh, all right. I got the impression you and he had had a row. He muttered something to the effect that it doesn't matter what he does he never gets it right. He was better after he'd played golf, and Kent won the cricket, but he seemed sort of lost without you. He took me out to dinner. I was going to go out with Leo but Dad seemed so lonely.'

She hoped Fiona hadn't talked about the Rainbow.

'He said I wasn't to worry about you and him, it was just you having a mid-life crisis thing and we all have bear with you until it's passed.'

'Well that's all right, then, isn't it,' she said, relieved but at the same time cross.

'That's what he said, Mum. I think ... Well ... Suzy said something that made me think, about you doing all you do for Dad, and the rest of us, and wanting just a couple of weeks to do your own thing. I told him that perhaps you were feeling unappreciated. I want you to know, Mum, that I do appreciate all you've done for us. And Suzy's right: the rest of us get at least two weeks holiday a year, so why shouldn't you?'

'Thank you, darling.' If only it were that simple.

'Did Suzy tell you about Grandpa?'

'She said that you and Dad had spent time with him. Is something wrong?'

'Nothing serious. At least, I don't think it is. But he's very low. He thought you'd be home this week. He gets so frustrated at not being able to do his garden or see things properly. I didn't realise that he can't even read the paper any more. Not even with a magnifying glass.'

Now that was emotional blackmail. That was Fiona's way, learned from her father: start by being nice and apparently understanding, then gently, gently, pull the guilt strings. What Fiona was really saying was that while she'd been away enjoying herself, everybody else was having to deal with poor old Fred. In all probability, he was no worse than he had been for the last year or so, and if Fiona cared that much about her grandfather she'd have known that his sight was failing: if not from personal observation she must have heard in conversations that both she and Suzy spent time reading articles from the newspaper to him. Being lectured by her daughter on the duty of care, albeit subliminally, really rattled her.

'I expect he was very pleased to see you dear, or nearly see you. It's not often you take the trouble.'

'Mum!' Fiona sounded offended. 'I'll have you know that I had to rearrange all sorts of things this weekend ... '

'How very noble of you. If you expect to make me feel guilty, Fi, you're onto a loser.'

'Why should I want to make you feel guilty? If you do, that's your conscience. All I was saying was that I'm concerned about Grandpa.'

'That's nice of you. I'm sure he appreciates it. I gather from that that you and your dad spent Saturday evening discussing your dad's plans to accommodate him at home, and you probably think it's a wonderful idea. Wonderful for you and Dad because you can then get on with your busy, busy lives and not worry about the poor old soul, or feel guilty about him being in a care home. Just think, you won't even have to go out of your way to visit him because you'll be able to kill two birds with one stone when you come to visit your mother, you know, that cranky woman who keeps house for your father, the one you expect to rearrange her entire life in order to look after said poor soul.'

'Excuse me, but if you'd like to backtrack to the beginning of this conversation ... '

'Yes, all right, Fiona, I remember you said you do appreciate all I do for everybody, but only, it seems, when I'm not there doing it.'

'I think I'm getting an inkling of what Dad's been going through. It doesn't matter what I say, it's going to be wrong.'

'It's not what you say, dear, it's what you do, or don't do. And now I shall leave you to think about that, and perhaps discuss it with your father, while I carry on with what I consider to be my well-deserved holiday.'

'Mum..?'

'Not now, dear. I'm meeting my friend for dinner and I'm already late. I'll call you when I get home.'

'Is this the friend ... '

'I must go. Goodnight.'

She put the heavy phone down sharply but her annoyance very quickly gave way to regret: regret that she'd let her own aggravation overrule her concern for her daughter's problem; regret, too, that Fiona still lived with the illusion that the sun shone from her father's backside; and further regret that by denying Rob the freedom to share his experience with his sisters, she had isolated him from the family.

*

She woke the following morning to low grey clouds concealing the mountains. Steady, drenching rain dripped heavily from lush foliage of trees and shrubs. After a quick but interesting visit to Wordsworth's cottage, they called in for a coffee with Pauline who had taken time off work to look after Gemma and Tim. She told them that her mother was with her sister in Newcastle. Nick's suspicion that Gillian's neck was broken was confirmed and now, following lengthy surgery, her condition was critical but stable. Gemma spent the entire half hour of their visit sitting on the window-seat of the first floor living-room, looking down into the street, absorbed in her own thoughts. Tim, pale and red-eyed, sat silently on the sofa, close to his aunt, stroking Jack's head. Linda felt for them all but there was nothing more she could do for them other than offer her good wishes.

Given the persistent rain, they took the precaution of pre-booking accommodation for the last two stops and decided to take the mostly low-level route to Rosthwaite in Borrowdale. It was, Nick said, reputedly the wettest place in England. She could believe it, but even though the fells were veiled by varying degrees of mist and cloud, and trees dripped, and house gutters spluttered, and the rivers rushed and overflowed onto the paths, it was still, in its way, beautiful and refreshing.

'Into every life a little rain must fall,' she said to Nick as they splashed along the stony path.

He grunted. 'I wonder how the author of that platitude quantified "a little".'

They had reverted to their earlier companionship. Nothing more had been said of their feelings for each other. She was glad now that she had resisted temptation because the feeling of guilt would have been unbearable when she arrived in Borrowdale and more memories of family holidays came flooding back. They were particularly powerful as she walked past the cottage they had rented for several years running. It seemed like yesterday: she almost expected to see Fiona, Rob and Suzy splashing about in their wellies and plastic macs with Jim in the beck helping them build a dam. He had been such a good dad, such fun to be with. As she came to a long large, deep puddle that covered the path for at least twenty paces, she had a sudden flashback to an incident when the family had been on a walk in pouring rain.

They'd come to just such a place where the path was deeply flooded, far too deep for the children's little wellies. It was decided that Jim would piggy-back them across, and naturally Fiona was the first. Jim had cautiously waded in with his daughter on his back. Rob, who would have been about seven at the time, had started to follow.

'No,' she had caught him by the hood to hold him back. 'Wait for Daddy to see how deep it is.'

'It isn't over Daddy's boots,' Rob insisted, pulling away from her restraining hand.

'That's because Daddy's boots are bigger than yours.'

'They're just below his knees, like mine are,' Rob argued.

'But Daddy's knees are higher.'

Rob looked down at his legs. 'No they're not.' And before she could stop him, he was wading confidently into the puddle. Linda, with little Suzy clinging to her hand, could do nothing. Jim stood in the middle with a big smile on his face, watching his son.

'You're going to get wet feet,' crowed Fiona from her superior position on her father's back. 'And then you'll moan all the way back to the cottage.'

'Won't,' insisted Rob. Inevitably he took the one step too far and the water gushed into his boots. The look of surprise on his face was priceless.

Jim laughed. 'Little lesson in life, son. Mother always knows best!'

But did she? For just a little while she felt a hollow sort of ache, and wished that the clock could be turned back and they could have that unity again.

Later that night, after a pleasant evening in the hotel bar chatting with other walkers, she phoned her son in New Zealand to tell him she was in Rosthwaite and they talked of the happy memories.

'It was a long time ago.' Rob said prosaically.

'It may seem like a lifetime to you, but for me it's like yesterday.'

'But it is yesterday. Past. History. You can't live in the past, Mum.'

'I don't, but the past influences the present.'

'Yeah, but it shouldn't dictate the future.'

'Umm,' she said, doubtfully. 'This is getting very deep.'

'I think about you a lot, you know.' He sounded very serious.

'I think about you, too. What are your plans?' What she really wanted to ask was: when are you coming home? She wished she could help him sort himself out but as she was struggling to sort herself out, she felt hardly qualified.

'I don't know yet. Guess you'll be heading for home in a couple of days' time, then?' he said, changing the subject. 'Back to business as usual.'

'Guess so.' She tried to sound enthusiastic and in that moment all her recent thoughts about Rob came together. Now she felt she understood her son's reluctance to come home. Home wasn't what it had been, wasn't what it should be and, to a large degree, it was her fault. In her effort to protect Rob from his father's wrath for having told her, and Fiona and Suzy from disillusionment, she had put him in a position where he felt dishonest. 'Rob,' she continued, tentatively. 'I've been doing a lot of thinking while I've been away ... '

'As you do,' he said in complete accord.

'I think I was wrong ... not letting you talk things over with your dad.'

'I understand why.'

'Thank you, but I see now it's been unfair on you. You've got something bottled that needs to come out. I think we both have.'

There was quite a long, thoughtful pause before Rob responded. 'Maybe, but is there any point now, raking over the coals?'

'If it would help you, yes.'

'It might still fracture the family.'

'The family *is* fractured. You're not here.'

'Let me think about it. Don't rush into something you might regret.'

'Me? Rush? Do I ever?' She laughed, knowing full well that the last thing she wanted to do was to blow on the embers of the pain of four years before.

'Well, no. Guess you don't.' She could hear the affectionate smile in his voice and it brought tears to her eyes. 'Anyway, I must get to work. Enjoy the rest of your holiday. I'm proud of you.'

'Thank you, darling.' She felt a tad dishonest accepting his admiration because she had done very little of the walk alone, but then, she hadn't set out to do it alone. That she'd made good her determination not to be manipulated by Jim was the achievement.

*

She woke the next day to find a text message from Rob. 'Call me. Love you. Rob.'

She called straight away.

'Hi, Mum. I've been thinking about what you said. If you're sure to want to have it out, then I'll come home. I should be there.'

'Thank you.' She felt sure now that whatever the consequences, the air had to be cleared: it wasn't fair that the innocent should be paying the price for the guilty and she did not want to spend the rest of her life feeling as empty as she had for the last four years.

'Don't say anything until I get there. We'll tackle it together, but I think we need to talk first.' He sounded so incredibly mature.

Tears welled in her eyes. He was coming home! 'All right, darling. When..?'

'I don't know. I've earned some leave. Might take a week or so to arrange flights.'

'Oh, Rob ... ' The thought that he would be home within a week or two made her feel fluttery inside.

'I gotta go now. I'm meeting someone.'

'Thank you, darling. Let me know as soon as you have your travel arrangements organised.'

'Will do. Love you.'

'Love you, too.'

*

The day was another very watery walk. There was a high-level option but in such appalling weather only a fool would contemplate it. As it was, most of the route followed water courses which were a wonderland of waterfalls, cataracts and rainbows of the like she had thought only Walt Disney cartoonists could depict. When they entered the beautiful

Ennerdale Forest they walked alongside a river that bounced and gurgled over boulders, running so fast that she could hear the stones rattling on the bed. It was the penultimate walk, and Ennerdale was the last and loveliest of the lakes.

She was one day short of the journey's end. It seemed impossible that it had taken only two weeks. She had met people, seen places, done things that were quite different from her usual daily life. She felt she had achieved something. It had been a real holiday away from all her responsibilities, if not entirely away from her inner feelings and fears. One thing the holiday had done for her was give her time to think and the one conclusion she had come to was that she had to make some changes. Quite what the changes would be she was still unsure: it all rather depended on what happened when she got home. Her feelings about going home were mixed, but that was the challenge for the day after tomorrow. More immediately she had to face that tomorrow would be her last in Nick's company, and about that her feelings were unequivocal: she was going to miss him dreadfully.

They had taken the precaution, whilst in Grasmere, of booking ahead for the nights in Rosthwaite and Ennerdale, primarily because the forecast was so awful and they didn't want to arrive and find there were no rooms in the inn and having to plod for miles out of their way for accommodation that would also accept Jack. Not that she could imagine any but the most heartless soul turning him away if he arrived on their doorstep. It was just as well, because they got the last two available rooms in the inn at Ennerdale and one of those was a recent cancellation.

They arrived at the Shepherd's Arms at about six o'clock and opted to have a swift pint in the bar before going to their rooms. This had the added advantage of giving Jack time to dry off. There were already quite a few walkers in the bar, several making their first stop, having set out that morning from St Bees. Very quickly they were drawn into the conversation and being pumped for information about watering holes and what was, or wasn't, worth seeing along the way. An hour later, they were about to leave to go to their rooms for a wash and brush up, when who should come into the bar looking like the proverbial drowned rat but Jacquie.

'Urghh,' Jacquie groaned and slid her rucksack from her back. 'Am I glad that leg's over. I tell you, I'm just doing this thing now out of pure determination not to be beaten. God! I hope they've got a room. My schedule got blown by my injury. I was supposed to have been here two nights ago.'

Linda smiled: blisters didn't qualify in her book as an injury. Her smile quickly vanished when she realised that in all likelihood there wasn't a room available, unless there'd been another cancellation. She waited while Jacquie made enquiries at the bar. When the barman came back shaking his head, Jacquie looked incredulous.

'Anything will do, a mattress in a store cupboard ... '

'Sorry. There's some B&B's around that might have something.'

Jacquie groaned. 'It's the first time this has happened. I've been lucky everywhere else. And it has to be on a night like this!' She looked beguilingly at Nick. 'I don't suppose a knight in shining armour is going to relinquish his room to a damsel in distress, is he?'

Linda was amazed at the girl's cheek: she really believed she could manipulate everything and everybody to her own advantage.

Nick grinned. 'Surely such chivalry is considered sexist in this day and age!'

Jacquie flicked her brows suggestively. 'Couldn't we share it?'

Nick shook his head. 'Three's a crowd.' He didn't elaborate that his sleeping partner was Jack and not Linda.

'Oh!' Jacquie looked wide-eyed at Linda as though she was the last person on earth that she could imagine any man wanting to go to bed with.

Linda didn't want to share her penultimate night with Nick with Jacquie as well, but nor would her conscience allow her to ignore the girl's plight when she did have a solution. She hesitated a bit, hoping that something else would magically solve the problem, but when it didn't she tentatively offered, 'My room's a twin room. You can share with me, if you like.'

'Oh Linda! You're an angel! You've saved my life.' Jacquie embraced her wildly.

Nick, who was standing behind Jacquie raised his eyes skyward and mouthed the words. 'Too bloody soft.' She lifted her shoulder a little as if to reply: what else could I do?

*

Jacquie was a person who took control. When they arrived at their room and began the process of unpacking and changing into something presentable for the evening meal, it didn't occur to her to ask Linda which bed she preferred: she instinctively commandeered the one closest to the window; she didn't ask if Linda would like to use the bathroom first, and it was assumed that she would be joining Linda and Nick in the dining-room. A stronger woman might have objected, but to Linda these were petty irritations not worthy of creating an unpleasant atmosphere. Her biggest fear was that they would be stuck with her for the last leg of the walk.

'Is somebody coming to collect you at St Bees?' Jacquie asked.

'No. I'm getting a train, from Carlisle.'

'I've got a friend coming to collect me. I'll give you a lift to London if you like.'

'That's kind, but I wouldn't want to intrude.' She couldn't think of anything worse than being stuck in the back of a car, and it would be the back, while Jacquie bragged about her adventure.

Jacquie laughed. 'It's a girl friend. She won't mind.'

'You're very kind, but I've already bought the ticket and actually, I like travelling by train.'

'You've never been a commuter, then!'

'No. I haven't.'

Jacquie stripped off her walking gear with no inhibitions. Her body was tight, her legs long and firm, her breasts neat in an under-wired bra. Linda's body was not bad for her age, but the fifteen years' difference between them showed. She picked up her clean shirt and crinkly skirt and took them to the bathroom to change in privacy.

When she came out of the bathroom, Jacquie was sitting on her bed talking to somebody on her mobile phone. Linda mouthed, 'See you later,' and left her to it.

Nick was already downstairs at a table in the bar.

'Where's the black widow spider then?'

'On the phone.'

'I suppose she'll be joining us for dinner?'

'I haven't invited her, if that's what you mean.'

'Can we avoid it?'

'Yes, if you want to make it obvious by having a table for two.'

'She'll latch on to us for the last leg, you realise that?'

'Yes, and like you, it isn't what I want, but on the other hand ... '

'On the other hand what?' He was clearly disappointed at the turn of events.

She met his eyes. 'Perhaps it's for the best ... a third party.'

His eyes held hers then he reached for her hand. 'I thought you knew you could trust me.'

'I can trust you, Nick. It's myself I have a problem with.'

He squeezed her hand. 'No you don't. You know what you have to do.' He scraped his chair back. 'Now, what can I get you to drink?'

'A glass of wine. Thank you.'

Jacquie joined them in the bar and for dinner, and afterwards the three of them sat with other walkers in the bar laughing at each others' stories. Curiously, neither she nor Nick mentioned their involvement in the incident on Helvellyn. Several times she glanced across at Nick and found him watching her and every time he smiled. Eventually he got up and announced that it was past an old man's bedtime and that he had to take the dog for a stroll. Linda got up, too, but fortunately Jacquie was far more interested in the attentions of the rest of the group.

When they stepped outside it was to find that the rain had stopped. Everything was dripping and glossy in the lights from windows, the air was warm, moist and earthy smelling. Jack trotted ahead of them, stopping to sniff and cock his leg at regular intervals. Nick pulled her hand out of her pocket and held it tightly.

'I just want to say this. I understand how you feel about your family and that your life is complicated, but if when you get back you find things have changed, that you want to change your life, remember me.' He squeezed her hand harder. 'I wouldn't want to take you away from the people you love. You don't have to move to Cumbria. I'll come to you.'

She felt a great lump rise in her throat. 'Oh, Nick. I feel so bad. I didn't mean to … ' She had to blink hard to stop the tears.

'Don't feel bad. I'm grateful for the days we've had.' She couldn't think of anything to say. There wasn't anything she could say. It seemed so contrary that she should feel guilty about the strength of his feelings when the whole walk thing had started because she had wanted Jim to express exactly those feelings. They reached the bridge over the bloated river and leaned for a while, watching the water rush under it.

He cleared his throat. 'I think it would be best if we said goodbye here. I think to walk together tomorrow would only make us sad.'

Her throat tightened with a feeling of panic. Her stomach ached but still she could do nothing, say nothing, to prevent the inevitable. He was right. If it had to be, then it was best that it was done quickly.

'Remember what I said. If you want me, you know where to find me.'

She leaned against him, unable to find anything to say that wouldn't raise false hopes.

He chuckled softly. 'Ironically, although it's what's holding you back, I admire you for your loyalty, and your honesty.'

'I'm sorry,' was all she could say.

He ruffled her hair then took her hand and they walked slowly back to the hotel, Jack trotting ahead of them, his white-tipped tail swinging. Nick held the door open for her. Jacquie was still holding court in the bar. They went up the stairs together. Outside her room, she bent to give Jack a final pat and kiss the white blade on his forehead while Nick took her key and unlocked her door. When she straightened, her vision was blurred and her throat painfully tight. Nick put his arm around her shoulders and pulled her head close to his chest, then lowered his face into her hair. She hugged him hard and felt his warm breath as he whispered. 'Goodbye, lovely lady. I'll see you in my dreams.' He hugged her again, nodded a final goodbye and moved on to the next door.

Inside her room she closed the door, leaned against it and allowed her tears to flow. She knew that to avoid seeing her again, he would be leaving very early in the morning.

CHAPTER 13

THE LAST FOURTEEN AND A HALF MILES of her walk she did alone beneath a sky that was as changeable as her mood: sometimes grey, sometimes bright, but mercifully dry. Fortunately, Jacquie had set a ridiculously ambitious time for her friend to collect her at St Bees, so she set off at a march leaving Linda to get there in her own good time. She was never more glad to see somebody's back disappearing into the distance as she was that one.

Jacquie had returned to their room about an hour after Linda, which was good because it had given her time to bring her feelings under control and get into bed. For a while she had lain on her back, aware of every sound: the muted voices from the bar, the occasional passing car, the creaking of floorboards as somebody walked along the corridor. In the morning, she felt certain, she would be awake to hear Nick and Jack creep past her door on their way out of her life.

Nothing like as quietly, Jacquie came back to the room. She bumped Linda's bed on her way to her own.

'Ooops! Sorry.' She turned on the bedside light. 'It's really good of you to let me share your room.' She talked as she pulled off her sweater and eased out of her snug slacks like a snake from its skin. 'You know, I've thought a lot about our conversation. About me having a baby. I heard where you were coming from but I still think I'll go for it.' She chuckled, 'Who knows, the bloke I met in Richmond might have done the trick for me. I do hope so.'

Linda feigned sleepiness with a yawn as she said, 'Just be prepared for it to change your life completely.' She turned her back to make it obvious that she was not in the mood for conversation. Jacquie didn't take the hint but nattered on through the open bathroom door and when she got into her bed, but Linda ignored her.

Right up to the moment of parting company, Jacquie didn't get the message that Linda didn't actually like her and it was interesting that, despite Jacquie's claim to having made good friends on the walk, especially Linda, she didn't make any arrangements to keep in touch, for which Linda was extremely grateful. She had little doubt that she would fade from Jacquie's mind a lot quicker than Jacquie would fade from hers, but that was only because she feared that Fiona was headed along that same path.

At first, as she set out on her own she felt lonely and sometimes, when thinking of Nick, she had to blink back tears, but within a few miles she began to feel glad that she was doing this last bit alone: it was giving her time to put her emotions in order. Tomorrow evening she would be back amongst her family, so twenty-four hours of solitude was a welcome break between the life she had made for herself for the last two weeks and the life she shared with them. So as not to dwell on Nick, she make a conscious effort to think forward and positively.

She was very much looking forward to seeing Suzy and the children again, and her days in the café with Jenny were usually great fun. One of the things she had been going to think about on holiday was Jenny's proposal that she buy the café: she had intended to reach a decision as to whether or not it was even worth discussing with Jim. Everything was against it: it wasn't a viable business, it would take too much of her time, but, and to her the but was a big one, if she didn't take it on, who would? Probably nobody and that precious little bit of their community would be lost.

The idea of a village consortium was quite a good one, but in reality, could she muster sufficient people, or even just one or two, who would be prepared to put time into it? Given her experience of people's unwillingness to take on committee responsibilities in the various village organisations, she doubted it.

What she really needed to consider was how *she* could make it work when there were so many other demands on her time. And that brought her thoughts to the problem of Fred: if Jim had his way, Fred would become a major responsibility. She visited him regularly and kept an eye on him, and when she didn't, Suzy did, so he was never neglected. As far as she was aware, whilst he readily accepted the help he was given, he was not in a hurry to move away from his house. At least, he'd said nothing to that effect to her. It occurred to her that perhaps Jim's plans for his father weren't so much for Fred's comfort, but so that Jim could feel he was doing something. But knowing Jim as she did, apart from making alterations to the house and perhaps pop in to his father's quarters on a daily rather than weekly basis, would he be doing much? How often would he find time to sit and read articles from a newspaper, cook and eat a meal with him, make his bed, see to his laundry? And Fiona's contribution would be once a month if they were lucky!

Recalling her last conversation with Fiona brought a little pang of guilt. Perhaps she had been a bit unfair but really, what did Fiona know of her grandfather's situation? What did Fiona know of anything that went on in the family these days? Come to that, how much did she know of what went on in Fiona's life? She knew of her career progress, her holidays, but it was a long time since they'd talked about the small everyday things that she talked about with Suzy. Fiona had grown away from her, which was fine, she was spreading her wings, but she would hate it if one day Fiona was to tell a stranger that she and her mother didn't get on. She realised that if she didn't want Fiona walking down Jacquie's path, then she had to make more of an effort to prevent it, and arguing with her wasn't the way. She resolved that at the first opportunity she would arrange to meet up with Fi for a girly chat.

Another thing she was keen to do was clear the air for Rob. The repercussions were unpredictable: it could bring the family back together, or, just as likely, the girls might stand in judgement on their father and the sense of family would be utterly lost, which had always been her biggest fear. As far as Jim was concerned, she couldn't untangle her feelings. It wasn't just the pain his fling had inflicted that still rankled, it was the fact that he had apparently swept it under the carpet and seemed totally unaware of how it had undermined her confidence in him. The whole business of the walk clearly demonstrated that he didn't recognise that she needed extra reassurance.

Going home wasn't going to be as easy as this last day's walk. There were a few small hills but mostly her way was across rather soggy but pleasant green pastures and golden harvested fields. Long before she reached the coast, she could smell the change in the air as sultry earthiness gave way to a strong salty breeze. Then she saw the lighthouse at North Head and felt a quiver of something that was part excitement, part trepidation. It was almost the same feeling she'd experienced when she'd set out. She was nearing journey's end, but had the uncomfortable feeling that it wasn't the end because nothing had been resolved. Technically, the walk wasn't finished until she reached St Bees bay, a couple of miles to the south, so she continued along the cliff-top path with the receding, choppy, grey-green sea pulling away to her right. Had the day been clear she should have been able to see the Isle of Man and the high lakeland fells, but the moisture in the atmosphere, drawn from the sea and rain-dampened ground by the heat of the sun, created a haze that blurred her horizons.

She had walked without a break and at just after three o'clock in the afternoon descended from the grassy cliff, down a flight of wooden steps, onto the sand and shale beach. She had done it: she had walked all the way from Robin Hood's Bay to St Bees on her own two feet. She took a moment to savour the sense of satisfaction before she bent down to pick up a small, red-grey stone and closed her fingers tightly around it.

The tide had already abandoned the shingle between the rows of wooden breakwaters and was going out, leaving ripples of muddy sand where gulls and seabirds poked. Beyond was the shimmering white curve of the shoreline. The bay was removed from the town and not over-busy: a few people were walking along the wide, concrete sea wall, throwing sticks for dogs to retrieve, and four or five families with small children were making sandcastles with moats. As she debated going the last few yards for the symbolic paddle, she felt more alone than she had felt on the entire walk.

She wondered if she would have done it without Nick, and decided she would, because she had been determined to do so. She had, for the most part, selected her own routes, read her own maps. Nick had sometimes queried her choices and recommended alternatives, but she didn't see accepting his help as any sign of weakness or diminishing her achievement. After all, what was so clever in turning down well-intentioned help and either ending up in trouble or missing out on something special? She understood that by his pre-emptive departure he had wanted to spare them both the agony of a whole day anticipating the inevitable, but it didn't spare her the heartache she felt just now. She took her mobile phone from the pocket of her rucksack and sent him a text message.

'After uneventful walk, am standing on the shore at St Bees. Thank you for everything.' She hoped he would know that 'everything' meant … well, everything: his company, his affection, his understanding, for giving her his undivided attention and making her feel she was important to him. She put her head back, feeling the warmth of the sun on her face, squeezing her eyes tight to hold back the tears: being important to him was a double-edged sword. She hadn't set out to be important to somebody new. If she had set out to do anything at all, it had been to regain something special she'd once had with Jim, and in that she had spectacularly failed.

It's over, she told herself. For now, anyway, the walk is over, Nick is over.

She sent text messages to Jim, Suzy, Fiona and Jenny: 'Mission accomplished. See you tomorrow.'

Her original plan had been to find somewhere to stay in St Bees village on the Friday night, then start the journey home on Saturday, but as she'd arrived earlier than anticipated, what was the point in hanging around? The walk was done, the time had come to go home. Turning her back on the disappearing tide, she walked purposefully up the beach towards the sea wall steps, with the intention of finding a taxi to take her to Carlisle station, but stopped when her telephone rang.

'Congratulations!' It was Jim.

'Thank you.'

'If you look up to the sea wall, you might see somebody you recognise waving to you.'

She looked up and scanned from right to left where people were walking. She saw a man in sage polo shirt and green chinos waving at her. It was Jim. His phone clicked off as he headed at speed toward the steps. Surprised beyond belief, she stayed rooted to the sand, watching him run down the steps, onto the shingle and come towards her, grinning widely with his arms open wide. How typical, she thought, how bloody, bloody typical: why couldn't he have done it a week ago?

As best he could with such a large rucksack on her back, he hugged her hard and pressed a firm kiss onto her lips. 'I've missed you. I don't think we've ever been apart for so long.' He looked so damned pleased with himself, which annoyed her even more.

'Haven't we?' Feeling they'd been apart for much longer than the two weeks he was referring to, she didn't respond to his embrace.

Ignoring her coolness, he smiled encouragingly. 'If your intention was to make me realise that I take for granted all the things you do to make my life easy, then you succeeded. I missed you more than you can imagine.'

'But not enough to meet me halfway.' She could feel a rumbling inside like a volcano about to erupt. She had missed him, too, to start with, but his personally-appointed understudy had filled the void and now the idea of responding to Jim made her feel unfaithful to Nick.

He smiled again, head appealingly on one side. 'I'm sorry. I didn't realise that's what you wanted.'

'Even though I told you what I'd been expecting? You didn't miss me so much that you wanted to drop everything to jump in the car and come to see me?'

'Is that what you expected me to do?' His dark brows raised above perplexed light brown eyes.

'It would have been a wonderfully romantic gesture, the sort of thing you might once have done, but no,' she sighed theatrically, 'I hoped, but I know better than to expect it.'

'I'm sorry I disappointed you.' He was trying very hard to conciliate, but it was a sham: he knew he was in the wrong but wasn't going to admit it.

'Never mind,' she smiled, meeting sham with sham, 'I had a wonderful holiday, which brought back all sorts of happy memories of our early days with the kids, and I had the unexpected pleasure of the undivided attention of a male companion.'

He abandoned insincerity with an almost audible sigh. 'But you're still angry with me.'

She couldn't contain it. 'Yes. I am. I'm bloody, bloody angry that you didn't recognise what I needed when I needed it, and that you sent somebody else to do what I wanted you to do, somebody I quickly formed a bond with and have had to say goodbye to. And now you turn up expecting me to fall into your arms with delight to see you? Too right I'm angry!' The look of confused dismay on his face was priceless. 'You seem to have this idea, Jim, that I'm a piece on a chessboard that stays put without a thought in my head until you're ready for the next move. Well you're wrong. I have a life. I have thoughts and feelings that operate independently of your control!'

That they were obviously arguing attracted some curious looks from passers-by. Jim looked uncomfortable.

'The car's in the car park. Let me take your pack.'

'I've carried it for nearly two hundred miles, I'm sure I can manage a few more yards.'

He led the way up the steps. When her pack was stowed in the boot, he opened the door but before she could get in, he folded his arms around her and hugged her again. 'I'm sorry I couldn't make it last weekend.'

She was damned if she was going to let him off that easily and remained stiff in his arms. He sighed and let her get into the car where the soft beige leather smelled warm and luxurious.

He got into the driving seat and ran his hands thoughtfully around the leather-covered steering wheel. 'Is there something you're trying to tell me?'

There was a lot she wanted to say, but she was unprepared for it. She settled back into the comfort of the seat, her head cushioned on the soft headrest, her eyes focused on the white billowing clouds. 'For the first half of my walk, much as I enjoyed Nick's company, it was you I wanted. I had even asked you, but you refused even to consider it.'

Calmly, she told him how easy Nick had been to get on with, about his inviting her to a campfire supper, their picnics on the moors, their suppers in the pubs, their breakfasts together. 'He paid me the huge compliment of enjoying my company, and I enjoyed his. It was easy and comfortable and we chatted and laughed and joked and I learned so much from him. And when you didn't turn up at the halfway point and told me that Nick was being paid, I can't tell you how hurt and furious I was. I felt deceived and utterly humiliated, like some daft stray sheep that needed a shepherd.' She told him how Nick had scoured the moors in the pouring rain trying to find her when he knew she was walking in anger, and of her two nights and day in Nick's house, their night together in a hotel room.

'Are you telling me that you had an affair?' he asked, his face deadly serious.

'It depends what constitutes an affair, doesn't it?' She met his anguished eyes and her anger flared again. 'What did you expect, Jim? What on earth possessed you to send somebody else to walk with me?'

'I was worried about you. For God's sake, Linda, you knew I didn't want you to do it, particularly alone, but for some reason I still don't understand you were bloody determined. I was worried, right? Sheena said she knew of this guide guy. It seemed like a good idea, to have somebody watch over you. I didn't expect him to … '

'Fall in love with me? Ha! What a preposterous idea! Who'd want to fall in love with a middle-aged woman having a mid-life crisis! You don't love me enough to put yourself out for me, so why on earth should anybody else, unless paid to do it!'

'I do love you. It just wasn't convenient.' His voice shook with emotion.

'Did you expect us to walk in silence?'

Silence followed for a moment or two before he asked. 'Where is Nick now? Why wasn't he with you at the end?'

'He's on his way home.' She turned her face away from him and felt a lump rise in her throat when she pictured Nick walking over the hills, alone with his dog and his disappointment.

He hesitated again then asked in a low voice that dreaded an answer but had to know. 'Did you sleep with him?'

'No. I was tempted, but no, I couldn't do it.'

'Why not?'

'Because with somebody like Nick it wouldn't have been a casual fling.'

He punched the steering wheel with a tightly clenched fist.

'Remember, Jim, it was you who brought Nick into my life. I can't help it if what he has to offer sounds more attractive.'

'What has he offered?'

'Himself. Totally and unreservedly.'

'Do … do you love him?'

She had to think for a moment before replying. The answer had to be yes, in a way, but … But what? But not in the same unreserved, passionate way she had once loved Jim. But then she was a lot older now, post-menopausal. Love in later life was different, not so hormone driven. But if that was the case, why did she still regret the loss of that passion?

'If that's how you feel, why didn't you go with him?'

'Because I stopped long enough to think about the effect on my children, Fred, my parents, my friends.' She turned to look at him. 'Did you ever think about the long-term effect of your actions on the rest of us?'

He shook his head as if not knowing what was hitting him. 'I thought we'd put all that behind us.'

'Did you? Really?'

He gripped the steering wheel then suddenly turned to reach for his seat belt and click it into position. 'We have to talk, but not here. It's too public.' He turned the key in the ignition, checked the road was clear and pulled out. His expression was one of controlled anger. She had never harped on his affair. After he'd heard that she knew, he'd given his reassurances and the subject had not been raised again. Being reminded of it now left him struggling to defend his current position. Driving was giving him time to think. She didn't ask where he was going.

Neither spoke as he drove away from St Bees without the aid of a map or satellite navigation, along a narrow winding lane that climbed between bracken-covered, rising fells. Either he'd travelled the route already that day or his recall of their motoring in the area was pretty amazing, or maybe he had no idea where he was going, he was just going. Eventually he pulled into an unoccupied grassy lay-by. He opened the windows to let the breeze blow through, turned off the engine and released his safety belt. There was not a soul in sight, the only sounds the swishing of the breeze in the green and gold bracken and a distant aircraft.

'As openers, I want to tell you that, contrary to what you obviously think, I do love you. I don't want our marriage to end.'

She wasn't ready to talk. She stared ahead, watching the grey herdwick sheep munching at the grass beside the road.

He plugged on with more determination than comfort. 'I don't need reminding of my ... transgression.' He paused and took another resolute breath. 'I always hoped that in time I'd convince you that it was you, and only you, that I love. I hoped that you'd forgive me, but you haven't, have you?' When she still didn't respond, he battled on, his jaw tight with controlled anger. 'I don't think the issue here is my love for you, but yours for me. Do you think I haven't noticed that you no longer instigate love-making? That your response to me is only a few degrees warmer than duty? Can you imagine how I feel for causing that change in you? Every time I make love to you I'm reminded that I've damaged something that was precious. It's not what it was, but because I love you, because I want you, the real you, I went on trying, hoping that one day ... ' He sighed heavily, acknowledging that he had virtually given up hope.

This wasn't easy for him. He had never been one to talk about his feelings: he didn't often have to because they were always apparent. The fact that he hugged, kissed, danced, caressed were things that she had loved most about him. She hadn't known how he'd felt about it, but couldn't deny that lovemaking hadn't been the same. Having made the decision to stay with him she had tried to make their marriage work in its fullest sense, but more often than not she had faked an orgasm so that he could feel free to reach his and thus get the job done quickly. Why had she done that? To protect herself, possibly, but now she saw that, subconsciously, it could have something to do with forgiving him being somehow disloyal to Rob.

'For God's sake, Linda, help me. Say something.'

Unprepared for this conversation, she started uncertainly. 'I tried, but it's not just about feeling physically betrayed … Doing what you did devalued everything I'd worked for. It created a hole in the family. I wanted to shield the girls from the truth … but Rob … '

'Hang on.' Jim twisted in his seat. 'You're not making any sense at all.'

'It was Rob who told me of your affair.' She saw the colour drain from his face. His eyes fixed on hers were so confused that she couldn't turn away. 'He saw you going into that woman's flat. He didn't want to believe it. He knew you had lied to me about working late but he kept it to himself. It tore him apart. He was in the middle of his exams and he couldn't concentrate because he didn't know how to handle it.'

Jim stared at her in disbelief.

'What could he do? He loves his mum, so should he save me the pain and not tell me? Let me go on being deceived? Or should he tackle you, and probably be told not to tell me? Knowing how much he admired you, can you imagine what that must have done to him?'

Jim's eyes flicked across hers with a look of absolute horror.

'You were probably too preoccupied to notice it, but I could see something was seriously wrong with him. He didn't seem able to tell me, but eventually one night when he was rip-roaring drunk he broke down in tears and told me all. I didn't know how to handle it either. *I* had to comfort *him*. I thought I was protecting him when I told him that you didn't need to know that it was him who told me. I told him not to tell his sisters.'

Jim sat as if paralysed, stony-faced. 'Why ... why didn't you want me to know it was him?'

'I didn't think you'd understand. I thought you'd be angry with him, feel betrayed by him, I don't know. It just seemed the right thing to do at the time. I didn't realise that what I was doing was isolating him. He didn't leave the country because he'd flunked his exams: he left because he can't live with hypocrisy. I didn't expect him to be gone for so long and now I feel so guilty, and I'm angry for feeling guilty because it was *your* fault.'

'Why the hell didn't you tell me?'

'There was too much angst in our lives already. Your mum ... '

'Jesus ... ' He turned away, looking up to the fells, anywhere but meet her accusing eyes. 'And you've kept all that bottled? Now I understand ... ' Whatever he thought he understood he didn't elaborate. After a while he leaned back against his headrest. 'I suppose in all this time Rob must have come to terms with it.' His voice sounded strange, almost husky with emotion. 'He's seen you carry on. He does at least talk to me.'

'You can ask him yourself when he comes home.'

'He's coming home?'

'In a week or two. I told him I'd decided to tell you. He felt he should be here but,' she lifted her shoulders, 'events have pre-empted his arrival.'

He shook his head as if unable to take it all in.

Now that they were talking about it, she felt the need to explain the coolness he'd detected. 'For a long time I thought your affair was my fault. People don't stray from happy marriages, do they? I couldn't understand *why*. But the things that were straining our marriage weren't *all* my fault, were they? What you failed to see was that your mother wasn't just my mother-in-law, she was my best friend. I was struggling to keep up the pretence that she would get better, for her, for Fred and the kids. Because of what you'd done, when she died, I had no one. I couldn't share it with my kids, nor Jenny. It probably sounds daft to you, but the only shoulder I had left to cry on was Dottie's.' There were no tears now, just an ache that she had thought she had come to terms with but now realised that she hadn't.

'And then she died ... ' He groaned. 'Now the whole walk thing begins to make sense.' He shook his head. 'You've learned to hide your feelings, even from me. I didn't realise ... '

Her anger flared again. 'How much feeling did I need to show? When I was planning my holiday I was practically begging you to make one small sacrifice for me! Not two weeks, or a week, just one weekend would have sufficed!'

'I misread it.'

'Because once again you were too wrapped up in your own life! The thing is Jim, somewhere along the way, sooner I think than I realised, we took different paths.' A picture of blue hills and misty horizons came to mind. 'When I was on top of Kidsty Pike I saw the world as you see it. All peaks. You don't see the valleys as you pass through them, all you see is the next challenge ahead of you. If you turned round, as I did, all you would see is the last peak you'd climbed, your starting point would be totally obscured: out of sight and out of mind.'

He was silent for quite a long time, his cheek twitching as his mind went over what had been said. Eventually he drew a deep breath as if weighing up the wisdom of what he was about to say.

'You're right ... I did drift away from you. My job had taken off. I can't deny that I enjoy being in the driving seat and when I clinch a deal or back a winner it's great. It's an old cliché to say my wife doesn't understand me, but, at the time ... ' He took another deep breath, bracing himself to talk about something he found hard to face. 'I was carried away on a high. I wouldn't even call it an affair ... it was just ... ' He moved his head slightly in a negative fashion. 'I can't believe I allowed it to happen ... ' He stared ahead, his eyes glazed, not seeing the fells but something inside his head. His voice dropped.

'My mother's last words to me were telling me that you were special and that you would need me when she'd gone.' He leaned forward, putting his head on his hands on the steering wheel. 'But it was too late. When you told me that you knew ... when you broke down in my arms, I can't tell you how much I despised myself. I didn't expect instant forgiveness. I knew it would take time to rebuild our relationship. I believed that as you'd stayed with me, didn't totally reject me, there was a chance it would come right again. But it hasn't. I still can't get near you, not properly, not like it was.'

There wasn't much she could say to that. It hadn't been the same because she had never felt the same. She had gone through the motions but her heart and mind had never fully engaged with her body. She had thought she had forgiven him, but as she'd discovered on her holiday, she hadn't.

As they both had plenty to think about she didn't interrupt the silence that followed, but her thoughts were jumbled. The truth was out now, and Rob was coming home, but how did that change things? Her yearning for Rob to come home had been because she wanted her family united, physically and spiritually, but how could that be if she and Jim parted company? It was still such a mess.

Eventually he drew a deep breath. 'I can see that I've fouled things up, big style. I can understand you finding it hard to live with.' He covered her hand with his so tightly that she couldn't withdraw it. 'What can I do to prove to you that you are the most important person in my life? That without you … ' His voice petered out as though the thought was unbearable. After a while he took a breath and started again, his voice determined but shaking. 'My job is demanding and sometimes it has to take precedence over everything. That's the way it is. But if it would make you happy, I'll resign.'

She had to laugh. 'I appreciate the offer but I wouldn't want you to do that. All I ever wanted was to feel that I mattered, too.'

'You do!' He crushed her fingers so hard that she yelped. 'Sorry.' He relaxed his grip but maintained possession, caressing her wrist with his thumb. 'Now that you've explained things, you have to give me another chance.' His hand tightened painfully around hers again. She wanted to pull free but couldn't.

'Why do I have to? How many chances do you need, Jim? For whose benefit, mine or yours?'

'Ours. All of us.'

All of us. The family. Her reason for being.

He squeezed her hand again. 'I've booked us into a hotel for the weekend. I had thought … '

She could imagine what he'd thought. He had imagined that she'd be so thrilled to bits see him, and impressed by his coming all that way to meet her at the end of her walk, that all the previous aggravation would melt from her mind. Well, now he knew just how wrong he could be!

CHAPTER 14

THE HOTEL WAS HIS SORT OF PLACE: a large country house hotel with award-winning restaurant, swimming pool and spa, set half-way up a hillside above the town of Keswick. She felt somewhat incongruous walking into the carpeted foyer in her travel-weary slacks and t-shirt, carrying her walking boots, alongside Jim in only slightly creased polo shirt, chinos and comfortable loafers. He, it transpired, had travelled up the night before and had already booked in.

He opened the door to their room where the first thing she saw was a bottle of champagne and glasses on a silver tray.

'I think your achievement's worthy of a bottle of champagne, don't you?' He was rising to the occasion in typical Jim fashion.

'To be honest, a tray of tea would be more welcome.' Despite her achievement, she was not in champagne mood.

Jim smiled. 'Tea it is then. We'll have the champagne later.'

Their room had a stunning view. One window looked down to the beautifully kept gardens with red squirrels hopping across colourful flowerbeds and lawns, the other overlooked the town and down the lengths of the Derwent and Newlands valleys to the mountains beyond Borrowdale.

Jim stood behind her pointing to and naming the mountains they'd climbed with the children. 'Cat Bells to

High Spy, Glaramara, High Raise. And between them is Langstrath Beck where we swam in deep clear pools. Do you remember that?'

'And Dottie fell asleep in the water, with her head resting on her paws on a rock and all her fur floating behind her.' Tears filled her eyes as the pictures filled her mind and an enormous sense of loss engulfed her. Jim moved to her side and put his arm across her shoulder, easing her into a gentle embrace, massaging her back between her shoulderblades.

'I'm sorry, darling. I didn't realise how important she had become to you.'

She stayed close to him until the tearfulness passed, his arms strong around her, the lingering scent of his aftershave familiar and warm.

'I'll run you a bath. Fi's packed some things for you. They're in the wardrobe.'

'Fi? Isn't she at work?'

He shook his head. 'She quit. She told me last weekend that she was having problems with her manager. Apparently she rejected his advances and since then he's made life difficult for her. I told her she should report the issue to his superior and apply for a transfer, or apply for another job, but she seems to have got it into her head that she wants to do something where she's her own boss. Anyway, she handed in her notice on Wednesday and was told by the manager to clear her desk and get out.'

'Oh ... poor Fi. She did sort of indicate, some time ago, that she might give up banking, but then dismissed it as a wobbly moment. I had no idea she was under such stress. I

... Oh, hell, and I sounded off at her on the phone on Tuesday.'

'She told me. She's been quite worried about you, too. Apparently she and Suzy had quite an in-depth chat about you on Saturday. They think you need another dog ... ' His eyes darted across hers. 'But it isn't a dog you need, is it?'

She could feel tears rising again but managed to smile and shrug. 'Amounts to the same thing, except a dog is more biddable, reliable, predicable and loves walks. A dog listens and wants to please ... '

He chuckled and pulled her close again, rocking her and breathing his warmth into her hair..

*

After her bath she studied her reflection in the full-length mirror. She hadn't seen that woman for two whole weeks. She'd become used to the one with windswept hair, minimal make-up, crumpled shirt, mud-splattered trousers and even muddier boots. The one she looked at now was in a simple blue shift dress, chunky opal necklace and not very comfortable high-heeled sandals, her blonde hair shining and swept behind her ears. She was Jim Challoner's wife.

He chose that moment to return to the room, having taken advantage of the indoor swimming pool.

'That's more like it,' he approved.

She returned the smile through the mirror. There was something slightly unreal about being in a hotel room with him as he tossed off his clothes in order to have a shower before going down to dinner. Twenty-four hours previously she had been in a humid bar drinking beer and surrounded by very damp walkers talking about walking, with a man she had been dangerously close to falling in love with. She had expected to spend this evening alone, preparing herself for going home, and now here she was, unexpectedly with Jim in a luxurious hotel room. He had taken control of her life again. But had he? He hadn't forced her to come with him: she was here with him of her own free will.

While he was in the shower, she tidied up the clothes he'd abandoned, then sat in the chair looking out over the panoramic view to check her phone for text messages, and to call Fiona. There were congratulatory messages from Suzy and Jenny and a message from Nick.

'Congratulations. Thank you too. Best wishes.' Thank you for what, she wondered, still feeling that she had given him more pain than he needed.

She pressed the numbers for Fiona, but her mobile was switched off.

Jim came back with a towel around his middle. 'Who are you calling?'

'Fi. Her mobile's off. That's unusual.'

He flicked his brows. 'She's at Leo's.' He shook his head in a confused way that was becoming familiar. 'I never expected to see her in love. Particularly not with somebody so laid back. I can't see it lasting.'

'Is she in love?' If she was it had happened very suddenly.

'So she says.'

Fiona had known Leo nearly all her life; perhaps she saw him as a safe harbour, somebody who wasn't going to think badly of her for jumping off her career ladder. Was that such a bad thing? Jacquie's image came into her mind. 'I think he'll be very good for her.' While he dressed, she told him about Jacquie and her attitude to life and relationships and her fears that Fiona could have gone the same route.

'Do you feel I pushed the kids?' he asked, turning from the mirror with a vaguely hurt and perplexed expression.

'No, not pushed, but you set a high standard and give the impression of being intolerant of failure.'

'Mmm. That's more or less was Fi said. I have to say I was surprised. I thought I'd been a good father, interested in their progress, encouraging.'

'When they're achieving. You don't identify with Suzy, or Rob.'

He thought about it for a bit then conceded, 'Perhaps I did bully Rob when he ducked out of university, but then I didn't understand his reasons. I feel … ' He heaved a great sigh. 'I let him down. I let my mum down and I let you down. I have to live with that.'

'We all have to.' She twiddled her wedding ring. 'When that woman fell from Helvellyn, I was struck by the thought that one person's wrong move has life-changing ramifications for their whole family. Yours did.' And hers could have.

His face had become serious again. 'Why has it taken us so long to talk about it?'

'I suppose, because neither of us wanted to.'

'Sometimes, you know, I see elements of your mother in you.'

'God forbid!'

'Seriously. You've locked all this inside you, and now I see that far from getting over it, it's ... sealed you in. And this thing about Rob. I'm astonished that you didn't feel I should know. I don't understand why.'

'I don't think there's one simple answer to that. At the time I thought I was protecting him because he'd come to me, not you. He was so wound up about it ... I thought it would create a clash and the girls would find out, and maybe everybody ... I just didn't want anybody to know. There was so much going on at the time. I couldn't cope with that exposure. I really don't know, exactly. It's taken me all this time to realise that it was keeping Rob away.'

He came to sit on the edge of the other chair by the window and took her hand in both of his. 'I'm glad he's coming home. It's not going to be easy for any of us, but if we're all willing, we can make it work.' He smiled and pulled her hand to his lips. 'We're going to be okay, aren't we?'

She nodded. 'I expect we'll muddle along.'

'I don't want to just muddle along. I don't want any more tip-toeing or mind-reading. I want things to be right.' His eyes were intense and loaded with meaning. She turned away, very aware now that she was the one who held the key to the barrier that existed between them. Over the last few years he had come to accept it as the price he had to pay, but now he was feeling for a way around it and it made her feel nervous.

He squeezed her hand again. 'Come on, let's go down to dinner.'

The slightly unreal feeling persisted. Jim was charming, attentive and conversational throughout their meal at the pink-draped table in a beautiful conservatory restaurant. It was all so different from the night before. She wondered where Nick was now. Had he organised transport home, or was he walking back? She didn't know. Already he seemed a long way away, withdrawing from her life just as surely as the tide had been receding from St Bees.

Deliberately, she pulled her attention back to Jim and realised that he was silently watching her. He smiled softly and she guessed that he knew she'd been thinking of Nick.

'Has Fiona said what she intends to do now?'

'She says it depends on you.' He looked across the table, quizzically hurt. 'Why didn't you tell me that? Jenny is selling the Rainbow and has offered it to you.'

'Because I knew what you'd say.'

'That it's hassle you can do without. You don't need the money. You don't have six days a week to put into it, and the financial return is not worth the effort. Right?'

'Precisely.'

He grinned infuriatingly. 'End of subject, then.'

'And what do you think to Fiona taking it on?'

'I think it'll be hard work for small financial return. However, as a bistro restaurant I think it'll make more money than the café. She's always enjoyed cooking, she would be her own boss, she has a good business head. If that's what she wants to do, I see no reason why she shouldn't have a crack at it.'

'I think when I get home I'm going to commit murder.' She joked but she was absolutely seething inside.

Jim smiled. 'You, however, still have first refusal.'

'Why can't I get through to you that it's not just about making money? The Rainbow café is a community asset that serves all sectors.'

'Not to mention giving you a huge amount of personal satisfaction.' He shrugged light-heartedly. 'If you feel that strongly about it, go for it.'

'Double murder. You know damned well I have other calls on my time. I have a home, a garden and family, none of which I want to compromise.' That was the problem in a nutshell.

He raised an eyebrow. 'I'm pleased to hear it.'

But she wasn't ready to give up. 'I've considered a village consortium.'

He smiled again. 'And like all the other organisations that the community desperately wants to preserve, they'll complain like buggery that some capitalist venture is going to deprive them, but they won't be prepared to put their time and money into keeping it going.'

'Your encouragement is predictably underwhelming.' The awful thing was that he was absolutely right. She was on a hiding to nothing and she knew it, but the idea of letting it go made her feel unbelievably bereft.

'Actually, Fi has a better idea.' Jim smiled softly. 'She knows it's important to you and she doesn't want to pull the rug from under your feet. Her idea is that she buys the business and continues to run it as a café six days a week, with your part-time help, if you're willing, and uses the facilities for a bistro three evenings a week. If it works, she can increase the number of evenings. I'd say it's a good business plan. It makes greater use of the existing facilities. The evening restaurant should be profitable, and the daytime café will continue to serve the community and keep you out of trouble.'

'Mmm. I'm not sure how I'll fare working for my daughter. She was always a bossy-boots.'

He chuckled. 'It's the best solution you're likely to get to your problem. Don't forget, you're the one with the experience. I think her idea is that you will run the café three or four days a week to give her time off.'

'Mmm. Did she say where she'll get the necessary capital from?'

'I said we'd back her.'

'Subject to discussing it with me, of course.'

'Of course.' Jim smiled and reached across the table for her hand. 'I'm sorry if I've appeared to belittle what you do. Until I was put right by our daughters, I didn't fully appreciate what it meant to you, and that you need more outlet for your talents than one selfish husband who takes it all for granted.'

'I don't believe Fi said that!'

'Not directly, she was quoting Jenny.'

'Not an opinion you usually value.'

'But when seconded by my daughter, I can take it on the chin.' He caressed her hand with his thumb. 'I wish you'd told me about Jenny's offer. I might have had an inkling of what all this has been about: you'd lost your dog, were in danger of losing your job … or even if I didn't twig, maybe the girls would have put two and two together sooner.'

'Poor Fi. I've misjudged her terribly.'

'There's a lot of me in her, but she's your daughter, too.' He smiled. 'I gather you had a go at her about Dad.'

'Only because she chose to lecture me on my duty of care.'

'Well you don't need to worry, he's adamant that he's not going to move.'

'I could have told you that. He's lived in that house all his adult life, he knows where everything is. I know he grumbles about not being able to see and do things for himself, but he's far from ready to relinquish his independence. He'd hate it if he wasn't free to totter across the green to the pub, or have his friends drop in as and when they felt like it.'

'But I do worry about him being alone at night.'

'He has a panic button.' She smiled. 'I tell you what, when you retire you can invite him to live with us, then you can be at his beck and call to ferry him back and forth to Melling so that he can have a pint and chat with his friends.'

He gave her a sideways look.

'Honestly, Jim, I'm not being selfish. I'd like to say that your concern does you credit, but what it shows is that you don't know your father very well.'

'I'm not doing too well, am I? I fouled up our marriage, all my children think I'm only interested in their successes, I don't understand my father. Is there anything else?'

'Probably, but I think your ego's taken a big enough bashing for one weekend.' She folded her napkin and put it on the table. 'Never mind, on Monday you can go back to work and put all your ruffled feathers back into place.'

He humphed a little laugh and pushed back his chair.

*

When they went to bed he snuggled into her back and his need to make love was like a fire up her spine, but, possibly afraid of rejection or a cool response, he didn't make any of the usual signals. She was relieved because she didn't yet feel relaxed enough to respond: too much had been said, too many memories revived, too many thoughts were still churning in her mind and the feeling of disloyalty to Nick persisted. After a while Jim's breathing slowed and she knew that he had fallen asleep with his arm still possessively around her. It was something he hadn't done for a very long time.

*

In the morning she was woken by Jim getting out of bed and opening the curtains to the glorious view bathed in sunshine. He smiled as he came to the bed to kiss her, gently, undemanding, but at the same time seductively, on the lips. A hot flush started in the small of her back and brought every pore of her skin, every hair follicle, to life.

'Good morning.'

'Good morning. What time is it?'

'An hour to breakfast.' He got back into bed. 'I'm going to phone Rob.'

She shuffled up the bed and he settled the pillows for her. He had taken the news of Rob's part in events very calmly but, she supposed, time had taken a lot of the sharp edges from the situation. When he was back in bed, he reached for his mobile phone and with the air of one braced for the worst, he pressed the quick-dial for Rob's mobile number. He had obviously rehearsed his piece.

'Hello, son. I'm in the Lake District with Mum. From our room we can see into Borrowdale. It's brought back all sorts of memories of family holidays.' She wondered if he had selected this hotel so that the happy memories would counter the bad. He was certainly now using it to set a scene.

Rob responded with something like, 'How nice. How's Mum?'

'As lovely as ever. Looking very fit. Look, son,' he said, diving straight in, 'she has told me that it was you that told her of my affair. I'm really sorry it screwed things up. For you as well as Mum. And for so long. I'm sorry. I can't excuse it but I swear it was a brief aberration, and that it's been bitterly regretted.'

She leaned close to Jim so that she could hear her son's reply. That he was surprised was apparent by the thoughtful delay before he said, 'Apology accepted.'

'I owe you, Rob, more than I can ever repay for not broadcasting the knowledge to all and sundry, particularly now that I know what it's cost you.'

'Yeah, well … it was for Mum.'

'I wish you'd told me. I wish one of you had. I hadn't realised I'd become so unapproachable.'

Again the pause was longer than the usual transworld telephonic delay. 'I suppose you didn't. For a time I couldn't face any of you without feeling dishonest or angry. Bloody daft really, but that's how it was.'

'And now?'

'Well, if you and Mum have got it sorted, then I guess that's it. Nothing more to be said.'

'If when you get back you find you do want to talk about it, I promise you, whatever I'm doing, I'll stop and listen.'

'Yeah?'

'Yeah.' Jim smiled. 'So, are you coming home with any ideas about your future?'

Rob laughed. 'Now you really sound like yourself!'

Jim became serious again. 'I owe you, Rob. If you need any help … '

'Thanks. I'll bear it in mind.' It bordered on being dismissive. Rob, it seemed, was ready to stuff the skeleton in the cupboard, but respect for his father was going to take a lot of rebuilding.

When the phone was handed to her, Rob asked, 'Are things really okay or is he just brave-facing it?'

'We're moving in the right direction. I'm sorry it took me so long to come to terms with things, to clear the way … '

'No need to apologise. I was thinking of coming home for Christmas anyway. Actually, I feel I should be apologising. I didn't realise that my being away made a difference.'

'Neither did I until I went walkabout.'

'I still find it hard to understand what he did.'

'We're all fallible.'

'You don't have to defend him.'

'I'm not defending, just accepting that he isn't perfect.' She might have added that she now understood how easy it was to get distracted when things were out of kilter at home, but decided against.

'That's all right then. I'm looking forward to seeing you again.'

'We're all looking forward to seeing you again, too.' Her throat tightened as, ironically, the heartache of missing him seemed stronger now that he was coming home.

'I hope you're fattening up a calf.'

'You bet.' She struggled against the cry in her voice and tears streamed down her face. Jim leaned out of bed for a tissue and dabbed her cheeks. 'Let me know when you expect to arrive. I'll be there to collect you.'

'No need.'

'I want to.'

'Okay. I'll call you. Gotta go now.'

'Okay, darling. See you soon.' The words brought more tears. Jim put his arms around her shoulders and rocked her. 'It'll be all right.'

*

They spent Saturday on the fells, or to be more precise, between the fells, walking up the valley at the back of Skiddaw. They'd done it a few times with the kids because they had been fascinated by the house in the middle of nowhere which had latterly become a walkers' hostel: their lively imaginations had created all sorts of *Wuthering Heights* type stories about it. To start with it felt weird. She had been married to Jim for twenty-eight years and known Nick for only two weeks, but despite their long history and happy holiday memories, walking with Jim seemed strange. She felt sad because had they done this the weekend before so much unhappiness might have been prevented. By mutual unspoken consent, and maybe habit, they didn't speak any more about their problem but focused on observations of the beautiful, bracken-covered fells and a tranquil meandering beck that slipped around and over boulders of granite. Always a positive thinker, he spoke of the future, of his hopes for the chairmanship of the company, the places he planned to visit, and his thoughts about the Rainbow venture.

At first she just listened but gradually she became motivated to join in. She was amazed to realise how things had changed in twenty-four hours. When she'd finished her long walk she'd had mixed feelings about going home, but now she was looking forward to it: she was looking forward to seeing Suzy and her children again, to discussing the future of the Rainbow with Fiona, and most especially to making a big welcome home for Rob.

When they returned to the hotel Jim said, 'You know, I really enjoyed that. We must do it more often.' He smiled apologetically. 'I wish I'd been with you last week. I'm sorry.'

She accepted the apology with a smile but felt he didn't fully appreciate the ramifications of his actions. He probably never would.

They followed the routine they would have had they been on holiday with the usual set of friends: retiring to their room after the day's activities to bath, shower and prepare for the evening's aperitif and dinner. Jim gave every impression of being comfortable, as though there'd never been any problem. Throughout their dinner he kept conversation going, covering diverse subjects from work, golf, Rotary, family and promoting the idea of buying one of the time-share apartments attached to the hotel to ensure a regular Lake District holiday. She liked the idea but wondered if the nearby golf course might eventually prove the stronger attraction.

They returned to their room and went through the routine procedure of her using the bathroom first, changing in privacy into her nightwear as she had done since his affair, while he undressed in the bedroom. When he'd finished his ritual splashing and gargling, he turned out the lights and came into the bed. He snuggled into her back and his hand found hers that was under her chin and clasped it tightly. It wasn't a sexual move but she knew that was what he wanted. She had the feeling that he was waiting for her to make the first move. After a while, when she didn't, he moved her hair and pressed a long soft kiss into her shoulder. 'Good night, darling.' He stayed close to her for a few minutes more, then turned over.

His travel clock ticked quietly and quickly, counting the seconds as they hurried through the night. He fidgeted, turning from his side to his back and then, with another readjustment of his pillows, onto his side again. She could feel his distress and his need for physical reassurance that she still loved him enough to give herself to him, but she was still holding back, just as she'd been doing for the last four years. But now something had changed, and it was she who had triggered the change, and why? Because she had wanted him to show her that she was loved. But how could he if she wouldn't let him do it the way that he knew best? The meaning of the words, 'With my body, I thee worship,' became suddenly clear. They weren't just about legalising sexual gratification, or the procreation of children and the giving and receiving joy, but also about reassurance and forgiveness, loving, body and soul. And wasn't that exactly what her cage-rattling had been about? And all she had to do to get it, was give it.

It was that simple, but even so, it was some time before she plucked up the courage to roll over and fill the space between them, stretch her arm around him and find his hand. As his fingers curled through hers and took them to his lips, she felt an involuntary tremble shake her whole body. He must have felt it, perhaps misread it, because he turned and pulled her tightly into his arms, locking her close to his body, entwining his legs around hers: there was no way he was going to let her change her mind. Kisses followed, hungry kisses, full of passion. His hands wandered, first skimming over her nightclothes then searching for more intimate contact. In the near dark she cried then laughed as their bodies worked up a sweat between them. Her lovemaking was as unrestrained as his, both wanting to show the other how loved and needed they were.

Afterwards, feeling a little bruised but still tingling deliciously, she lay close to him while his pulse thumped healthily in her ear and his hand retained possession of her breast, refusing to let her nipple relax, teasing her as he used to until she could stand it no more and stopped him. He chuckled triumphantly and transferred his caress from her breast to her face and pressed a long kiss onto her lips.

'Things are going to get better, my darling. I promise.'

'Mmm,' she said, feeling very relaxed and sleepy. Even in post-coital glow she was realist enough to know that he wasn't going to change dramatically, but their mutual willingness to try was the most vital first step to recovery.

*

The next day they travelled home to be welcomed by Fiona and Leo, Suzy, Phil and a rapturous Daniel. Jim cracked open a bottle or two of champagne and they all raised their glasses to a chorus of 'Welcome home.' And she felt she had come home, but home from a journey that had taken far longer than two weeks.

On Monday she saw Jim off to work with a hug and heartfelt kiss that made him glow like the one of the kids in the porridge advertisement. As he drove off, waving his arm high through the car window, she wondered if once in the office he'd forget all about it until he came home again. A smug little smile moved through her body: somehow, she thought not, any more than she would. After seeing him off she had domestic chores to do before going to work, but first she had to phone Nick. She felt she owed him a real voice communication.

'Hi, Linda! How'yer doin'?' He answered, obviously recognising her number.

'Good,' she replied. 'Really good.'

'I'm pleased to hear it,' he responded, sounding a little less enthusiastic than he had at first.

'Nick, I wanted to speak to you because ... well, you ... '

He interrupted. 'Because I told you that I was here for you and now you're going to say that you don't need me?'

'I wouldn't have put it so bluntly. I'll always value your friendship.'

'I suspected I was on a hiding to nothing but you were too good to pass up without trying.'

'I'm sorry.'

'You're a lovely lady. He doesn't deserve you.'

'I'm sorry. I didn't intend to use you.'

'I know you didn't. It's the way it went.'

'How was your journey home?'

'Okay. We walked, a different route. We didn't get back until last night.'

'How's Jack?'

'Fine.' There was a pause, which out on the fells would have been comfortable, but on the phone had to be filled. 'It was good of you to call.' He signalled the natural end. She would have liked to suggest that they stay in touch but knew it wouldn't be fair, not to him nor to Jim.

She didn't hear from him again, but sent him a Christmas card and received one in return with a note to say that he'd had a letter from Pauline to say that Gillian had died and, as willed by her sister, Pauline had taken in Gemma and Tim. He was planning to visit them during the Christmas holiday.

Christmas had always been the highlight of her year. In the fifteen years since they'd moved to their house, their home had become the focal point of the annual family feast, but since Nan's passing there had always been the feeling that something vital was missing, and she'd always known that it wasn't just Nan. Suzy had introduced Phil and the children, and Fiona had always made a point of coming home, but Rob's absence had been a constant reminder of Jim's infidelity. This year was the first year since the bad times that all her children were present. If there were such a thing as angels in heaven, then Linda knew that Nan would be looking down and feeling as proud and happy as she was that all the family were at home.

It was a wonderfully satisfying moment, walking into the sitting-room on Christmas morning and seeing them all sitting expectantly around the glittering Christmas tree. Fred was in Jim's chair with thin, lanky Rob concertinaed on a stool by his side. Rob still hadn't sorted out his future beyond being certain that he didn't want to be stuck in an office, and it seemed likely that he might return to university to do some sort of geography degree. Phil was on the sofa restraining an over-excited Dan between his long legs, with Suzy beside him holding a bedazzled baby Ruth on her lap. Leo was a new addition, looking somewhat bemused, while Fiona held a tray of champagne glasses alongside Jim, who was poised to commence festivities with the popping of a cork now that Toots, her new dog, was safely in the utility room. Thus far, the café bistro idea seemed to be working; she and Fiona were working well together with not too many differences of opinion. Jim had rediscovered the joy of walking and usually managed a mile or two with her and the dog at weekends, but how long that would last remained to be seen. They were none of them perfect, they had their differences, but they were her family, and they were together, and her cup runneth over.

Ceremonial present giving was something she hadn't experienced until she'd become part of Jim's family, and she still found it childishly exciting to see the gaily-wrapped parcels in all shapes and sizes under the tree. She could usually tell whose pile was whose: Jim's and Fiona's were always superbly packaged in shiny paper with extravagant bows; Suzy's were modestly wrapped in recycled paper; Fred's in somewhat creased paper salvaged from the previous year.

Rob's presents for the last three Christmases had arrived in envelopes, usually book tokens as the cost of post and packing had been prohibitive on his limited budget, but this year he had reverted to his old style of buying only things that would fit into a shoe box so that all his gifts appeared to be the same size and were easily wrapped. Her gifts were usually packaged to a theme that changed from year to year; this year her colour scheme was green and gold. One parcel, obviously one of Jim's, dominated all the others. It was a box that stood about three feet high by two feet wide and across, wrapped in shiny snowflake design paper with a huge silver ribbon. It hadn't been there with the others when she'd come down for a sneak preview early in the morning.

Jim popped the cork and they all sang *'We wish you a merry Christmas,'* to get the party going; then, as per tradition, Fred handed his presents first and, as Nan had decreed, the children gave theirs so that they learned the joy of giving before receiving. Then Suzy gave hers, then Rob, Fiona and then it was Linda's turn and finally Jim's, by which time the floor was littered with colourful paper and little piles of books and toys and smellies.

With his usual panache he handed her a small box. She unwrapped it and found a beautiful diamond eternity ring which he ceremoniously put on her finger with a kiss that had more value to her than the jewel. He then handed gifts to all the others until only the big box remained in the corner. She looked around and saw that everybody had received a gift from him and was puzzled. But not for long, as he then pulled it out and brought it to her.

'I wasn't sure that diamonds would please you, but this I know you'll like.' His eyes twinkled with certainty.

It was a box, so there was absolutely no guessing what could be inside it. It was also quite heavy. The rest of the family were fascinated and watched in silence as she pulled the ends of the great big bow then carefully eased apart the seams of the paper.

'What is it, Ganna?' Dan wanted to know.

'I can't imagine,' she said, being none the wiser when the wrapper was removed and only a plain white box was exposed. She opened the top and peered in, keeping the rest of the family in suspense.

'What is it?' Dan was getting impatient.

'I'm not rightly sure … ' It looked like … a rucksack. A big one. She looked up at Jim who was smiling widely.

'For heaven's sake,' he said, 'open it properly.' He took hold of the box and pulled it apart so that its contents were revealed. It was a very large rucksack, far too big for their occasional Sunday outings, far too big, she thought, for her to carry. 'Look inside,' he encouraged. She opened the top flap and pulled out several lumps of screwed up paper, then found something else. A pair of walking boots. She pulled them out. They were far too big. Not her size. Her heart did a little somersault when she realised that neither the rucksack nor boots were meant for her: they were for Jim. She looked up and found his smile. 'Front pocket,' he instructed. She opened that and found a book, *The Long Distance Footpaths of Great Britain*.

'I thought we'd start with a spring assault on Offa's Dyke,' he said as she pressed herself against him and his arms wrapped tightly around her.